*Crazy, Sexy,
Revenge*

Crazy, Sexy,
Revenge

Also by J. D. Mason

J. D. Mason

Crazy, Sexy, Revenge

St. Martin's Griffin ✶ New York ≋

CRAZY, SEXY, REVENGE. Copyright © 2014 by J. D. Mason. All rights reserved. Printed in the United States of America. For information, address St. Martin's Press, 175 Fifth Avenue, New York, N.Y. 10010.

www.stmartins.com

The Library of Congress Cataloging-in-Publication Data is available upon request.

ISBN 978-1-250-05224-7 (trade paperback)
ISBN 978-1-4668-5374-4 (e-book)

St. Martin's Griffin books may be purchased for educational, business, or promotional use. For information on bulk purchases, please contact Macmillan Corporate and Premium Sales Department at 1-800-221-7945, extension 5442, or write specialmarkets@macmillan.com.

First Edition: October 2014

10 9 8 7 6 5 4 3 2 1

To the perceived notion of happy endings

Acknowledgments

This emotional journey has finally come to an end and I've enjoyed walking this road with each and every one of you. Life and every good story are filled with ups and downs, revelations, discoveries, and confrontations. Relationships have been formed, love has been lost, and the truth revealed.

I am going to miss these people: Desi Green, Lonnie Adebayo, Jordan and Claire Gatewood, Olivia, and finally, her ghosts, Julian Gatewood and Ida Green. They have all served me well and I hope that I have done the same for them.

Thank you as always, Monique Patterson, for your vision, patience, and encouragement. You are and have always been that angel (and sometimes devil) sitting on my shoulder, whispering in my ear, as I have told my stories. Thank you, Sara Camilli. I consider myself fortunate to have a warrior like you on my side. And my heartfelt gratitude and appreciation goes out to my readers, some who have been on this road with me since the beginning and others who've joined me along the way. Your encouragement is what keeps me going.

Now it's time to put this baby to bed. Read on and enjoy! And while you're doing that, I'll be hard at work on the next project and looking forward to starting a brand-new adventure with all of you.

Crazy, Sexy, Revenge

Crazy, Sexy, Revenge

Prologue

Jordan's eyes locked onto Lonnie's and suddenly the world was void of everyone and everything except for the two of them. He turned and walked toward her. She needed him.

"Don't you dare!" his wife, Claire, commanded from behind him.

For some reason he would never understand, Jordan froze in his tracks.

Lonnie held on to the stair rail and slowly dropped to a seated position on one of the steps, lowered her head, and raised a trembling hand to her chest.

"Oh!" she cried out as she saw blood seeping from her chest through her silk blouse.

Lonnie! he screamed in his head. Or maybe he'd said it out loud—he didn't know. It didn't matter. She needed him and he needed to be with her!

"You made me do it!" Claire called out. "I wouldn't have—I did it for you! I did it because of you!"

"Shit! Go back! Go back inside! Hurry the fuck up!" he heard a man say.

He looked over his shoulder and saw a couple, a white woman and a black man, run back toward a room at the other end of the building and all of a sudden he remembered where he was and most importantly, who he was.

He was Jordan Gatewood!

Jordan turned to look at Lonnie who lay back on the steps, clutching her chest, crying, gasping. . . .

Out of the corner of his eye he noticed curtains to one of the other motel rooms suddenly close. From some faraway place, he could hear Claire crying, sobbing like a child. And if he listened intently enough, if he truly focused, he could've sworn that he heard Lonnie fighting to take her last breath.

He was Jordan Gatewood!

Jordan stood in that spot long enough to watch the woman he'd loved die. Lonnie lay still, her hand dropping from the railing she'd clung to so desperately. Claire cried in the background. And—there were witnesses.

He was Jordan fuckin' Gatewood!

Jordan turned and marched over to Claire, picked up the gun she'd dropped at her feet, grabbed hold of her arm, and dragged her back to his car parked next to hers in the lot.

He flung open the passenger door. "Get in!" he commanded, shoving her forcibly into the vehicle.

The lump in his throat was as big as a fist and it threatened to choke him to death.

"I did it for us!" she protested, looking up at him tearfully. "I did it . . . You drove me to do this!"

"Get the fuck in the car!" Jordan shoved her so hard that Claire hit her head on the way in. He slammed the door shut and marched over to the driver's side.

He was Jordan Gatewood and he could not be here! He could not be a part of this—this—murder!

Claire had shot Lonnie! She'd pulled that trigger, not him!

Instinct kicked in, shoving reason out of the way. Jordan climbed in behind the steering wheel, and glanced into his rearview mirror. People had seen him here! They watched him get into the car and they saw what Claire had done to Lonnie. He started the engine, put the car in reverse, and backed out at a dangerous speed, then peeled out of the parking lot with tires squealing.

She was gone! He didn't need to see her again to know it! Jordan could feel it. His gut told him that Lonnie Adebayo was dead and it warned him, tortured him with the truth that he had been seen by too many people, which was fuckin' unacceptable because he was Jordan Gatewood, goddamnit!

Claire's sobbing was driving him crazy. "Shut up, Claire!"

"Oh God! I didn't mean—"

"Shut the fuck up!" He wanted so desperately to hit her, to punch her hard in the face for what she'd done! He wanted to punish her, to make her bleed, to feel bone break under his fist!

The rage bleeding from his psyche was terrifying, even to him. Jordan had to do something and he had to do it quick, and beating the shit out of Claire was not the best use of time.

He pressed the Bluetooth button on his steering wheel.

"Call Edgar!" he demanded the phone system.

"It's late!" the old man answered gruffly.

"I need you," Jordan said, gritting his teeth.

"What? What is it?"

He glanced at Claire in disgust, and then chose his words carefully. "Lonnie's been shot!"

"What? You shot her?"

"No! She's been shot! She's dead, Edgar." He swallowed, and unexpected tears clouded his vision. Jordan blinked them away. "She's at the Fairmont Motel off 635," he explained, choking up.

"What the hell happened, Jordan? Who's that?" he asked, referring to the sound of Claire crying uncontrollably. "Is that . . . Claire?"

Jordan ignored the question. "People were there and they saw us, Edgar! Too many people saw what happened."

Edgar would know what to do. The old man was cunning and capable and Jordan would bet his last dollar that Edgar had been in predicaments like this before and had come out shining like a new penny on the other side.

"Nobody can know that I was there. Do you understand?"

He didn't know how it could be done, but it could be done, and he didn't give a damn how!

"I need to be a fuckin' figment of those people's imagination, Edgar! I need to not exist to any of them! And Claire . . ."

"She was never there either," the old man finished wearily.

If ever this old man were to prove his loyalty to the Gatewood family, this was the time to do it. Jordan had never needed someone so much in his life until now. Edgar was all he had.

"Whatever it takes," Jordan continued, as he took a deep breath and slowed his speed. He didn't need to be pulled over. Not now.

"Hang up," Edgar said, hanging up before Jordan had a chance to.

Edgar could fix this. Jordan took another breath and held it before finally releasing it through his nostrils. If anyone could fix it, Edgar could. Edgar would.

If you're going through hell—keep going.

WINSTON CHURCHILL

Crazy
Crazy

Chapter 1

Who was he? Plato could see the questioning looks coming from all of them as he climbed out of the car. Was he a detective? That dead woman lying on the steps of that shitty motel looked expensive enough to command an investigation from the grave, even from where he was standing. Maybe he was her husband, who'd somehow known that his woman was here and in trouble. Was he like the rest of them, just passing through, stopping here to sleep for the night? Hardly.

He studied each of them intently: hoes, addicts, homeless. These were desperate people, and desperate people were one of two things: afraid . . . or dangerous.

"Damn, he got here quick," he heard someone murmur.

"That the po-po?"

"Too clean to be the po-po."

"A pimp? Her pimp?"

"Maybe."

Plato walked over to the woman. Beautiful! Even in death, or especially.

Waves of ebony hair fanned out on the steps beneath her. Red-stained lips parted slightly, making her look as if she was just about to whisper a secret. Dark eyes fixed on the stars above. Damn shame. Plato didn't have much time, ten, maybe fifteen minutes at the most before the Dallas Police Department started to arrive. It was an expensive fifteen minutes, but if you had the money and the power, you could afford it.

There was a door open on the second floor. Had she come from there? Plato stepped over the lovely figure and casually climbed the stairs. He looked inside and saw crumpled bedsheets and a towel tossed on the floor. Plato went into the bathroom to get another towel, then began wiping down every surface that could possibly contain a fingerprint, the faucets in the shower and bathroom sink, the linoleum counter, a small table and chairs in the main room, along with the headboard, nightstands, and finally, the doorknob, inside and out. He threw the towel on the bed and closed the door behind him.

He was down to eight minutes.

The crowd had begun closing in on the dead woman's body. Curiosity drew them to her, that and greed. Some of them eyed those gold bangles on her arm like they were candy. Diamond earrings called to them like sirens from the sea. Shit like that could buy a lot of nights in this dump or some good-ass hits of whatever it was these fools shot into themselves.

"Anybody see what happened?" he asked, eyeing them all suspiciously.

"I did." An overachieving, dirty white girl spoke up.

"Shut up, Lisa," her dirty black boy said, sliding up to her from behind.

Plato focused on the girl. Tracks had left her arms bruised and looking like someone had been chewing on them. "What did you see?"

"A black man, kinda tall, like you. He went inside that room you just came out of and then she came and went in. I think I heard them getting it on, but . . ." She rolled her eyes. "He came out and she was screaming and then this other broad came out of nowhere and shot her."

There was no sound. The silencer stole the sound. There was just the gun. And blood. And wide eyes that had probably been ocean blue before the drugs, now gray, staring back at him in disbelief, before rolling back into her head. Her body fell at her dirty man's feet.

Plato looked at each of them. "Anybody else see anything?"

An old man with one leg, balancing on one crooked and socked foot, wearily shook his head, and slowly began backing up toward what was probably his room. The dirty black boyfriend of the dirty white girl held his mouth open to release a scream that refused to come. Two young prostitutes held on to each other's hands and stared wide-eyed and shocked at Plato.

He had five minutes.

"Can we go?" one of them asked helplessly. "Please don't kill us."

He started walking toward the front office. The two girls took off running.

The dude behind the counter was a relic, tethered to this place by some ungodly connection that only made sense to him. The portly man played some kind of game in his mind, make-believing that he ran a five-star hotel in the heart of Dallas instead of a dump on the edge. The green-and-gold bow tie he wore threatened to choke the breath out of him as it clashed violently against the brown-and-lilac button-down, short-sleeved shirt. His khakis were perfectly pressed, with sharp creases running down the front of his legs.

Plato could read it in his eyes that the man was afraid. He'd seen too much. He knew too much, and this fool would start talking to the first cop who showed up on the scene. Hell, he'd probably been the one to call them.

Plato stood across from the man with the counter separating the two. Being six-five, just about every man he came into contact with was shorter than he was. Plato's size struck fear into people who had something to hide. And this one looked like he had plenty, but Plato only cared about one thing.

"Y-yes . . . sir?" he asked Plato nervously. "May I h-help you?"

He contemplated the man, realizing as he studied him that this man's fate was sealed the day he took his first breath from his momma's womb. Plato could see the recognition in the man's eyes, as the revelation slowly took root in his own mind, and he began to panic at the thought of his impending death.

"Room 204," Plato said. "Who was it registered to?"

The man hesitated. Ethics made him do it. "I'm sorry, s-sir, but I'm not at liberty to say."

Plato almost admired his conviction. Almost.

He took a step closer to him and slowly repeated the question. "Who was it registered to?"

Conviction took hold of ethics' hand and dragged its ass right out of the front door. The man frantically began typing on the keyboard to his computer.

"Smith," he said quickly. "John Smith."

"Who paid for it?" Plato probed.

The man swallowed. "Ross. Franklin Ross. He paid over the phone by credit card."

Plato had no idea who Franklin Ross was, but he knew that the man was a goddamned idiot using his own credit card to pay for a room registered to John Smith.

Plato turned to leave, and then he turned back to face the man, one last time.

Time was up.

Plato stepped out into the parking lot and could hear the sirens whirring in the distance.

"Only the dead have seen the end of war," he murmured, quoting his namesake.

Now the police didn't have just one murder to solve. They had three. They had no witnesses. Maybe they'd find the killer of that beautiful woman someday. Maybe not. Maybe they'd even catch up with Plato's ass. Maybe not. But for a while, the police would stumble and scratch their heads trying to figure out what these three people could've possibly had in common. They'd wonder why they'd all been shot on this night at this place. Naturally, the first thing the cops would try to do was to connect the three killings, but Plato knew that any detective worth his badge would soon see that there was no connection between the murder of the woman and the desk clerk or the junkie in the parking lot.

Plato climbed back into his car and turned on the engine, but before backing out of the parking space, he pulled out his cell phone and made a call.

"How bad is it?" Edgar Beckman asked as soon as he answered the phone.

"There's a woman lying dead on the steps. I'd say that's pretty bad," he said coolly.

"Witnesses?"

"Several."

"Should we be worried?"

"Death should always leave you worried."

The old man sighed irritably. "Do you think anyone will say anything to the police?" he asked impatiently.

Plato knew people, and he especially knew these kinds of people. They were the throwaways, the forgotten-abouts, the kind of people that were on their way to someplace else. The woman lying on those steps wasn't one of them. He could tell by the clothes she wore, the perfection to which her hair and makeup were done. He glanced back in the rearview mirror and saw the small scattering of the motel residents crouch around her body, begin riffling through her purse, and take whatever jewelry she wore.

"No," he finally said, satisfied in the affirmation he'd been so divinely blessed with in this moment as he watched those people that he truly did understand them. "I don't think you have to worry about any of them saying a goddamned thing."

"Who was registered in that room?"

"John Smith, but he's not the one who paid for it," Plato said.

The man paused. "Who paid for it? How?"

"Franklin Ross paid for it with his credit card. You know that fool?"

The old man sighed. "Thankfully, no, not personally." He hesitated and then continued. "And what about the car?"

"What about it?" Plato asked unemotionally.

"You have to take it. You have to get rid of it," he demanded. "I told you there'd be a car parked there and that you had to get rid of it."

Plato surveyed the parking lot.

"A Mercedes? A white Mercedes?" Beckman said frantically. "In the parking—"

"Ain't no Mercedes out here, boss," he said, hanging up his phone without waiting for a response. Plato's fifteen minutes were up.

Chapter 2

Adrenaline had dissipated and Jordan was suddenly exhausted. Ten hours had passed since Lonnie had been killed. Jordan still couldn't believe it. It still didn't seem real that Claire had actually pulled that trigger. Two years ago Jordan had walked away from Lonnie, believing he'd killed her. He'd tortured her, and he'd meant for her to die that night. But he couldn't remember feeling the way he did now. He hadn't killed her and two years later she came back into his life, pissed as hell and bent on making him pay for what he'd done to her, but she was alive, and something inside him was relieved. The world was different without her—his world was different.

If it wasn't for this board meeting first thing this morning, he wouldn't have come into the office, but this meeting was too important to miss. Under normal circumstances, he wouldn't have missed it, and Jordan had to keep up appearances. He'd been calling

Edgar for hours, worried that the old man might've finally let him down. Edgar wasn't answering his phone, though. And Jordan had spent the better part of the night pacing the floor and trying to drown out the sound of Claire's incessant crying. He'd spent the night expecting that knock belonging to the police to come to his door. Without even trying or meaning to, Jordan played out scenes in his mind of being taken into custody.

"Call my lawyer!" It would be the first thing he'd say to them, the only thing he'd say.

For some reason, he couldn't fathom scenarios of Claire's arrest. He'd be the one they'd take. He'd be the one they'd believe had shot her. And he'd let them because Claire was weak and she'd make him end up looking like a messy fool.

"There he is! Bravo, Jordan! Bravo!"

All thirty officers of the Gatewood Industries Board of Directors stood up and applauded as he entered the room. Jordan Gatewood was caught off guard by the reception and for a moment, Jordan forgot that a woman was dead—that Lonnie was dead.

"We did it, big brother." His sister, June, came over to him, smiling and wrapping her arms around him. "It's official. With the merger, Gatewood Industries is now the third largest oil company in the world!" She laughed and kissed his cheek.

He'd been awake all night. Jordan hadn't eaten since . . . since . . . It wasn't until dawn that he remembered about the board meeting, that he remembered how important it was to keep up appearances.

Forcing that smile was damn near impossible. "Yes! We did it!" He looked lovingly at his sister, and then appreciatively around the room at everyone else. Jordan had no choice. He had to hold it together. He had to be that confident leader, that CEO that everyone was expecting to show up this morning to this meeting. His wife had shot and killed a woman the night before, and he'd spent all night long expecting the police to show up on his property to make an arrest.

"Check it out, big guy!" one board member said, holding up the newspaper with a headline that read, Gatewood Industries—Big Oil's Next Giant?

A grainy photo of him speaking at some event was below it. For a moment, he felt proud. He felt strong and confident and on top of the fuckin' world. But on that page was another headline, smaller, and it damn near screamed at him above the cheers.

Award-Winning Reporter Found Dead

The sound of his sister's laughter broke through the fog engulfing him.

June gently grabbed him by his elbow. "Sit down, Jordan, before you fall. I know. I still can't believe it either."

"Do you have any idea how much the estimated worth of Gatewood Industries has increased since yesterday?" Bev Jackson, the controller, looked around the room and asked.

"Double!" someone shouted.

"Triple!" a few others chimed in.

"Try four times what we were worth this time yesterday and you'll be close to right," she finally said, holding up four fingers. Bev leaned back in her seat. "It's unprecedented."

It was true. If he were ever going to actually let that fact sink in, now was the time to do it. Lonnie Adebayo was dead, but the world had definitely not stopped turning because of it, and the very real fact remained that he was now head of one of the largest, most powerful corporations in the world, and that meant something. That ball that he'd had in his gut all night slowly began to unravel. The magnitude of that began to creep back to the surface. He hadn't killed anyone. Claire had shot Lonnie. Jordan was an innocent man. And today, in this moment, he was a very important man. If he didn't believe it himself, he could look at these people and see in their faces that he was their hero. They worshipped and adored him now, more than ever, and last night was behind him. Lonnie was gone.

"I'm meeting with the event planner this afternoon," June announced to the group. "The event is going to be the talk of the town, a black-tie ball, exclusive to all shareholders. I suspect there'll even be a few celebrities there," she said excitedly.

A party? Jordan felt an explosion go off inside him. *With all that had happened, this fool wanted to have a party? Stop! Catch yourself!* Jordan had to control himself. He was exhausted. Too much was happening too fast.

"Don't forget to send me an invitation," he quipped. The room roared with laughter.

June looked at him proudly. "You're the guest of honor, Jordan Gatewood," she said lovingly. "You'll get the first invitation, big brother."

Jordan needed to rest. He needed time to clear the thoughts clamoring in his head. He needed to calm the fuck down and work like hell not to appear guilty of something he hadn't even done. He needed to talk to Edgar to make sure that the man really had taken care of the situation like he'd promised. And he'd left Claire in a fuckin' mess this morning before he left the house. Claire was a liability, a problem, and no longer a priority.

Jordan was CEO of Gatewood Industries, and damnit, he needed to man up and act like it. All eyes were on him, waiting for him to give the marching orders. He was used to that. And he was damn good at it.

Jordan swallowed. "The easy part's done," he began, looking each person in the room in the eyes. "We've taken Anton Oil and made it ours, but now the real work begins," he said, sternly. "We've got two vastly different corporate cultures that we need to turn into one. Some offices will close, some new ones will open, jobs will be lost, new ones made." Everyone in that room hung on his every word, as Jordan pushed the events from the previous night back into the dark recesses of his mind to focus on the task at hand. "Anton had a nasty little oil spill in the Gulf that we're responsible for now, and for all the billions we've made, it's going to cost us at least that much to clean up the mess we've inherited."

The jubilation wafted out of that room like smoke, but as much as he needed to keep it real, this wasn't the time to douse the fire of these people. "But if anyone can turn that shit around, it's us," he said confidently. "The world's watching, people." Jordan stood up and adjusted his tie. "Let's give them a fuckin' show they won't soon forget."

Every back straightened, every chin raised, and as he turned to leave, they applauded him, again. Jordan was most definitely the man of the hour—for the time being.

Chapter 3

The sonofabitch did it!

"No," she murmured in disbelief, watching the news reporter on television. Lonnie's picture flashed in a box as the woman spoke. *No! No! No! This can't be happening! Lord, please! Don't let this be true!* Her knees began to buckle and she slowly began to sink to the floor. "No! Oh God! No!" she cried out as the reporter drove the point of that news story deep into Desi's heart.

"Yolanda Adebayo's body was found late last night at the Fairmont Motel on the outskirts of Dallas. Ms. Adebayo, an award-winning and Pulitzer-nominated photojournalist, is believed to have died from a gunshot wound to the chest."

Desi willed the television reporter's mouth to stop moving. That woman was a fool if she thought that Lonnie could possibly be dead! "Shut up," Desi commanded, clenching her teeth. "Shut up! Shut up! Shut up!"

Jordan . . . He shot . . . "Jordan," she muttered, tears clouding her vision. But Lonnie couldn't be dead. Not her. Lonnie was too smart to let herself get caught up by Jordan again.

"Desi? Baby?"

Desi didn't even hear Solomon come into the room.

"Police are stumped by the triple murder at the Fairmont Motel and the connection, if any, between the three victims," the reporter continued. "Detective," she said to the man suddenly appearing beside her. "Detective, I know it's early in the investigation, but is there anything you can tell us about the victims that might lead you to understand any connection between the three murders?"

The connection was Jordan Gatewood. His name burned the back of her throat. Desi struggled to catch her breath and scream it at the top of her lungs.

"Desi?" She felt Solomon's arms around her, raising her up off the floor.

"He did this," she murmured, sobbing and unable to take her eyes off the television.

Solomon lifted her up and led her over to the bed. His voice broke through the trance she was in, and Desi looked into his eyes.

"Jordan killed her, Solomon," she repeated over and over again, forcing the words to take root. "He did this! I know it, Solomon! I know he killed her!"

"You're shaking, baby," he said.

Dear God! Her friend was dead and Jordan Gatewood had finally killed her! "She was going after him for what he did to her." The words spilled from her lips quickly. "I warned her—I told her not to, but she wouldn't listen, and he did this. He killed her, Solomon!"

"Desi . . ."

She pointed to the television. "Jordan did it. Don't ask me how I know. I just know. I know he did this."

Solomon stared at the television to understand the connection between the news story and Desi's hysteria. "Desi, calm down. You don't know . . ."

"Of course I know it was him because I know him, Solomon!" she shouted. "I know what he's capable of. Jordan did this! He shot Lonnie and he's going to get away with it if I don't do something!" Desi cried, struggling to break free of his grasp.

Solomon was determined not to let her go. "You don't know that he killed her."

"It was him!" she shouted. "Can't nobody tell me that Jordan didn't do this!"

"Even if he did, how can you prove it?" he asked.

The knot tightened in her stomach. Desi stared back at him in disbelief. "I'm going to the police," she blurted out. "I'll tell them what he did to her two years ago—that he tried to kill her back then, and that he wanted her dead!"

"Proof, Desi," Solomon responded. "You accuse a man like Gatewood of murder you'd better have proof, baby, and you don't have any."

She was angry at Solomon for the things he was saying. Desi wanted to lash out at him, but . . . he was right. Desi suddenly found herself in old territory, that feeling of helplessness, where an eighteen-year-old girl was left to suffer for someone else's crime.

Desi was flooded with that same fear she'd had back then, when Olivia Gatewood put that gun in her hands after the woman had shot and killed Julian Gatewood in Desi's living room. Desi was paralyzed then, too afraid to open her mouth to tell the police the truth, that she didn't shoot Gatewood. While her mother, Ida, cried and begged for them not to arrest Desi, Desi said nothing and it had cost her twenty-five years of her life.

"He's going to get away with it," she murmured, more to herself than to Solomon. It was a revelation that grew with each passing second.

Even if she went to the police and told them what she knew about Lonnie's relationship with Jordan, it was still Desi's word against his. Desi had come a long way since her release, but even she didn't believe she'd come far enough to go head-to-head with a Gatewood and win.

The tears flowed down her cheeks, and the lump in her throat swelled until she felt herself suffocating. "He's going to get away with it. Isn't he? Just like his mother . . . Jordan's going to get away with killing somebody I love."

Desi broke down crying in Solomon's arms. Despite everything—the money, the secrets she'd revealed in her memoir about her past and being set up to take the fall for Julian's murder—despite it all, she was still that same girl inside, crushed under the weight of the Gatewoods and helpless to do anything about it.

Chapter 4

Detective Bobby Randolph had been called into a triple homicide early this morning. Shit like this put a knot in his stomach the size of a basketball. Three bodies of three people who didn't look as if they could possibly have anything in common and not one damn witness to speak of.

"All three were shot in the chest," reported one of the police officers who'd arrived at the scene earlier. "Not sure who was shot first."

"Any idea what Miss Designer Jeans was doing in a dump like this?"

"Nobody's ever seen her before."

He rolled his eyes in frustration. "And the girl in the pink top?"

"Her boyfriend is the guy in the green pants. Said she went out to the gas station to get some smokes. Claimed he was sleeping."

"The sound of the gunshot woke him up?"

The officer shook his head. "He didn't wake up until he heard the sirens."

"Figures," he said. "Motive?" he asked.

"The woman on the stairs was robbed."

"What about the desk clerk?"

"He had two hundred in cash in the drawer and twenty bucks and a credit card in his pocket."

Bobby glanced at his watch and rubbed his burning eyes. The call came into the station at midnight, but he'd been on the scene since just after five in the morning. It was just now going on nine.

The bodies had been removed, and all that was left meandering around the crime scene were a few of the motel residents and the last of the crime scene investigation crew. Lack of sleep made his less-than-pleasant demeanor even more unlikeable.

"Fifteen goddamned people staying in this place and ain't nobody seen or heard nothing," he grumbled miserably.

"I'll bet if we check a couple of them we might find a few of the dead woman's missing belongings."

"Don't tempt me," he said, glaring at an old man who was staring out of his doorway back at Bobby. The woman had been robbed, but the fools had been kind enough to leave her wallet and ID.

A quick Internet search on his cell phone told him that Yolanda Adebayo had been in a place she didn't belong. The woman was five-star, and this dive was a no-star. Even lying dead and covered in blood, she looked like she could've bought and sold a place like this ten times over. Had she been the target?

His phone was buzzing in his pocket, but Bobby refused to answer it just yet. He knew who it was. The media was all over this story already. "How the hell did the media get wind of this so fast?" he questioned angrily.

A young, beautiful, successful journalist found murdered in his city was bound to make national headlines, and the brass was going to ride his ass like a mule to hurry up and get this case solved.

He fixed his gaze on the spot where her body had been found. What the hell was she doing here? What business could a woman like that possibly have in a joint like this? They'd asked every single person staying at this motel if they'd seen her before and every last one of them said the same thing. They had never seen the woman, and they "didn't know nothing."

"We're done here," a young CSI team member said to him.

"Did you go through all the empty rooms?"

Had the woman been coming or going? Had she been staying or visiting in one of those rooms? Had she talked to any of these people?

"We've been through every last one of them. Collected about a million prints and some other unsavory things but we won't know if we have anything of any importance until we get it back to the lab."

He nodded as she passed.

"Did we pull the security camera from the front office?"

"Yes."

Bobby looked around the surrounding area outside of the motel, hoping to see a camera on one of the streetlights or on top of the building.

"We searched, Detective," the police officer finally said. "The only working camera was in the front office."

"Shit," Bobby muttered. Maybe that's why the clerk had been killed. He'd seen the perp.

The cell phone was starting to wear a hole in his pants pocket, so he finally gave in and answered it. "Yes." It was his lieutenant. "Yes, sir. We're done here. Wrapping it up now."

Bobby waited patiently while the man stated the obvious on the other end of the phone. This was a high-profile case. Ms. Adebayo was a very important and notable person and it was imperative that they find the killer quickly. The world was watching.

"Understood," Bobby said curtly. He wanted to tell the man that he had shit for evidence and that short of water boarding, these good folks living at this establishment were not going to offer any information of their own free will. But that's not what the man wanted to hear. "I'm all over it, Lieutenant," he stated firmly. "Yes, sir. I'll wrap it up nice and tight before you know it."

He hung up knowing good and damn well he'd just lied to that man.

Chapter 5

Jordan's day had been filled with meetings, interviews, and press conferences detailing the news of the Gatewood Industries' merger with Anton Oil. It had taken all of his energy to stay focused, to be present in the whirlwind that was his corporation, and to ignore the incessant vibrating of his cell phone and messages from his assistant, telling him that his wife had left another urgent and frantic message, demanding he return her calls, until finally, he took matters to another level and called on a different kind of babysitter.

"Whatever it takes," he told Warner, head of security at his estate, "get that goddamned phone out of her hands. I don't care how!" he ordered angrily. "And lock her ass in a room or something. But keep her in that house and make sure she has access to nothing—not a phone, a laptop, not even the fuckin' television!"

Jordan had no idea what to expect when he walked into his

house. The eerie quiet unnerved him and was nothing like the chaotic scene he'd left behind this morning. Claire had been a wretched mess, hysterical, screaming, cursing, and fully expecting to die in the electric chair, and according to her, it was all his fault.

"You fuckin' couldn't keep your hands off of the bitch!" she'd screamed all the way home in the car. "You couldn't keep away from her! No matter what I did, how much I loved you or how many sacrifices I made for you . . . it was always her! I'm glad I shot her! I took her from you! I took the one thing you cared about more than me! I did what you failed to do, Jordan! I killed her! I got rid of her once and for all!"

Warner met him in the living room. "She's in the bedroom," the large, bearded man told Jordan. He looked more like someone who should've been wrestling bears in the wilderness than like one of the most sought-after and well-respected security men in the state. "It's been quiet. Louisa packed her things, like you asked."

"Good," Jordan responded curtly, brushing past the man. "Have Lux bring the car around."

Jordan begrudgingly made his way up the stairs and down to the end of the hallway to the double doors of the master suite. For all he knew, Claire was standing on the other side of it with a pistol pointed at his head—or her own.

She was just sitting there, in the dark, curled up on the chaise next to the window that led out onto the balcony. Claire didn't budge when he opened the door, letting the light from the hallway flood in behind him. Jordan reached over to the wall to turn on the light. Claire grimaced, pulled the top of her robe to cover her face, and turned away from him.

Their marriage was over. Standing in the middle of that room, staring at the mess she was, Jordan knew that there was no way for the two of them to recover from this.

"You need to get dressed," he finally said to her.

Jordan loosened his tie, pulled off his blazer, tossed it onto the bed next to him as he sat down. He took a long, deep breath and let it out slowly, slumping and rubbing the burn from his eyes. He was beyond tired, and carrying the weight of the world around all day long on his shoulders had finally caught up with him.

He closed his eyes, and locked onto Lonnie's face when she'd looked at him before she died. It took a moment for her, for either of them to realize what had happened. In his mind's eye, he saw the disbelief on her face when she realized that she'd been shot.

"Claire, get dressed," he repeated, wearily. Jordan had been operating on adrenaline all day. He'd moved methodically through each moment, robotically, doing what needed to be done, saying what needed to be said, knowing all the while that it was only a matter of time before everything caught up with him. It was the anticipation that was the worst, the anticipation of some cop coming into his building, accusing him or Claire of murder.

"Claire!"

"Fuck you, Jordan," she finally responded, unemotionally.

The sound of her voice was all it took to push him completely over that ledge he'd been balancing on all damn day.

Jordan bolted to his feet, stormed across the room to where she sat, grabbed her by the arms, and forced her up onto the floor.

"Get your hands off me!" she screamed. "Don't touch me! You bastard! Get your hands . . ." Claire broke free of his grasp and struck him hard across the face.

Jordan stared at her, stunned, and she hit him again, and again, and again, until finally, he'd had enough.

"I could put you in the fuckin' trunk of my car and make you disappear like smoke," he growled.

"Do it!" she dared him.

He grabbed ahold of her wrists, holding on so tightly that Claire cried out.

In that moment, it became crystal clear to him just how much of a liability Claire was, and had always been.

"Your weak ass has been a waste of my time since I met you," he blurted out.

Tears filled her eyes, and Claire spat in his face.

Jordan grabbed her face, covering almost all of it with his hand, forcing her back down onto the chaise. She clawed at him, kicked at him, but he was numb to her defenses. In that moment, he wanted her gone. Whatever that meant, he wanted Claire to disappear from his sight. Her muffled cries escaping from between his fingers snapped him out of the fantasy he'd become immersed in.

He let her go and backed away. "Get your clothes on," he demanded again.

"Why couldn't you have just left her alone?" she sobbed. "Why couldn't it have just been me and you, Jordan? And our baby?" Claire swallowed and took a step toward him. "Why wasn't I enough for you?"

They had talked about having a baby, but that's as far as it had gone. Just talk.

"You can't stay here," he said, fighting to keep what little was left of his composure.

"You called the police?" she asked, standing up. "You called them!"

He turned to her.

"Are they coming, Jordan?" Claire finally sounded afraid. "Wh-what did you . . . You told them that I killed Lonnie? Oh God!"

Claire collapsed to her knees on the floor.

She disgusted him. "Get up and get dressed, Claire," he said coldly.

"I can't go to prison!" she cried uncontrollably. "Oh, God . . . I can't . . ."

Jordan had no sympathy. He went to her, grabbed her by the arm, and jerked her to her feet. "Put your shit on so that I can get you out of this house!"

She tried to talk, but Claire's lips moved without sound.

"I'm putting you on a plane, Claire," he finally began to explain. "I'm getting you out of the country."

She looked confused. "But the police . . ."

"For now, they know nothing," he said, almost believing it himself. "But you can't stay here." He relaxed his grip on her. "I've got a car waiting downstairs. Louisa packed some of your things. I can send you whatever else you need, but the sooner you get out of Dallas, the better."

She gradually began to comprehend what he was telling her. Claire nodded helplessly and began to peel out of her robe, letting it drop to the floor as she stepped over it to go to the closet.

Years ago he'd bought a château in Lisbon, Spain. The two of them had spent an anniversary there. Jordan had had his assistant call ahead to have the villa prepared for her. The farther away she was from him, the better. He couldn't stand the sight of her or the sound of her voice. Jordan had coddled that woman with kid gloves and hated it. It was over. Their marriage was finally over. Jordan started to leave the room.

"I'm not going . . . to be arrested?" she asked meekly, glancing at him from over her shoulder.

He stopped in the doorway. Jesus! He was tired. "Not tonight, Claire," he reluctantly said.

Claire slipped a blouse over her head and turned to her husband. "Jordan?"

He stopped and faced her.

Claire trembled. "I made a mess of things." Her voice cracked. "Didn't I?"

She stood there, expecting him to say something—anything. But there was nothing to say, and Jordan left her standing there.

Chapter 6

Solomon came from inside the house, handed her a cup of hot tea, and sat down next to her on the sofa in his courtyard next to the pool. Desi loved his home, an eight-thousand-square-foot master-piece in Hyland Park that felt like it had been lifted out of the Mediterranean and dropped in Dallas, Texas, by accident. He pulled her back into his arms. The sun was starting to set, and soft lights illuminated the pool from under the water and filtered through the shrubbery landscaping on the other side of the yard.

Solomon was well off in his own right. He was one of the most sought-after lawyers in the professional sports and entertainment community, and made millions representing some of the most famous people in the world. He and Desi had met when she'd asked him if he'd review a publishing contract for her from a publisher offering her a book deal to write her life story. When he found out who she was, he refused on the basis that he believed she had been guilty of murder like everyone else. But he eventually realized the truth: that Desi had been set up by the Gatewoods for Julian Gatewood's murder.

Desi had spent all day crying and he'd been here, offering a shoulder, or just letting her cry her eyes out until they were swollen to the size of golf balls. Solomon had proposed. A few months ago, he'd given her a ring, and asked her to be his wife. That was the only thing that had kept Desi from crying herself to death. When she showed up at his door a few days ago on her way back from Tyler, he welcomed her with open arms, picked up her bags, grabbed hold of her hand, and practically dragged her inside.

"Come on in, girl! Look around. Get used to the digs. This is going to be the place you call home if I have anything to say about it."

She didn't have the heart to tell him she had no intentions of ever living in Texas again. Desi figured they could have a bicoastal type of relationship. Dallas was a nice place to visit, but Texas wasn't home anymore.

She took a sip of her tea.

"You need to eat," he suggested tenderly.

Desi tried her best to smile. "Don't you ever get sick of bacon?" she asked.

He looked at her like she was crazy. "Who the hell gets sick of bacon?"

"Obviously not you."

He'd made bacon for dinner. He'd made a BLT for lunch. And of course, he'd made bacon and eggs for breakfast.

"Keeps me strong," he bragged, flexing his biceps behind her. "You know you like your man strong."

Desi laughed for the first time all day and Solomon looked pleased with himself. But the very real fact remained that Lonnie truly was dead. Jordan had been the one to kill her and would more than likely get away with it.

"I warned her not to come back here," Desi said wearily. Just thinking about Lonnie and the fact that things could've worked out so differently had she just listened to Desi and taken her advice. "I warned her to leave him alone."

"If what you tell me about her is true, then you know she was going to do what she wanted to do anyway, Desi."

He was right. Lonnie was determined and bullheaded. She had grand ideas of herself, believing that she was invincible, even after what Jordan had done to her two years ago. He'd beaten her nearly to death, but somehow, she'd survived and come back more determined than ever to make him pay for what he'd done to her. The first time he'd tried to kill her a miracle had saved her life. But this time Lonnie was all out of miracles. Desi ached knowing that her friend was gone for good, knowing that her death was real and headline news.

"Jesus, Solomon!" she said, squeezing her eyes shut. "Lonnie was there for me in ways that don't even seem real." She looked at him. "She showed up in my life long before we ever met face-to-face and she kept me going, she kept me alive," she tearfully explained.

Solomon listened patiently.

"She wrote me a letter not long after I was sent to prison, and she was the first friendly face I saw twenty-five years later when I was released. Lonnie was the one who made sure I got my inheritance when the Gatewoods were bound and determined to fight me for it. And they would've won had it not been for her."

Lonnie had hooked Desi up with a lawyer friend of hers, who put together an entire team of lawyers every bit as cunning and powerful as the Gatewoods' team and they fought tooth and nail to make sure she received the twenty million dollars from her mother's estate, left to her by Julian Gatewood.

"She was the one who uncovered all the lies and secrets behind my conviction. All those people took Gatewood money to make sure I went to prison—the judge, the sheriff, the jury—and she uncovered the shit they were hiding in their own lives so that I had something to fight back with." Desi was crying again. "I don't know what would've happened to me when I got out of prison if it wasn't for her."

He pulled her close and held her against his chest. Solomon had never been a Lonnie Adebayo superfan, but he understood that Desi was, and why. So much had happened these last few days, weeks. So many revelations about her past, strange new twists in her future, and of course, Lonnie's death. Desi had spent the last few hours trying to sort it all out in her mind. She hadn't been ready to talk about it until now. And well, he was here, and if he was going to be her husband, she was going to have to learn to be open with him. She was going to have to tell him everything.

"Do you know why I came back to Texas, Solomon?" Desi had flown to Dallas, rented a car, and driven to Tyler without ever mentioning it to him. He didn't know she was even in town until she called and asked if he was up for a sleepover.

"I'd like to think it was to see me," he said unabashedly.

"I wouldn't have left without seeing you," she admitted. "But that's not why I came."

He looked hurt, but quickly recovered. At least, he recovered on the surface. "So, why'd you come to Texas?"

"To see a woman named Gloria Dawson in Tyler."

"And who's Gloria Dawson in Tyler?"

"Her mother used to work for Julian Gatewood," she explained. "She was his personal secretary."

He rolled his eyes at the mention of Gatewood and then looked at her. "So? How does that tie in with you going to Tyler to see Gloria Dawson?"

"Her mother had given Gloria some things to keep. Things that belonged to Julian. Personal things."

He waited.

Desi couldn't believe she was actually going to tell someone. Until now, the only people who knew were her and Gloria Dawson. "She gave me my birth certificate, Solomon." She choked up. "My real one."

He looked skeptical. "Not another birth certificate," he said sarcastically.

His tone stung a little, but she understood where he was coming from. It seemed that the Gatewoods played a game of musical birth certificates. There were birth certificates and then there was the truth. Desi had gotten ahold of Jordan's real birth certificate that showed Joel Tunson as his father. She'd gotten it from Joel himself, and thought she could use it as leverage against Jordan. Lonnie had thought the same thing, and now she was dead.

"He was my father, Solomon," she continued tearfully. "The man I was accused of killing, the man I grew up loving, was my father—my real father."

The lawyer wheels started spinning in his head. "How do you know it's valid, Desi? How do you know it's real? Maybe it's what he wanted. Maybe he had planned on making it official, baby, but . . ."

Desi couldn't blame Solomon for being doubtful. With everything those people were capable of, deciphering fact from fiction would take a PhD to figure out, but this was different. This made sense. "Gloria's mother loved Julian. She cared for him like a son, and according to Gloria, they had no secrets between them. She looked after him, Solomon. And she made her daughter promise to keep the things she left behind in case I ever came looking for them. If they were false, why would she care?"

He was trying to understand. She could see it in his eyes.

"There's more," she continued.

He raised his eyebrows in surprise. "More?"

She nodded. "It's probably going to end up in the news."

"What?"

"You've heard about Gatewood Industries taking over that oil company, Anton?"

"Yeah." He sighed.

This was going to be tougher for him to swallow than finding out Julian Gatewood was her father. "I bought stock." She shrugged.

Now he just looked pissed. "In Gatewood Industries?"

She shook her head. "In Anton Oil."

"When? Didn't that merger happen already?"

She nodded. "I bought stock back when it was cheap."

He sat up and leaned forward. "How much stock, Desi?"

"A lot, Solomon."

Solomon raked his hand across his head. "So that means . . ."

"That means I'm a shareholder in Gatewood Industries."

She expected him to curse, but he didn't. He did, however, stand up and start pacing back and forth in the courtyard. Desi knew he wouldn't be happy about it, but it was better that he find out from her than read it in the morning paper. Solomon wanted her to have nothing to do with the Gatewoods. And she got that. They'd damn near ruined her life, they were toxic, and they hated her. He wanted to protect her from all that, but he didn't understand. Lonnie understood, and now with her death, Desi understood too.

"Why would you do something like this?" He stopped and stared at her. "Desi—baby, you know . . . Do they know?"

"I'm sure they do," she said calmly.

"I don't get it," he said, frustrated. "I don't get why you'd want to put yourself in this situation. You know how they feel about you. You know that those people are fuckin' crazy, Desi! You might as well have put yourself in front of a moving train! Why? Why the hell would you make a move like that?"

"When I lost Mr. J, who I loved, I had no time to grieve. I had no chance to grieve, and as far as everyone around me was concerned, I had no right to grieve." She'd started crying. "When I lost my mother, I was too far away to grieve. She died alone, Solomon, and she died afraid for me. And I detached myself from her because as far as I knew I was going to spend the rest of my life in that place. Lonnie was like my sister. We didn't always get along, or even like each other, but I knew she had my back, from a thousand miles away, and deep down, she knew I had hers. Losing her brings up all of those times before, when I couldn't cry, couldn't process losing someone close to me—it's not just her I've been crying about all day."

He took her hands in his. "Alright. So, now I do get it. But why would you want to be all up in the Gatewood mix like this, Des? They took Julian from you, and your mother, and according to you— even Lonnie. Why put yourself in their faces like this? You doing this for yourself or for Lonnie? You trying to finish what she started?"

She swallowed. "I need to do this. Lonnie started this for me. She tried to fight this battle for me, Solomon, and she's dead because of it."

"That's not your fault. And if what you say is true, and Jordan did kill her, then what's to stop him from doing the same thing to you?" he asked, the fear showing in his eyes.

"Me," she whispered. "I can't make you understand this. I can't make you like it. And I hope to God you stay on my side, Solomon. But this has got to end, and in my soul, I know that I've got to be the one to end it."

"What the hell does that mean?"

"This started with me and the Gatewoods, Solomon." Desi shrugged. "That's the only way it can end."

Chapter 7

Frank held the barrel of the gun in his mouth. Damn! He'd fucked up! Jesus! He'd fucked up! Lonnie was dead because of him. Ed Brewer was dead because of him, and Colette was going to prison—because of him. They had him dead to rights on Ed's murder. The only thing keeping his ass out of the electric chair was that high-priced lawyer Gatewood had sent to post his bail and represent Frank when it came time to go to trial. He'd been a fool believing that Gatewood gave a damn about his ass. Deep down Frank had talked himself into believing that Jordan felt some kind of loyalty because they were blood and all, but shit! Gatewood had set him up.

Pull the trigger, man! Frank cursed in his head. *Pull the god-damned trigger and get this shit over with!*

He couldn't go to prison. An ex-cop in prison was a dead man already. What choice did he have? What the fuck did he have to live for?

Metal clanked against his teeth. Frank pressed his thumb to the trigger and squeezed his eyes shut. He was done.

Just then his phone rang. He tried ignoring it, but then made the mistake of glancing at the screen and seeing Jordan Gatewood's name come up. Frank pulled the gun from his mouth. This was one call he had to take. He'd blow his head off after he finished saying what he had to say.

"What the hell you want, motha fucka?" he blurted out over the phone.

"Shut the fuck up and listen!" Jordan retorted.

"Fuck you, man! I ain't gotta listen to shit coming out of your mouth! You set me up, motha fucka!"

"You set yourself up, Frank. Who the hell told you to pay for the room with your own damn card?"

"The room needed to be paid for in advance. How the hell else could I pay for it? Hell, it wasn't like I could drive over there and pay cash for it. I've got the police sitting right outside my door twenty-four/seven! I'm damn near five hundred miles from Dallas! What the hell was I supposed to do?"

Jordan didn't say anything and Frank thought he might've hung up. His life was fucking worthless now. Frank rubbed frustration from his eyes. "Why'd you have to kill her, man?" he asked, starting to choke up. "What the fuck? I mean, was this what you had planned all along? You got my ass out of jail for this?" he asked, desperate to understand.

"I didn't kill Lonnie," Jordan finally said.

Frank burst out laughing. "Yeah, man. I didn't kill anybody either. That's my story and I'm sticking to it."

"Your name's on that motel registry, Frank. You're in their computer system."

"Tell me something I don't know."

"Call your credit card company and report your card stolen."

What did he just say?

"Do it today," he continued. "As soon as you get off the phone."

Frank's head was beginning to throb. What was Jordan up to this time? What was he planning?

"Why would you tell me that?" Frank demanded to know. "Why the hell would you say that to me?"

"To save your ass, idiot!"

"For what, man?" he yelled back. "Why the hell would your ass be so interested in saving my ass?"

"Fine!" Jordan shot back. "You do what you want to do. "Fuckin' rot in prison for all I care, man!" Jordan hung up.

Frank put the phone on the coffee table, stood up, and started pacing the room. If the police hadn't found out he'd paid for that room yet, they would. It was only a matter of time. Even if Frank did have an alibi sitting out in front of his house in a squad car the night Lonnie was killed, he could still be held as an accomplice to murder even if he didn't pull the trigger. And with his track record—well, it was highly unlikely that they'd believe anything he had to tell them.

He'd been a decorated officer of the Cotton, Texas, Police Department for years. Frank had gotten caught up. He'd needed money and getting it was too damn easy, so he and his partner, Colette Fisher, started extorting it from a meth dealer named Reggie Rodriguez. It wasn't much, a couple of thousand here and there, but two other cops got wind of what they were doing and decided that they wanted in on some of that action.

He and Colette got stupid. Ed Brewer's dumb-ass partner, Jake Boston, pulled his gun, Colette pulled hers, and Frank pulled his. All of a sudden, two cops were dead. Soon after, Frank left the force, leaving Colette to fend for herself. Drug addiction had gotten ahold of her and added fuel to an already desperate woman in a desperate situation. Every day she worked at that police department while they looked for the two people who'd killed those cops.

"Be cool," he'd told her. "Don't do anything to make them suspicious and it'll pass."

Colette flipped the fuck out and shot Rodriguez when they started to get close to him. She thought he'd open his mouth about the money he'd been paying her and Frank, so one night, she found him and shot him. And there was a witness. She was arrested, and soon after, implicated Frank in the cop killings. He was brought in and fully expected this thing to be a slam dunk, sending both of them to the electric chair. But Gatewood had other plans, at least for Frank. He sent the fanciest, most expensive lawyer in the state of Texas to Frank's rescue, got him bailed out of jail to await trial, if there was a trial. And then Gatewood called him.

"Call Lonnie," Jordan instructed him. "Tell her you're back in town just for a night, but that you want to see her."

Frank was quiet for a few moments. "Where?"

"That motel you were staying at, outside of town." Jordan's mind moved like methodical pieces of a machine. "She knows that I paid your bail, so don't act like you still believe that it was her."

"She's going to ask me what I want."

"Make it up, Frank. Make it good. And make sure she believes you."

Frank sighed. "What time?"

"An hour. Text me the room number."

That conversation happened last night, and now the woman

was dead. Frank was as guilty as if he'd pulled the trigger his damn self.

He picked up his wallet and took out his credit card. Frank flipped it over, looked at the number on the back, picked up his phone, and started dialing the 800 number. He pressed a bunch of numbers, responding to electronic voice prompts before finally getting a human being on the other line.

"Yeah, uh . . . I need to report my card stolen. Yeah. A few days ago, I guess. I went to use it this morning and it was missing." He paused and waited for the woman to finish asking him a question. "The last time I used it? Probably to get gas, day before yesterday."

Chapter 8

Bullshit was slamming into him from every direction. Jordan felt like a stone rolling down the side of a hill that had no bottom. Given the circumstances, he should've been feeling like king of that damn hill, a king who was now head of one of the largest, most powerful corporations in the world. But no matter how hard he tried, Jordan couldn't pretend that his personal life wasn't crumbling to pieces all around him.

Ever since Lonnie's death a few nights ago, he lived this same routine. Jordan would leave his office a few floors down and come up to his penthouse and drink until he was too numb to move, inviting Lonnie's lovely ass into his heart, mind, and soul to torture his memories in her own delicious way.

"Are you living your dream?"

He laughed. "What?"

Lonnie rolled on top of him and straddled him. They were still brand new to each other, still exploring and discovering each other.

"Is this what you wanted to be when you grew up?"

She wore her hair cut short back then. Lonnie was beautiful, dark, and smooth. She challenged him, tempted him, and intrigued him.

"Did I want to be lying naked in bed with a beautiful woman on top of me when I grew up?" He laughed and kissed her. "Hell yes."

"That's a given, smart-ass. And hell, if it wasn't me, it would be some other beautiful woman, but that's not what I mean." She rolled her eyes. "Men like you have everything, looks, money, power, tons of pussy."

"Tons," he moaned, rubbing her luscious ass.

"You were born into this life, Jordan, like royalty, a prince who was a prince, wealthy and privileged—long before he was anything. You never had a choice but to be who you are now. But what if you did?"

"This must be a trick question." He raised his head to try and steal a kiss, but Lonnie dodged him. "With everything you just said, why would I want to be anyone else?"

Lonnie laughed and shook her head. "Silly boy," she said condescendingly. Had anyone else called him that he'd have had them exiled from the kingdom.

"Do you know how many men out there want to be me?"

Lonnie batted big brown eyes. "All of them."

"Damn right, all of them," he retorted. "And can you blame them?"

Thinking back to that conversation now, Jordan suddenly couldn't stomach himself. Had he always been so vain, so embarrassingly ignorant and clueless?

"Are you living your dream?" she'd asked him. Lonnie wouldn't have asked such a question lightly. She wouldn't ask it in jest and there would be nothing casual about it. She was testing him. She

was searching for something more to him than just that meathead shit he came back with, and Jordan realized how foolish he must've seemed to her in that moment.

The real answer to that question was no. Jordan had no real dreams of his own. He'd stepped into some other man's dream and decided that it was the only one that mattered. That's the answer he should've given her.

Lonnie suddenly turned introspective. "I met a boy once in Sierra Leone. He was twelve and he thought that because I was American, I was rich. 'All Americans are wealthy,' he said."

Jordan groaned. "Don't do this, baby."

"Don't do what?"

"Don't tell me some sob story about some poor kid in Africa who didn't have a pot to piss in, but how thankful he was to be alive. I was just starting to get hard."

She licked her lips. "Like . . . I can't get you hard anytime I feel like it?" Lonnie ground her hips against his.

Jordan moaned. His cock pulsed uncontrollably.

"Can I finish my story?"

"Hurry."

"So, I asked this boy what he wanted to be when he grew up, and do you know what he said?"

He rolled his eyes in frustration. "What did he say?"

"He said that . . . he wanted to be free to choose."

Free to choose. Jordan laid his head back on the edge of the sofa and stared out at the city lights through the balcony across from him. *Shouldn't every man choose this?* he thought, looking out from his penthouse perched on top of the world. Jordan took a sip of cognac. If he was truly going to be honest with himself, then he had to admit that all this glitter certainly wasn't golden. A woman was dead because of him, the one woman he had ever truly been able to convince himself that he had loved. And another woman—the one he'd married—had been the one to kill her. Jordan didn't pull that trigger, but he might as well have.

"Men like you believe you're happy," Lonnie continued, *"and you believe you're free, but are you? Or, are you bound to someone else's destiny?"*

"You saying I'm not happy and I'm not free?"

She shrugged. "I'm just making conversation." Lonnie seductively began to slither down the length of him.

Deep down, he knew the truth. "No you're not," he said to her.

"Do you want a blow job?" she asked.

Jordan got up and stepped out onto the balcony of his living room, still wearing the towel he'd wrapped around his waist after getting out of the shower. Jordan wasn't happy and he certainly wasn't free. Had he ever been?

Desi Green had somehow managed to weasel her way into Gatewood Industries, and he had been too preoccupied to even see it coming. The woman he had tried to love had shot and killed the woman he'd tried to stop loving, and in a strange twist of fate, he had lost them both.

Jordan was alone with his secrets, sleep was a rare commodity, and peace was impossible to come by. If this was paradise, then it was hell.

As if on cue, the phone rang. It was Claire. He stared at it, watching it ring several times before absently answering it.

"I've been calling," she said.

It was the first time he'd heard her voice since she left.

"I know."

"I hoped you'd call me back."

Jordan finished his drink and poured another one. He closed his eyes and searched inside of himself to feel something for this woman, but came up empty.

"Has anything . . . Has anyone . . ."

Jordan sighed. "No, Claire. No one's come asking about what happened."

He was cautious by nature with everyone. He hadn't been cautious enough with Lonnie, though. He hadn't been nearly as cautious as he should've been.

Claire was quiet on the other end of the phone and Jordan gave serious thought to hanging up.

"I still can't believe I did what I did. I didn't mean to . . . I was just so confused, Jordan, and so angry. I thought you were going to leave me for her and I couldn't live with that. I couldn't lose you."

Claire waited for a response from him. What did she want to hear? What did she think he should say? He wasn't in the mood to try and appease her. And he certainly wasn't in the mood to lie.

"We're both at fault. Between the two of us, we ruined everything, Jordan. . . ." Her voice trailed off. "I knew you wanted her." Claire was crying. "I knew that you couldn't stay away from her, and it tortured me."

Jordan had tried to stay away from Lonnie. She'd come back to town with an agenda to get even, to make him pay for his trespasses against her two years earlier. The Lonnie he had loved had turned into a woman with a vendetta bent on destroying him and he couldn't let that happen. But as bitter as their relationship had become, she still stirred feelings in him like no other woman ever could.

"You're right, Claire," he said bitingly. "I couldn't keep my hands off of her."

Claire started to cry. "You're a fucking pig, Jordan," she said dismally.

Jordan was impressed. In all the years he'd known his wife, Claire had never openly insulted him. Maybe if she had, he'd have had more respect for her.

"Good girl," he grunted.

"Why can't you love me and tell me that you loved me more, Jordan? Why can't you say that you will do everything to protect me until this whole mess blows over so that we can begin to try and put our marriage back on track?"

"Because I'd be fuckin' lying, Claire," he said dryly.

Claire was quiet on the other end of the phone.

He had no sympathy left for Claire or anyone. Jordan was running on empty in the emotions department.

"Did you like it better when you were cheating on me with her? Is that it? If I hadn't killed that bitch and she was still alive, would she still be your side chick that you could fuck whenever you wanted? Would that make you happy?"

"Happier—yes," he eventually admitted. "Much, much happier, Claire." He would sell his soul if he thought it would bring Lonnie back. "I'd be happier not having a woman's murder hanging over my head," Jordan continued. "Happier not having a woman's death hanging over my head because you pulled the trigger over some dumb shit. I'd be happier knowing that my family's name and reputation was safe from the scandal this'll bring if it ever gets out. Yes, Claire. There are quite a few things that would make my ass happier right now."

"Would you have been happier if I'd killed myself, Jordan?" she questioned meekly.

And there it was—that elephant in the room. Jordan was tired. He was exhausted and his eyes burned from lack of sleep.

"Jordan?" she prodded. "Would you have preferred it was me who died that night instead of Lonnie?"

Was he really so cruel? Claire was vulnerable. She had always been vulnerable. Jordan knew that. He had to choose his next words carefully. But, in the end, would it really matter what or how he said it? She'd been perched on that proverbial cliff, balancing precariously for all these many years. Maybe what Claire needed was the one thing he'd been reluctant to give her, that gentle push over the edge. Sometimes, the most humane thing a man could do for a wounded animal is to put it out of its misery.

Jordan rubbed his tired eyes. He desperately needed to sleep. She wanted to hear him say it. Claire was practically begging for the word to part his lips.

"Just say it." She sobbed pitifully.

No. Not tonight.

Jordan sighed. "Good night, Claire," he finally said before hanging up the phone.

Chapter 9

Bobby Randolph dressed in the dark, trying not to wake up his wife. It didn't work.

"What're you doing?" she asked, half sitting up in bed. "Where are you going?"

"To work." He sighed, frustrated.

"It's Friday. It's your day off."

He sat on the side of the bed and slipped on his shoes, then leaned across the bed and kissed her on the forehead. "Baby, I stopped getting days off when I caught this case."

The sun was just starting to come up by the time he pulled out onto the highway. Bobby drove with the radio off because it seemed like the only thing anybody could talk about was the murder of that reporter, Lonnie Adebayo. Folks seemed to forget that three people were killed that night. One was famous, the other two, George

Cook and Lisa Feldman weren't, but that didn't make their deaths any less important. His lieutenant had been riding him like a horse about closing this case of the Adebayo woman. The man hadn't so much as said two words about the other victims.

Sitting at his desk, Bobby studied the profiles of all three victims on his computer screen. The only thing these three people had in common was the fact that they were all at that motel that night and all three had been shot in the chest.

The most logical question was why. Adebayo was the only victim who was robbed. Had the girl, Lisa Feldman, walked up on the perps and been shot because of it? Was it as simple as her being in the wrong place at the wrong time? Feldman had a record—possession, possession with intent, prostitution, and shoplifting. So, maybe she had been in on robbing Adebayo too, and her partner or crew turned on her.

Where did George Cook, the desk clerk, fit into all of this? He was shot in the front office and nothing was taken, not the money in the register and not the money or credit card in his pocket.

"Just like you like it," his partner, Iris Fenway said, setting a little cup of heaven on his desk. "Caramel soy latte with a splash of vanilla, and extra whipped cream."

All of a sudden, the world didn't seem like such a bad place after all.

He grinned as she sat down across from him. "If me and you weren't already married to other people . . ." He removed the lid from the cup and raised the sweet nectar to his lips.

"I would never marry a man who drinks soy lattes," she said with a smirk.

Iris wasn't his type either, too tall, too skinny, no titties, she smoked, and she was blond. Bobby never really cared for blondes but her ass was cute. Besides all that, she was his partner and he never saw anything remotely physically appealing about her except in times like these when she came to his rescue in his darkest, most desperate hour of need.

"So I spoke to George Cook's wife yesterday," she volunteered.

"And?"

She shrugged. "She said about as much as we already suspected. Cook was pretty unremarkable. He went to work, to church, liked to fish, and he was unnaturally close to his mother, but I didn't probe."

He didn't expect her to find much, but they owed it to the man and his family to not let him disappear in the whirlwind of the Yolanda Adebayo media circus.

"She said he barely had any friends, let alone enemies."

"'Bout what I figured," he said dismally.

"So that brings us back full circle," Iris said, leaning back in her chair. "Who killed these people and why?"

"And what was she doing there?"

"Maybe she was covering a story?"

"What story?"

"I don't know. She did a lot of documentary type shit; investigative stuff, political coups, sex trafficking, stuff that took some digging and in the process could piss off some very dangerous people. Maybe somebody wanted to shut her up?"

He shook his head. "I don't know. I checked with some news people and they all said that she'd pretty much been on hiatus for the last few years. As far as any of them knew, she wasn't working on anything or with anyone."

"It wasn't like she was short on money or needed a place to stay. She was living in a loft downtown, an expensive one."

"Yeah, but it wasn't hers," Bobby concluded. "It belonged to some corporation out of Europe."

"She had friends in high places, that's for sure. I came across a few articles on the Internet, and I could've sworn I read a quote from Angelina Jolie paying her respects."

"She wasn't registered in any of the rooms at that dump."

"We questioned almost everyone who was registered that night and out of those twelve people, nobody saw anything, not even an expensive-looking black woman who might look like she knew Angelina Jolie."

Bobby laughed. "They ain't talking because they ripped her off."

"Still. Take the woman's wallet, but at least tell us what you saw. Shit. That's just mean, Bobby."

It was mean. Or maybe it was something else. Maybe it was the fact that it wasn't only that fancy black woman lying dead on that property. Two other people were dead, too, and all that killing had left people with a strong case of amnesia.

"You said you questioned almost everyone who was registered there," he reminded her. "Who'd you miss?"

Iris pulled out her notes. "John Smith, a.k.a. Franklin Ross. Obviously John Smith's not bright enough to realize that it's taboo to register under an alias if you're going to pay using your own credit card."

Bobby thought for a moment. "Franklin Ross. Why does that name sound familiar?" He looked at Iris.

She shrugged. "Hadn't had a chance to check it out, but I'll do it now." She began typing in the name into her database.

"Ballistics should have some news for us later today on the caliber of the weapon used," he added while she searched the database.

"Well, I'll be damned." Iris sat back and scratched her head. "Whatdya get?"

"Franklin Ross?" She looked over the top of her screen at him. "Frank Ross, ex-cop in west Texas awaiting trial for killing another cop."

Bobby's chin dropped. "Seriously?"

She nodded. "Yeah. That's exactly what I was about to say."

Chapter 10

Every manner of celebrity and dignitary from around the world converged on Omaha, Nebraska, flying into town in private jets and pulling up at the city convention center to pay homage to Yolanda Adebayo a week after her death. Desi's breath was taken away by the sheer number of people in attendance: political leaders, musicians, actors, reporters, heads of corporations. She'd always known that Lonnie was big-time, but until now, she had no idea how big. Lonnie's family sat up front, while one prominent person after another stood at the podium to sing Lonnie's praises as a journalist and photographer.

Stunning images of Lonnie flashed around the massive room on large screens, images of Lonnie at work, behind a desk, but more often than not, out in the trenches—Sudan, Iraq, Afghanistan, even the Arctic Circle. In a matter of hours, Desi learned more about her friend than she'd learned in the nearly thirty years they'd known each other. Her heart tore in two as she soaked in the life of this woman who'd reached out to Desi when they were just girls. Desi had just been sent to prison for murdering Julian Gatewood, the man she now knew was her father, when Lonnie did the unthinkable and reached out to her in a letter.

"I live in Omaha and I saw you on the news. You looked scared. I'd be scared too . . . I don't expect for you to write me back. I just wanted you to know that there is somebody out here who is on your side no matter what . . ."

Even when the two of them didn't agree, Lonnie was on her side. Until the very end, Lonnie had her back.

Desi hadn't planned on staying at the reception for long. She felt like a fish out of water with these people, but surprisingly, there were a few of them who recognized her.

"Desi Green. Right? I read your book. Tragic, tragic story, but I'm so happy to see you've managed to get back on your feet and were able to tell your side of the story. What was it like in prison?"

"Please say you're going to open up a store in Miami! I found a pair of your shoes in a boutique in New York City . . . Oh, what was it called . . . ? You know! The little place on Forty-Seventh Street."

In one surreal moment, Desi walked over to the small urn and stared at it. In so many ways, Lonnie had saved her life and it seemed a shame that Desi couldn't have saved Lonnie's.

"It seems criminal, doesn't it? Almost sinful."

She glanced up at the tall, thin Englishman standing next to her.

"That a life as big as Lonnie's could fit in so small a jar." He looked at Desi and forced a smile.

Shit. When he summed it up like that, yeah . . . it just seemed wrong.

"You are her friend? Desi Green?"

Desi nodded. "Yes."

"I am her friend too." He held out his bony hand for Desi to shake. "Phillip. Phillip Durham."

Phillip Durham looked like he hadn't slept or eaten in days. He wore a wrinkled white shirt under a sport coat that looked as if he'd pulled it out from the trunk of his car just before the service started. Thick stubble covered his face, and dark half-moon circles nested his eyes.

"Can I buy you a cup of coffee?"

"I was just about to leave," she told him.

Suddenly tears filled his eyes, and he leaned toward her. "Please," he begged, gently cupping her elbow. "I am one of the reasons she's dead, after all."

Phillip Durham was a man with way too much money and time on his hands, and Desi listened with disgust as he explained what he meant by that statement he'd made at the memorial service.

He slumped over a cup of black coffee at a coffee shop a few blocks away.

"When I pulled her out of that hospital," he explained quietly, "she was so afraid . . . so helpless." His gaze darted across to Desi. "In all the years I'd known Lonnie, I'd never seen her like that. The Lonnie I knew was fearless, and tough, a real fighter." He made a fist. "But all she wanted to do was to get as far away from Dallas . . . and him as possible."

"Jordan," Desi murmured.

He nodded. "Lonnie Adebayo had finally met her match."

"Rape and torture will do that to a woman," she blurted out. "She wasn't superwoman. You saw what he did to her. He nearly killed her."

"Lonnie retreated inside herself," he continued as if he hadn't heard Desi. "She barely ate, slept, or even spoke for months."

He looked to Desi for a response, but she was speechless.

"She was better than that! My Lonnie was a warrior and nothing, absolutely nothing had ever terrified her like that!"

Desi was stunned. "Do you hear yourself? You sonofabitch. You selfish, self-centered asshole!"

Lonnie had no business going after Jordan but she did because of this maniac? Was that where this conversation was headed? "You talked her into getting back at him? You convinced her that going after the man who damn near killed her was a good idea?"

His face flushed red as he averted his gaze back to the cup in front of him. "She'd lost her fire," he muttered.

"She damn near lost her life," Desi growled, leaning toward him. "Jordan is evil! He's a fuckin' demon in an Armani suit and you set her loose on him? My God, Phillip! You don't know shit!" She struggled to keep her voice down. "You had no idea of the kind of man he was or what he was capable of and you set her up to confront him?"

"I promised I'd help her! I was there for—"

"Yeah and now Lonnie's dead." Tears flooded her eyes. Jesus! Desi felt overwhelmed with emotion and a very real conclusion came to her. "If you'd left her alone . . ."

"And if you'd had the courage to fight your own battles . . ." he said, unblinking.

An icy silence rushed past the two of them. Did he really just go there? Desi was stunned.

"Lonnie's fight with Jordan should've never been hers," he continued boldly. "Some part of me believes that if she hadn't stepped in on your behalf, she'd still be alive today, but she's dead now because that's exactly what she did."

He might as well have thrown that ceramic coffee cup at her head. Desi swallowed. "She's dead because she fucked Jordan and he got pissed when he found out that she knew me."

"Exactly!" he said, quickly reeling in his emotions. "And I pushed her to go too far." His voice cracked. "But this fight was never hers, Desi. It was always yours, and you let her step out in front of you and take that bullet."

Was he wrong? Was he out of line? No. "You're not telling me anything I don't already know," she murmured.

Desi had been a coward her whole life. She'd let the Gatewoods railroad her on murder charges. She'd let them walk all over her and everything that had ever mattered to her in her life, for longer than she could remember. Her answer—take their money. Write a book and after more than twenty-five years, tell her side of the story, but what did it matter? Lonnie had provided the fuel she'd needed to fill the pages of that book. Lonnie had investigated the judge, the jury, even the Gatewoods, and uncovered every dirty detail, putting her ass on the line for Desi's cause. Not a day had gone by that Desi didn't feel guilty about it. Not a day had gone by that Desi didn't feel afraid to push the boundaries even further than Lonnie had already done.

"It wasn't my intent to place blame," he said sullenly.

"You're right," she muttered. "I'm to blame as much as anyone."

"Between the two of us"—Phillip cleared his throat—"Lonnie never stood a chance."

"So, you wanted to tell me how shitty I should feel. Is that why you asked me here?"

"She left you with ammunition, Desi, and an obligation."

Desi stared tearfully at him. She knew where this was going, and she knew that it was past time for it to go there.

"You're a Gatewood," he continued. "You have the name Jordan wished he'd been born with. And you have a huge financial stake in your father's corporation, Gatewood Industries."

She looked surprised. "Lonnie told you all this?"

"I helped her to uncover the truth that Julian was your father. The rest was easy enough to come by." He smiled.

"I have a name, but no claim to it. And I own some stocks." She shrugged. "I'd love to kick Jordan in the ass, but honestly . . ." Desi's enthusiasm deflated. "I don't know how."

"I do."

She stared at him. Phillip Durham was crazy and he'd talked Lonnie into doing some crazy shit. Desi doubted that he had anything of value to offer, but she decided to ask anyway.

"Tell me," she said.

If he did have some answers then she needed them before she got back on that plane to Dallas.

"It's simple, Desi," he said earnestly. "You go back to the beginning, back to where it all started."

She had no idea what he meant by that.

Phillip continued. "This war with the Gatewoods started long before you and Jordan ever laid eyes on each other. It began long before Lonnie ever made love to him."

Either his crazy was contagious or the implications of what he was saying were starting to come together.

"Are you talking about—"

"I'm talking about the love triangle between your mother, Julian Gatewood, and his wife, Olivia."

She stared skeptically at him. "Now you're reaching."

"Back to the past, yes, but that's where the answer lies, Desi. Who is the one common denominator in every terrible thing that's ever happened to you in your life?"

One name immediately came to mind. "Olivia."

"Going after Jordan has never been the answer, and had I seen it sooner maybe Lonnie would still be alive." He choked up. "If you want him, you have to get her."

"But I thought he'd had her put in a home somewhere. I'd heard she was crazy."

"As a fox!" His blue eyes sparkled. "She's a brilliant strategist. History shows that. Olivia took a poor man's son, erased the boy's name, and gave him a new one—a rich man's name. It's the best-kept secret in the country and she's held on tight to it for close to fifty years!" He said it almost as if he admired the woman. "She killed her husband right in front of his mistress and her child, and sent you to prison for the murder, Desi. And she got away with it! Shakespeare would've had a field day with a story based on this woman's life, and now she's one of the wealthiest women in the world because of this merger."

Desi thought about all that he'd said. Olivia Gatewood had always seemed larger than life to Desi. Even the night when she stormed into their home, pulled that gun and pointed it at Desi's mother, the woman seemed like a beautiful ghost, and for years, Desi had almost believed that she'd imagined her. All of a sudden, Jordan didn't seem so big and bad—not compared to his mother.

"You're her husband's love child, Desi," Phillip continued. "And now, a major shareholder in her company. You are everything she hates and we only hate what we're afraid of."

Desi met his gaze with her own. "You think that woman's afraid of me?" She swallowed.

He nodded. "More than even she knows." Phillip reached across the table and took hold of Desi's hand. "To take out the puppet you have to take out the puppet master," he explained, smiling. "It really is that simple."

He was an idiot if he really thought that anything about Olivia Gatewood was simple.

"What it comes down to is you against a little old lady." He forced a crooked and vulnerable smile. "I'm betting on you."

"Why?" she asked, perplexed.

"Because Lonnie would have."

Chapter 11

DESI GREEN—
Gatewood Industries Newest Shareholder

How does the woman convicted of murdering Julian Gatewood become a major shareholder in his company? Let this reporter count the ways.

First, she's got to somehow avoid being sentenced to the death penalty for shooting one of the oil business's biggest trailblazing icons. Next, she's got to survive a twenty-five-year stint in one of Texas's most notorious prisons. Upon her release, she's got to inherit more than twenty million dollars from her mother's estate, by way of Mr. Gatewood himself (her mother's lover and the same man she was sentenced to prison for killing). Shortly after her receiving her inheritance, she's got to write a

New York Times bestselling memoir, call it *Beautiful, Dirty, Rich,* and expose a conspiracy theory behind her conviction so ripe with controversy that Hollywood is ready to start World War III in a bidding war for the movie rights. And finally, she's got to buy up nearly a third of the remaining stock in a failing oil company being eyed for hostile takeover by none other than Gatewood Industries, thereby sneaking in the back door, so to speak, and becoming one of Gatewood Industries' biggest share-holders. I couldn't make this stuff up if I tried, folks.

"Tell me you saw this?"

Olivia tossed the newspaper down on the coffee table, as if touching it dirtied her hands.

Edgar Beckman sat across from her. "I did."

"How the hell did that happen, Edgar?" Her light-brown eyes blinked back heated tears. "How could he let that happen?"

Olivia's children had betrayed her. Nearly a week ago, June had come here gloating over the news that Desi Green had bought into Gatewood Industries. Olivia didn't want to believe that girl's lies, but her calls to Jordan had gone unanswered. Edgar was her only true friend, and she'd called, asking him to come in the hopes that he could shed light on this catastrophe.

"My nerves are frayed," she said, smoothing her hair. "I feel myself unraveling, Edgar, and it shouldn't be this way." A tear escaped down her cheek. "Jordan is supposed to be the gatekeeper for this company. Either he doesn't care as much about it as he says he does, or he's no longer up to the task." She looked at him, searching for some sign in his expression that perhaps she was right.

Edgar's stoic expression gave nothing away.

"Why would she do this?" she murmured, knowing the answer was already there, deep inside her soul. Olivia blinked. "To get back at me? To punish me?" she asked weakly.

Edgar took a deep breath. "She's the only one who knows the answer to that question, Olivia," he said wearily.

"Why would he let her?" she barked. "How could he not know, Edgar? Was he so anxious to take over that damn oil company that he was blind to everything else? Did he not care? Did he not see this glaring atrocity sitting right in front of his face?"

"I don't know, Olivia," he shot back tensely. "I'm not your son's keeper. I don't know what he was thinking!"

"Desi Green is making us look like fools! The reporter in this article all but says it. She's turning our name into a mockery, and I won't have it!"

"What can you do about it, Olivia?" he shot back, flushing red. "What the hell can anybody do about it?"

A chill washed over her body. "Surely you're not that naïve," she said coolly. "She's been a tick under my collar ever since she got out of prison."

"You made that possible, my friend."

Olivia took offense at his tone, but not at his comment. Edgar was right. She'd made sure that the judge presiding over Desi's murder trial didn't hand down the death penalty to that child. Back then, that's what she was. Desi was all of eighteen, just a girl, frightened and helpless. It had never been Olivia's intention to make that girl suffer, only Ida Green, and of course, Julian. Guilt gnawed on Olivia's conscience during that trial. Yes, she'd shot her husband, but Ida was the one she had aimed for. Julian died protecting Ida, and in that moment Olivia condemned that woman in the worst way possible. She placed that gun in the hands of Ida Green's child and called the police. Olivia was never quite clear on how the details of that production came together. She was the grieving widow. Lawyers spoke on her behalf for the most part, but it was she who told that judge not to put that girl in the chair.

"*She's a child,*" she'd told him. "*Children shouldn't have to die like that. She won't die like that.*"

"The biggest mistake I ever made was killing my husband." It was the first time she'd ever said that to anyone. "The second biggest mistake was not making sure that she got the death penalty for his murder when she was convicted."

He leaned his heavy frame in her direction. "If she dies now, Olivia, why she died will be as plain as the nose on my face," he explained earnestly. "If anything happens to that woman that doesn't come by way of natural causes or—hell, a plane falling out of the sky—the whole world is going to look to the Gatewoods as being responsible."

He was right. Olivia felt helpless because Edgar was so right.

She swallowed. "So, what should we do?" she asked humbly. Edgar was the voice of reason. Even before Julian's death, he had been the one who she trusted with her well-being more than anyone.

"For now, nothing." He shrugged. "We ride it out. We keep our heads down, ignore the media—don't even make a statement, short of acknowledging that Desi Green is indeed a stakeholder in Gatewood Industries. But let's not glorify an undignified situation. At the end of the day, all money is green, even hers."

Olivia clenched her teeth. "Her money is mine! Julian gave that whore Gatewood money!" she snapped, referring to Ida Green.

"Then consider this," he said calmly. "Her Gatewood money is back where it belongs—in Gatewood Industries."

She looked surprised to hear him say that, but a sense of something akin to revelation and even relief began to settle on her. "That's the most enlightened thing you've said since I've known you, Edgar."

He sighed. "It's simply the truth, Olivia."

He was right. Desi had brought Olivia's money, with interest, back into the fold. Now the trick would be figuring out a way to get it out of her control. But how?

"When was the last time you spoke to my son?" she asked.

Edgar shrugged. "It's been a while."

"I feel he's been distracted, aloof, and maybe even secretive."

The man showed no emotion, but Olivia's instincts were better than people knew. Edgar was being coy.

"I'm beginning to question whether or not Jordan still belongs at the helm of this ship, Edgar."

"Because of this slipup with Desi Green?"

"It's bigger than a slip, my friend. He's avoiding his mother and it's my power of attorney that's put him in the position that he clings so passionately to."

"Jordan's made some mistakes, Olivia, but I hardly think that you should be questioning his leadership over this. Look at how he's grown this company."

"His sister helped."

"June?" Edgar laughed. "She helped with the merger, yes, but before that she was hiding out in Atlanta somewhere nursing a piss-poor marriage. I hardly think you can compare the two." He waited for a response. "You're not really thinking of replacing Jordan with June, are you?" he asked, stunned.

Olivia smiled. "I'm thinking of giving my son a wake-up call, of reminding him who the real head of Gatewood Industries and this family is."

Jordan had forced Olivia into this retirement community and placed her under a doctor's care for her protection. That's what he told her. Desi Green's accusations in her book that Olivia had pulled the trigger and shot Julian had made Olivia's son nervous, and he said that sending her here was the only way he could keep the police from reopening the investigation of her husband's murder.

"He's put me here and forgotten about me, Edgar," she said impassively. "I'm not a threat to anyone here, especially to him."

"He put you in this situation to protect his mother," Edgar emphasized.

She was no fool. Olivia had foolish moments. She had moments when she lost track of time, but when her mind was clear, it was crystal clear.

"I think it's time for me to go home, Edgar. I think I've rested long enough."

Chapter 12

"Señor Gatewood! Señor . . . You can't . . . Señor Beckman is not . . . Señor Gatewood! No!"

Edgar Beckman pushed his fat ass up off that couch as fast as he could when he saw Jordan Gatewood charging toward him.

"What the hell are you doing in my goddamned house?" he growled.

Rage had consumed Jordan and before he realized it, he had a handful of Beckman's collar and had palmed the back of the man's head like a basketball. Edgar was too old and too stunned to fight him, and his body struck a pose as rigid as a tree trunk in Jordan's grasp.

Edgar's housekeeper screamed at Jordan in Spanish and fought with all of her strength to get him to release his hold on Beckman.

"Seven days!" Jordan spat in Beckman's face. "You've been dodging my ass for seven motha fuckin' days, you sonofabitch!"

"I'm calling the police!" the housekeeper yelled, running from the room.

Beckman's eyes bulged from his skull. "Amelia!" he shouted to her. "Get your hands off me," he commanded, peeling Jordan's fingers from the collar of his shirt.

Jordan gradually began to release his grip.

"Amelia." Beckman swallowed. "Take the rest of the day off."

Amelia spoke frantically in Spanish.

"Just . . . go," he said more calmly. He took a step back from Jordan's towering frame and glanced up at him. "I'll be fine."

The woman nodded apprehensively, and then finally turned to leave. The two men stared each other down until the sound of the door closing signaled that the woman had left.

"Seven goddamned days!" Jordan said, gritting his teeth and glaring at Beckman. That's how long it had been since the night Claire shot and killed Lonnie. That's how long it had been since Jordan made that call to Beckman. "I've called. I left messages. And I called again! You picked a fine time to fall off the face of the earth, Edgar!"

The old man took his sweet time making his way over to the bar to pour himself a drink. Jordan inhaled deeply, forcing himself to calm the hell down. He'd gotten Claire out of the country, but he'd been damn near drowning in the formalities of getting this merger with Anton closed out. Jordan wasn't CEO of one larger corporation. He was the CEO of two big-ass corporations with very different corporate cultures, systems, and politics, and the stress of bringing the two together in the midst of a woman's murder was like dragging this whole damn state of Texas up the side of a mountain.

He paced back and forth as Edgar poured that drink down his throat, taking a long, slow exhale before finally feeling calm enough to hold a rational conversation with Beckman.

"Want one?" Beckman offered, filling two glasses this time. The man visibly trembled.

"Why the hell have you been avoiding me, Edgar?" Jordan asked, openly perplexed by Edgar's behavior. "I have been living on the precipice of disaster, man, waiting for a knock at the door to my home, or for the police to come storming into my office, ready to handcuff me and haul my ass off to prison!" He walked over to Edgar. "With everything that's going on, now is not the time to turn your back on me. I need to know what happened after Claire and I left that motel. I need to know if—if you took care of it. Do the police know we were there?"

"You're standing in my living room talking to me, Jordan," Edgar said wearily. "If the police knew you were there that night, do you think I'd be offering you a cocktail?" He raised his glass in a mock toast.

"Your flippancy is unsolicited," Jordan said coolly.

"In lieu of the fact that a woman's dead because of you, and my friend and I covered your ass—again—I don't give a damn about your solicitation."

"Careful, old man," Jordan warned.

"Or what?" Edgar shot back, glaring at Jordan and laughing. "I'm not the one who killed that bitch! I'm not the one worried about the police showing up at my door ready to put handcuffs on me! What do I have to be careful about?"

Edgar had always been the one person he could count on since he had taken over Gatewood Industries. Even before that, Edgar was the one who came to all of Jordan's football games, talked to him about girls, even taught him how to drive and how to shoot. "I'll always be there for you, boy," he'd told Jordan back when Jordan was feeling particularly dejected because of Julian. When did that change?

The amused expression faded from Edgar's face. "He may not be your daddy biologically, but I swear to God you're just like him," he said dismally, shaking his head. "Led by your dick instead of your head. You had a woman at home! A woman who loved you! Cared about you! Would do any damn thing you wanted her to do for you! You took her for granted, son. How long did you think she'd let you get away with it? How long did you think she was going to let you keep humiliating her like that?"

"Who're you talking about, Edgar?" Jordan asked, studying the man. Of course. All of a sudden, it was obvious. "Are you talking about Claire?" Jordan stepped toward him. "Or are you talking about my mother?"

Edgar nodded erratically. "You see the similarities too?" he asked, wild eyed. "You see it, don't you? Olivia loved Julian in ways that weren't natural. I couldn't understand it. Why did she put up with it as long as she did? She knew about that woman. Julian rubbed her face in his affair, and still she remained devoted to him. She's still devoted to him."

"Of course I've seen it." Jordan finally spoke up. He'd lost his mind over Lonnie, and Claire had lost her mind over Jordan. "Is it any wonder that somebody ended up dead?"

Suddenly, Beckman slammed the glass down so hard on the marble bar that the glass shattered in his hand. "I'm through with you, boy!" Edgar turned a violent shade of red.

Jordan raised a brow. "You're through with me? What the hell is that supposed to mean? You promised you'd always be there for me, Edgar." He felt the need to explain, because, surely, Edgar had lost sight of the bigger picture. "There's no one else I trust more than you. There's no one else who's got my back the way you do."

"What the fuck else do you want from me?" Blood gushed

from his palm. "You fucked up, Jordan! You call me and just like I always do, I came and cleaned up behind your shitty ass!"

"And my shitty ass appreciates it. Believe me." Jordan knew Edgar's secrets too. The last thing he'd ever felt the need to do was to remind his friend of those secrets, but a gentle reminder couldn't hurt. "None of us is perfect," he continued, treading carefully. "Between the two of us, Edgar, we've got a lot of regrets."

Edgar's expression darkened. "Sure we do. But I'm an old man, Jordan. And I'm dying."

He was right. Edgar was old and he was dying. That wasn't news.

"I've got cancer, Jordan. Terminal." Edgar shrugged. "So you see, I have the advantage of not having to live with my regrets too much longer." Edgar tilted his glass in Jordan's direction. "You, on the other hand, are still a young man." He laughed. "And as far as I'm concerned, you can take both our regrets and shove them up your ass. I'm through."

The words "cancer" and "terminal" hung heavy in the air between the two men. All color washed from Edgar's face.

"How long?" Jordan asked reluctantly.

Edgar shrugged. "Too damn long if you ask me," he grunted. "If I was smart, I'd put a bullet in my head and get this shit over with."

Jordan reached for his drink and took a sip. "Tell me what happened after I called you."

Edgar huffed. "What difference does it make? You're still walking around free. You asked me to take care of it." He shrugged. "I did."

"How?"

"I covered your tracks, son," Edgar retorted. "I covered your ass! That's it."

"How?" Jordan demanded.

"I made a call, and the person I called made a call," he explained impatiently. "There's nothing to tie you to that place with that woman that night, Jordan. Is that what you want to hear? You weren't there."

He didn't go into details and Jordan didn't push for them. Edgar's conviction spoke for itself.

The old man squinted. "This is the last favor I'm doing for you, Jordan," he warned. "I told you before, I'm getting too old for this shit, and by now, you should know how to wipe your own ass, son. Don't call me again. You understand me?"

Jordan finished his drink and set his glass down on the bar before turning to leave. "I didn't kill Lonnie, Edgar. I'm not the one who pulled the trigger."

Edgar nodded. "There are triggers and there are triggers, Jordan, even some that aren't on guns. Breathe easy, son," he continued. "Your life will go on as it always has, despite the circumstances of something as silly as the truth."

Chapter 13

Solomon slowly rounded the turn in his white Bentley GT leading to the main gate of the community where he lived. A uniformed police officer standing in the middle of the street motioned for him to stop.

Hordes of reporters, camera crews, and vans crowded around the gates leading into his community.

The officer leaned down to the window. "Are you a resident here, sir?"

"Yes." Solomon pushed a button on the steering wheel, and the main gate slowly began to open.

"Thank you, sir," the officer said, allowing him to pass.

"Hey, baby." Desi greeted him at the door in her bare feet, wearing a pair of cutoff jean shorts, a white tank top, her thick tresses pulled back into a bushy ponytail. She looked like a college student instead of a fortysomething-year-old magnet for scandal.

He wasn't happy. Solomon made sure to let her know that he wasn't happy.

She forced a smile and rose up onto her toes to try and kiss him. He brushed past her, loosened his tie, and walked down the long foyer to the stairs.

"They followed me home, Solomon!" she called after him. "I went to the store and they followed me . . ."

He closed the bedroom door behind him, undressed, and climbed into the shower. This was not going to work. In his line of work, Solomon wasn't intimidated by the media. His list of clientele often required him to engage reporters. Solomon had given more interviews on a national and even international level than he could count. But this . . . this was different. This was personal. This was unacceptable, putting him and his family in harm's way.

Desi was waiting in the kitchen for him when he got out of the shower. "I cooked," she said, standing at the table over what was supposed to have been his meal. He could count on one hand how many times that woman had actually cooked for him.

Word of Desi's investment was blowing up the airwaves, the Internet, Twitter, and Facebook. Solomon had spent the day at his office trying to ignore the stares and whispers from his colleagues. Even one of his clients, Ryan Wood, one of the NBA's rising stars, had sent him an e-mail.

Whoa, man! What's up wit yo girl? Daaaaaaayuuuummm!

"We need to talk about this," she said nervously, pulling out his chair for him.

"All I could think about was my kid, Des," he finally said. Solomon's eighteen-year-old daughter was a freshman at UCLA. She'd called him this morning.

"Daddy? I don't get this. What does it mean? I mean, is this even legal? Can Desi do that? It's all over the news. People keep asking me weird questions. I don't—I don't know what to tell them."

"Tell them to stop asking you weird questions," he told her, and before hanging up, he reassured her that Desi hadn't broken the law and that he had no idea what it all meant.

Sonya was not a big fan of Desi's. She'd made it a point not to spend too much time around his fiancée. Her mother, Tracy, had a lot to do with that. Sonya's mom knew of Desi Green, the felon. And she was not happy with the idea of her daughter being around a convict.

"She was set up, Tracy," he'd argued. "Desi was a kid at the time. She didn't do it, and she would never hurt Sonya. I would never let anyone hurt my daughter."

"You say she's innocent. She says she's innocent, but the court said otherwise, Solomon," the woman argued. "I trust you, but I don't trust her and I never will."

"Did you think about that, Des?" he asked. "Did you think about me and how this would affect me? Did you think about Sonya? My clients? Did it even matter?"

Desi had gone into this mess dragging everybody else along with her. Not only was she on the radar from the media and the Gatewoods, but so was he. So were the people in his life.

She shrugged. "I guess not," she admitted. "I didn't think this through at all, Solomon."

This was bigger than Dallas, Texas. It was bigger than the state of Texas. This shit had gone viral.

"What did you expect, Desi? You, being who you are now, and this merger turning the Gatewoods into . . ." Hell! That corporation had tripled in size, literally overnight, and was the hottest commodity on the stock exchange now. That, in and of itself was news, but Desi buying into it, reportedly for pennies on the dollar—of course it was larger-than-life news.

"I'm sorry," she said. "I didn't mean to—"

"Because you still believe it's just you," he told her.

She'd spent most of her life living in the bubble that contained just her. Desi learned at a young age to cut herself off from everybody, including her own mother, which was why, when Ida Green passed away and the warden offered to let Desi attend the funeral, she refused.

"It's not just you anymore, baby," Solomon said. "What you do affects me, and vice versa. We're together, and when two people are together, then each of them has to take the other into account before they make decisions."

"So—what do you want me to do?" she asked, frustrated.

He shook his head. "No. No, don't you even go there. Don't you get pissed at me. This is your doing, Des. Not mine."

"What have I done that's so wrong, Solomon?"

He couldn't believe she'd asked that dumb question. "According to you, Jordan Gatewood is a killer?" he blurted out. "According to you, the man's capable of anything, hell, his whole family are gangsters, capable of getting away with murder and you ask me what you've done wrong?" He took a step toward her. "If they're so damn dangerous then why mess with them, Des? Why fuck around with the Gatewoods or that holy grail of theirs, which is that damn corporation, if you think those people are the monsters you say they are?"

The Gatewoods were either pit bulls or shih tzus. If they were pit bulls, then what the hell made her believe she could take them on by herself? Or maybe they weren't so badass.

"You think I've made it all up?" she said, raising her chin in defiance. "You think I lied about Olivia—about Jordan?"

"I don't know anymore. But I don't think you're as afraid of those people as you claim to be. And that's got me wondering. If I were you, I'd want to get and stay as far away from their asses or anything to do with them as I could, because, according to you, doing anything else would be like putting a gun to your own head. Making a move like this could cost you your life, Desi, and maybe it could cost me my life. I don't know. But why play with fire if you don't want to get burned? Unless . . . it's really not that hot."

"What do you expect me to do?" she yelled. "Sell my shares?"

Finally! She'd said something that actually made sense.

"Yes! Sell your shares, Desi. Sell every last one of them so that you and I can move forward with our lives!"

"I can't move on until this is over," she admitted.

It didn't take a genius to figure out what she was really saying. Solomon gathered his hurt feelings and tucked them away behind his pride. "Then I guess I was wrong. I thought what we had meant as much to you as it does to me. I made a mistake."

"You believe what you want to believe, Solomon."

There she was. The real Desi. The ice-cold one. The queen of detachment. He'd been wondering when she was going to show up.

"Those people took everything from me. They took my father, whether he was mine by blood or not doesn't matter, because I loved him like he was. They took me from my mother, and ultimately, they took her from me. They took me from my freedom, and finally, they took my best friend. But they made the mistake of leaving me my life, at least for now." Desi swallowed. "Maybe they will kill me. But I'm tired of running and I'm tired as hell of them being able to bounce me around like a ball and not doing anything about it. They have trespassed on me for the last time. By the time the dust settles only one of us might be standing but they're going to know that I was here and that I was in this fight."

"And what I think doesn't mean shit?"

"What you think means everything. But it won't change anything. Not now. It's too late. I'm in it. I'll either win or lose, but if I back down now, then they'll always know that they beat me. They've known that for too long. I can't live with that. Not anymore."

Solomon didn't eat the dinner she'd prepared for him. And he didn't stop her from packing up her things and leaving. Desi had made her choice. And it wasn't him.

Chapter 14

Why was it so much easier to be alone than to be with someone? Desi left Solomon's place and had been staying in the Four Seasons Hotel for a second night. She knew he didn't understand, but the argument the two of them had had really showed her how far removed they were from each other. And now she was losing him because of it. He wasn't a soldier in this war, and she was a fool for still fighting it at all. Desi had no idea what she was doing. She was clueless as to how she planned to get even with the Gatewoods for all that they'd taken from her life. And when it was all said and done, deep down, Desi knew that it wasn't going to end well for her.

Lonnie would've had a plan. Desi closed her eyes and imagined some of the things Lonnie might say if she were here now.

"You've got a shitload of ammo, girl. Think about it, Des. You've got the name, Gatewood, and the blood flowing through your veins. Jordan's

got a fake piece of paper. He's a puppet and his momma is pulling the strings."

She had a certified and sealed copy of a birth certificate that listed Julian Gatewood as her father. But her father was dead. She had proof that Jordan Gatewood was not who the world believed he was. But he'd use every resource he had to discredit her claims and he had his mother watching over him like always, who'd no doubt pull out all the stops to make Desi look like a lying convicted felon. Desi had money, and she had Gatewood stocks—but so what? She wasn't a board member. She didn't own controlling stocks, and other than the temporary scandal and uproar the news had caused in the media, after all the hoopla passed, she'd be just another stockholder. She had a whole lot of nothing and no idea what to do with it. And, she was alone.

Desi shook her head frantically back and forth. "Stop it!" she commanded herself. "You're not going to do this now," she muttered.

She wasn't going to allow herself the luxury of crawling back into the hole of self pity and worthlessness simply because it was the thing she'd always done. It was easier to feel like the victim and to run and hide. Desi had to think. There was so much to do, and she had no idea where to start or how. But that nagging grind in her gut wouldn't let her walk away this time. Jordan had murdered her friend. Olivia had murdered Desi's father, Julian, and in a roundabout way, she'd killed Desi's mother, Ida. Desi was alive for a reason. She had a purpose and if that purpose was to finally make those people pay for all their transgressions against those she'd loved most, then she had no choice but to see this through to whatever end it came to.

Her phone rang. Desi looked at it and saw Solomon's name. Leaving his house had been the best gift she could've possibly given him. Those reporters that had been camped out at his place were now camped outside the Four Seasons, waiting to get a glimpse of her and some kind of statement. Desi had made reservations to fly back to California the day after tomorrow. As usual, Texas had been a big, old, ugly bust.

After several rings, she finally answered it. "Hi," she said softly.

"I want to see you," he said.

"Okay," she reluctantly answered. "When?"

"Now. I'm downstairs in the lobby."

Solomon meant well. He was worried about her. And in her heart, she knew that his was the voice of reason. He wanted her to walk away from any fight she might be thinking of taking on with the Gatewoods. But she'd passed some invisible point of no return and Desi felt as if she was stuck somewhere in the middle of hell and high water. She couldn't go backward, and she had no idea how to move forward either.

"I know how you feel, Solomon. I just—I don't want to make any trouble for you or Sonya."

"Let me come up. Please."

Desi was staying in one of the penthouse suites. Solomon took the elevator that opened up directly inside the living room. He looked like he hadn't shaved since she'd last seen him. He wore his favorite dingy Earth, Wind, and Fire tee shirt, faded, baggy jeans, and sneakers. He'd even brought his laptop carried in a backpack slung over his shoulder.

He paused as the door closed behind him and sighed at the sight of her. He was such a beautiful man, and she hated putting him through this. Desi wished she was a different kind of woman, the kind that made his life easy, who could make him happy all the damn time, never dragging home any drama or reporters. She wished she could be that woman who baked, looked good in a bikini, and loved playing tennis as much as he did. Desi wished she liked golf.

Solomon walked over to her. He stopped and stood close.

"I'm so sorry I can't be who you want me to be, Solo—"

He bent and kissed her.

Lord have mercy! He tasted good! What was this? Her mind raced. Was this an apology? He had nothing to apologize for. She was the one who needed to . . .

He pulled his lips from hers, looked into her eyes, and whispered, "I can't sleep without you next to me."

Desi surprised herself and laughed. "I thought you were mad at me."

He sighed. "I am mad at you. But I need you." He slipped his backpack off his shoulder and set it on the coffee table. "I have a feeling that's never going to change, and I'm mad about that too."

He wasn't the only one caught in that trap. The thought of living without him soured inside her. "I really don't know what to do," she finally said.

Solomon took both of her hands in his, kissed them, and then led the way to the bedroom.

He was a fighter. Solomon had spent years training as a boxer and in the martial arts. His body conveyed his dedication to the sports he loved. She loved his long, lean, muscular frame and he always seemed to be fascinated by her lack of muscles. Desi wasn't fat, but she was allergic to the gym. It made her break out in a sweat.

He missed her. In just two days, he missed her, and it showed in the way he touched her, pulling her as close to him as he could. Solomon cupped her behind in his hand and nuzzled his face in the crook of her neck, taking long, slow breaths, inhaling her. She craved his dick inside her, but he refused, taking his time to savor other things about her, strange things, like the scent of her hair, the flavor of her mouth, the hardening of her nipples on the heels of his palms.

Solomon sat up on his knees while Desi lay on her back, spread her thighs, and pulled her to him until the lips of her pussy grazed his rigid cock standing up at attention. Solomon leaned forward until she thought he'd kiss her. She opened her mouth expecting his to mate with hers, but he kissed her forehead, the tip of her nose, her chin. He moaned low in the back of his throat as he trailed down her torso, grazing her skin with his nose, inhaling.

Solomon's tongue found her nipple and flicked against it until it swelled and threatened to burst in his mouth. He slipped his fingers inside the folds of her pussy, starting with the tips, massaging around the opening while Desi moaned and squirmed, thrusting her hips forward for more of him.

"Solomon," she moaned, almost pleading.

He drove his fingers inside her, pushing as far as he could. Desi bucked against his hand. As good as it felt, that's not what she wanted.

"I want you," she whispered, cupping his face with her hands to look into his eyes.

"You have me, sweetheart," he said, smiling. "I thought you knew that."

He pulled his fingers from inside her, opened his mouth, and licked her essence from them. Then, without warning, Solomon drove the length of his shaft inside her, and lowered his body down on top of her until the two of them were one unit. Desi closed her eyes and wrapped both arms around him. She wasn't alone. It was so hard to believe sometimes, and maybe she did things on purpose to push him away because being alone was easy. But loving someone like this, needing someone like this, took her breath away. It scared the hell out of her. And it made her happier than she ever thought possible.

He didn't move. Solomon lay on top of her, and held himself there, mating with her as if he were staking a claim, branding her, making sure that he left his scent on her, and that hers soaked into him. Desi felt the walls of her vagina begin to contract uncontrollably.

He moaned. "Don't."

Desi bucked into him. "I can't . . . I can't . . ."

Was she coming? Was he?

Chapter 15

Frank sat in the interrogation room across from one of the officers he used to work with.

"When'd you make detective, Floyd?" he asked. Back when Frank worked for the department, the two of them had been friends. Every now and then they'd catch a game of pool after work, throw back a few beers and a couple of pounds of hot wings, talk about work and women. Now, Floyd could barely even look at him.

"Few months back," he responded indifferently.

Frank had been sitting in this room for nearly an hour before Floyd showed up.

"Do you know why you're here, Frank?"

Frank knew, but he shook his head and played dumb. "Nah, man. I got a knock at the door and a couple of uniforms showed up and hauled me down here to ask me some questions."

Floyd took a long, deep breath before starting to explain. "The

Dallas Police Department contacted us with some questions about you."

Frank's heart sank into his stomach, but the last thing he needed to do was to let these fools see him sweat. Floyd wasn't the only one watching. He knew for a fact that they were watching him on the other side of that door.

"The Dallas PD?" He feigned surprise. "About what?"

Floyd flipped open a folder on the table in front of him. "The Fairmont Motel." He looked across to Frank. "Ever heard of it?"

Frank shrugged and shook his head. He laced his fingers together and rested his hands on top of the table. His palms were sweating rivers. He had to be careful. He had to be convincing, because his ass was on the line all over again. "I mean, I don't know. Why?"

Floyd chose to ignore the question. "Do you know a woman named Yolanda Adebayo?" Floyd stared at Frank, looking for a twitch, an indication that he was hiding something.

Frank had never considered himself an actor, but right here, right now, his life depended on him being able to act his ass off. "Doesn't ring a bell," he said thoughtfully. But then, just as coolly, he flipped the script on his buddy Floyd. "Oh, wait! That's the woman on the news." He acted out his revelation. "That reporter woman they found dead in . . ." Frank's eyes widened. He leaned back and looked disgusted. "Y'all think I had something to do with that? Really, Floyd? Is that what this is about?"

"Your credit card turned up in the motel registry, Frank," he explained, emotionless. "Seems it was used to pay for one of the rooms. A room registered to a John Smith."

Frank feigned frustration. "So, tell me this, man. When the hell did I have a chance to sneak off to Dallas with y'all motha fuckas sitting parked outside my door twenty-four/seven?"

"Nobody said you went to Dallas, Frank. I just want to know why your card would be on file."

Frank didn't know what to think. Floyd was playing it too damn cool and wasn't giving him nothing. Of course he believed Frank had something to do with that woman's murder. But right now, all he had was a credit card. Jordan's advice was paying off. For the second time, he'd saved Frank's ass. But just like before, Frank didn't know if that was a good thing, or something he'd come to regret down the road. But for now, he'd play that hand, at least long enough for him to get the hell out of this place.

"I reported my card stolen, Floyd," he finally said, locking gazes with the man. "I called the bank—shit—a few days ago and told them I'd lost it, or that it was stolen," he said calmly. He couldn't help noticing the gradual deflation of the man, as all the fight started to leave his body.

Floyd wrote something in the file.

"You can call the bank if you want to. I got my new card this morning and the number's on the back." He started to reach for his wallet. Frank handed the new card to the man. It still had that big-ass sticker on the front with an 800 number for him to call to activate it.

Floyd jotted down the number and handed it back to Frank.

Something in him felt compelled to plead his case. "I haven't left the city, Floyd, and with this trial hanging over my head—well, I'm not trying to do anything to fuck up my life even more. I didn't do whatever you think I might have done." This time he wasn't talking to a police detective. He was talking to the man who used to be his friend.

They weren't always watching him. There was usually a fifteen-minute window between the time one asshole left and another showed up, and this time, despite every instinct in him telling him to stay put, Frank took advantage of that small window of opportunity. Call it panic. Call it stupidity. It didn't matter what you called it, Frank had to get his ass out of town. Hell, he had to get out of the state, and eventually, out of the country if that was even possible. This whole damn town was closing in on him, and with Lonnie's death hovering over his head, he felt like he was in a pressure cooker. He'd missed the chance before when Colette had begged him to run away with her. Frank had been a fool thinking that shit with killing those cops would blow over. He knew better than that. Murder didn't just blow over. Karma wouldn't let it.

Frank had ditched his car, and talked a friend of his, Warren Mitchell, an old cat in his sixties, into letting him take his car, which hadn't been started in five years. They had to use Frank's car to give it a jump, and miraculously the piece of shit started. Four hours later he'd pulled up in front of his father's house. It was after midnight and thankfully, Joel had let him sleep. The old man even made him some bacon and eggs in the morning and poured him a cup of coffee before he finally asked the question.

"Why are you here, son?"

Frank shoved the last piece of bacon in his mouth, which gave him time to figure out how to answer that question. Joel was patient and waited.

Shit! The truth was the only answer he had to give. "The police are after me." He glanced nervously at Joel sitting across from him. "They think I killed a man. And they might think I had something to do with somebody else's being killed too." There. He'd said it. He'd blurted out every word of the truth.

Joel just looked at him and sighed. "Well? Did you?"

He wished to God he could say no, that the police had it all wrong, and it was a case of mistaken identity. But the conviction of that old man's eyes wouldn't let him. "Yeah."

Frank knew of his brothers, Malcolm and Woody, but he'd never known them. By the way they acted when they walked into that house later that morning, they knew of him too. This wasn't what he wanted. Frank hadn't asked to be dragged into an inquisition of men he didn't even know, judging him while Joel coaxed his story from him. This wasn't how he'd ever planned on getting to know his so-called family. Frank was an outsider, and he felt like it. And none of them had any intention of making him feel any other way.

"Why the hell did you bring your ass here, man?" Malcolm Tunson stood across the room looking at Frank like he was a damn alien. Malcolm was younger than Woody, and he was the more unforgiving too. Woody was born after Jordan, who was older than all of them, but that shit didn't matter.

They'd grunted, cussed, shaken their heads, and cussed some more listening to Frank tell them about the two cops he and his partner, Colette, had shot and killed. He had hoped for some sympathy when he told them that those dudes were bad news and pulled their weapons first, but he got nothing. They did show some interest, though, when he told them that he'd gotten some fancy, expensive lawyer assigned to represent him who got him off on bail and who probably would've gotten him off altogether if he hadn't run.

"How'd you afford a fancy lawyer?" Woody asked. Woody was a reverend at the Baptist church in town.

Joel leaned forward, resting his elbows on his knees, and stared intently at Frank. "How'd you pay for that attorney, son?" The old man asked as if he already knew the answer.

A few months back, Frank had come here to ask the man a question. Frank wanted to know if it was true that Jordan Gatewood was Joel's son, and Frank's half brother. Joel warned him to leave it alone, and to leave Jordan alone. Frank didn't listen.

He felt like he was six years old, in trouble for pulling some girl's hair in class or something. "Did you pull that little girl's hair, Frank?" Lord! He wished it were that simple.

"Jordan Gatewood paid for him. . . ." His voice trailed off.

"Awwww . . . shiiiiii . . ." Malcolm groaned.

Woody shook his head.

"Y'all know?" Frank asked, surprised. Malcolm and Woody weren't the least bit surprised by the mention of that dude's name. He looked at Joel. "They know?"

Joel frowned. "Of course they know." He grunted. "Why the hell wouldn't they? He's their brother too."

"You let Gatewood pay for your lawyer?" Woody asked, looking like Frank had just told them he'd licked the bottoms of Jordan's cowboy boots.

"I didn't let him do anything, man. I was there, and the dude showed up out of the blue. What the hell was I supposed to do? He had bail! Ain't no way in hell I could've come up with that kind of money."

"Alright . . . alright . . . so, you had a lawyer, out on bail . . . like I said, what the fuck are you doing here?" Malcolm demanded to know.

Frank was sick of this motha fucka's tone. He was sick of his attitude. "Fuck it, man!" He stood up to leave. "I don't need this shit."

Frank headed toward the door, but Malcolm stood in front of it, blocking it. "Sit yo' ass down!"

Frank and Malcolm stood eye to eye. "Fuck you, man! You ain't my goddamned daddy!"

Frank pushed Malcolm. Malcolm pushed back.

"Nah, but I am!" Joel stood up and yelled. He pointed at Frank and then at the chair. "Sit down!"

Frank couldn't believe it. This old dude had never been more than an occasional ice-cream cone and a child support check. Now all of a sudden he wanted to step in and try and tell somebody what to do?

Woody slowly stood up too. "Frank," he said calmly, "I think you'd better take a seat."

Frank had always prided himself on his size, but now all of a sudden, he felt like a little brother, and reluctantly did as he was told.

Joel sat down and took a deep breath. "Why'd you leave Cotton, son?"

Frank was cornered, but hell, he didn't have anywhere to go or anyone to turn to and as fucked up as this situation was, these people were all the family he had.

"That reporter they found in Dallas . . . the one all over the news?"

"You shot her too," Malcolm said matter-of-factly.

Frank rolled his eyes. "Nah, motha fucka! I didn't!"

"But you had something to do with it?" Woody probed with more finesse than Malcolm.

Frank nodded. "She had a beef with Gatewood and wanted me to help . . . get back at him," he reluctantly admitted.

"Lord." Joel groaned. The old man knew. The other two were trying to put the pieces together.

"How?" Woody asked.

Frank shrugged. "She wanted me to push on him," he admitted. "I needed money, and she knew it. She figured we could kill two birds with one stone. I could get money I needed from him, and we could put the word out that he ain't who he says he is."

Malcolm burst out laughing. "What the hell kind of cops they got in Cotton? Yo' ass really that dumb?"

Frank shot to his feet and bowed up on Malcolm.

Woody got between the two of them before any blows could be thrown. "Sit down, Frank!" he commanded. "And Malcolm, shut yo' goddamned mouth for once!"

Frank hesitated, but eventually he sat down again. Malcolm backed off.

"What happened, Frank?" Joel asked gently. "How'd that woman die?"

Frank hadn't pulled the trigger, but he might as well have. It was hard enough telling them about killing a cop, but to say he'd had a hand in this . . .

"You shoot her, Frank?" Woody finally asked.

Frank shook his head. "I owed him," he said, looking at Woody. "He got me that lawyer, and bail, and I think he would've gotten me off without having to spend a day in prison," he shamefully admitted.

"Gatewood?" Woody asked.

Frank nodded. "He wanted me to call her and have her meet me at that motel. I was in Cotton, but I made the call." His voice faded and he choked up. "I didn't know what he was going to do. I didn't think he'd kill her. Next thing I know . . . it's all over the news and I'm neck deep in this shit."

The room was quiet while everyone let what Frank had told them soak in. Hearing it out loud, even Frank couldn't believe how dumb he'd been.

"So—you gonna run?" Joel finally asked.

Frank looked at him. "What choice do I have, pop?" He'd never called the old man anything other than his name his whole life. "Do you know what they'd do to a man like me in prison? I'm an ex-cop. They'll kill my ass."

Malcolm shoved open the screen door and went outside. Woody leaned back on the couch and raked his hand across his bald head.

"That motha fucka set you up!" Malcolm yelled from outside on the porch.

Frank was speechless.

"Yes, he did," Woody muttered.

Chapter 16

Bobby's murder investigation was heading into its third week. And the shit just kept on rolling down the proverbial hill, landing on top of his head. The lieutenant was getting beat up by the division chief, who was getting his ass kicked by the chief of police, who was being butt raped by the media on a daily basis, damn near. They were all living in a pressure cooker to find the killer of that woman, Yolanda Adebayo, and Bobby had absolutely nothing except evidence that a sexual act had taken place in the room registered to John Smith. Some of the DNA from the bedspread matched Ms. Adebayo's. But the male DNA didn't match any damn DNA on file.

"You look like a dog who could use a bone." His partner, Iris, tossed a manila file folder down on his desk in front of him.

"What's this?" he asked, flipping open the cover.

"Got it from the Auto Theft unit," she explained. "Maham at

Spring Valley in Richardson, they pulled some plate numbers from cars they weren't registered to. One of those plates was registered to Ace Rental Cars."

Bobby stopped flipping through pages and looked at her. "The same company Adebayo rented her car from?"

She nodded. "They filed a report that the car hadn't been turned back in when it was supposed to have been. Auto Theft found the tag pinned to a 2012 Cherokee."

"She'd rented a black Mustang." If he wasn't so cynical, Bobby would've jumped up and danced the Cabbage Patch on top of his desk. But it was still too soon for all that.

Iris nodded, "Yep, and get this. In the backseat of that Cherokee was another license plate." She leaned back in her chair. "And I'll bet you my next paycheck that you will never guess who that tag was registered to."

"I don't feel like guessing, Iris," he said impatiently.

"C'mon, Bobby. The least you could do is humor me."

"President Obama," he blurted out.

"Close." She smirked. "Jordan Gatewood."

Bobby raked his hands across his head and face, and sighed. "I told you I'm not in the mood for this."

"And I just told you who that other plate was registered to," she responded, looking pretty damn serious.

They had what was called a Mexican standoff, looking each other in the eyes, daring one of them to blink first. Iris wasn't playing. But even if she was serious about that other tag, so what? Tags were stolen off cars all the time. Maybe some idiot had just gotten lucky to get one from the king of Dallas.

"So, it's registered to Gatewood," he said eventually. "Tags get stolen, cars get stolen all the time. Anybody check to see if there's a report on file for the missing tag or vehicle?"

"Of course the Auto Theft guys checked," she said irritably. "And no. No one from the Gatewood camp ever reported a missing car or tags."

Iris was anxious to make something out of what was probably nothing. Bobby wasn't as eager to connect to two; after all, they were talking license plates, one of which was associated with one of the victims. The other, as far as he was concerned, was too far damned removed from a situation like that to even matter.

"The Cherokee was stolen?"

"No. Turns out the perp owns the truck, but he'd had his license revoked for DUIs and was looking for a work-around."

"He stole the tags to the rental car?"

She shook her head. "Bought them off some guy at a chop shop for a grand."

"Has Mr. Chop Shop been arrested?"

"Not to my knowledge, but Auto Theft is working on it."

Bobby's phone rang. "Keep me posted when they do." Bobby planned on talking to the cat to try and find out how he got his hands on the tags to that rental car.

"Randolph," he said, answering his phone. "You sending it now?" he asked, pushing buttons on his keyboard to bring up his computer screen. "Thanks," he said, hanging up.

"Whatcha got?" Iris asked.

"I've got a ghost. A John Smith had been registered for room 204," he explained.

"Still no match on the John Smith DNA even after the national search."

"Well, we know that Frank Ross was accounted for that night, being babysat by Cotton, Texas's, finest. And, he reported his credit card stolen the next day."

"Convenient," Bobby said irritably.

Ballistics had reported that ammunition from two different-caliber weapons were used in the shootings. Adebayo had been shot with a different gun than the other two victims, but all had died within minutes of each other.

"Call the Cotton PD," he told Iris. "Find out how we can get ahold of our boy," he said, referring to Ross. Stolen credit card or not, Frank Ross was the only connection they had to John Smith.

Iris immediately got on the phone and started making calls. After the third one, she stared wide-eyed at Bobby.

"They'd been keeping an eye on him after he made bail," she began to explain. "Turns out, he skipped town, Bobby. Vanished. They don't know where he is."

Guilty men ran. Dumb-ass men paid for rooms at a murder scene with their own credit cards while registering under an alias. Frank Ross had the disadvantage of being guilty and dumb, and all of a sudden, Bobby saw the light shining bright as day at the end of this long, long tunnel.

Chapter 17

"For all the money we've made, we've inherited a hundred million in pending lawsuits and damages stemming from the Anton Gulf spill." Jordan stood in front of his executive staff, finally putting the good, bad, and ugly into perspective from the Anton merger.

"We can make that money back in less than five years in revenue, Jordan."

He looked at his sister. June had been the one to pull the trigger on this takeover entirely too soon. But now was not the time to scold his little sister. Jordan had a hundred-million-plus problem on his hands that he had to contend with sooner rather than later.

"We can't afford to wait five years, June," he said sternly, sitting down and motioning to Paul Blanche, VP of public relations, to pick up where Jordan left off.

"Between the Feds and environmentalists, our ass is on the line," the man explained, pacing the room. "Anton drilling licenses have been put on hold until the Gulf mess was cleaned up, fines were paid, and they promised never to spill oil in the Gulf again, so help them God," he said sarcastically. "We took them over before any of them had a chance to finish what they started, so . . . it's on us to clean up their mess, boys and girls. Under the Gatewood Industries moniker, we have to come in looking like the cavalry, ready to save the day like superheroes, and here's how we're going to do it."

After the four-hour meeting ended, Jordan headed back to his office with June hot on his heels. "I know you think we moved too quickly with this merger, Jordan, but the Europeans were moving in fast," she said, practically running to keep pace with him. "I had it on good intel that we beat the Brits by a day—one day! If we'd have waited—"

"If we'd have waited"—he stopped suddenly in the middle of the corridor and bared down on his sister—"we'd have seen Desi Green's name all over Anton stocks."

"And you'd have let that stop you from making this deal?" she challenged.

Jordan had nothing to say. Would he have let Desi stop him from taking over Anton? No. But he would've been better prepared for her going in. He left June standing there. Jordan had let distractions get the best of him, which is why this merger happened the way it did. He'd been missing in action, playing games with Lonnie, when he should've been paying attention. June took the ball and ran with it. It was a good business deal with bad timing. Jordan could've staved off the Europeans, and maybe even dealt with Desi Green, but Jordan wasn't doing his job back then. He had to be careful not to make that mistake again.

"Mr. Gatewood." His assistant stopped him on the way into his office. "A detective called." She handed him a slip of paper with a name and number on it. Bobby Randolph. "He said he needed to speak to you about an urgent matter. Your calendar is open between three and three-thirty this afternoon. Would you like me . . ."

A rigid chill ran up his spine. A detective wanted to speak with him. With . . . him?

"Mr. Gatewood? Sir?"

The woman finally managed to get his attention. "Would you like me to call him to set up a meeting at three?"

Jordan paused. He had to face this. He hadn't done anything wrong. He wasn't guilty, but . . .

"Sir?"

He couldn't afford to look guilty. "Yes," he said, forcing the anxiety from him. "Three's fine," he said, disappearing into his office. Did they know? Jordan felt the weight of Lonnie's murder pressing on him. Did they fuckin' know already? Jordan's first instinct was to call Edgar. Edgar had promised that nothing had been left behind to tie Jordan or Claire to that motel. He'd assured him that his man had gotten there well before the police and made sure that he cleaned up behind Jordan. Had he missed something? Had Edgar been completely truthful with him?

He was just about to dial Edgar's number when his own phone rang. It was his assistant. "Mr. Gatewood. Your one o'clock is on the line."

Jordan had a phone conference with his lawyers. He wasn't in the mood . . . Jordan pressed buttons on his laptop and pulled up the videoconference link.

"Jordan," his lawyer said from the screen. "We've got a lot of ground to cover in a very short period of time."

Jordan leaned back and took a deep breath to help calm himself. "Yes. We do."

Calling Edgar would have to wait. For the next two hours, Jordan would be tied up with his attorneys. Coincidence? Irony? Yes to both.

Three o'clock came much too quickly. Detective Bobby Randolph was prompt. Short, slightly overweight, light-skinned with a salt-and-pepper goatee and cheap shirt and tie, he sat across from Jordan in his office like a kid who'd been called to the principal's office.

Jordan pretended to have the upper hand, the one with the power and the one in control. The truth was, he was shaking in his shoes.

"We found a license plate registered to your car in somebody else's car." He cupped his hands together and spoke matter-of-factly. The man was nervous.

Jordan needed for him to be nervous. The detective waited for a response. Jordan didn't give him one.

The detective cleared his throat. "I'm uh . . . a bit curious, Mr. Gatewood."

"About?" Jordan said coolly.

Randolph shrugged. "Why you didn't report a theft. An auto theft is a pretty serious crime, but we found no indication that the vehicle was ever reported missing."

Edgar was supposed to see to it that night that Claire's car was not at that crime scene. "You found the car?"

The detective shook his head. "No, sir. Not yet. We may never find it. When did you discover it was missing?"

Jordan shifted in his chair. "The car was actually my wife's car, Detective," he calmly explained. "I vaguely remember her mentioning something about it being stolen and assumed she'd be the one to report it."

Did it sound like bullshit? He studied the detective for any evidence that he found something strange about Jordan's explanation.

"Would you happen to know where she'd been when the car went missing?" he probed.

Jordan looked thoughtful, and slowly shook his head back and forth. "I can't recall."

"If you don't mind me saying, Mr. Gatewood, most people would remember losing an eighty-thousand-dollar Mercedes." He chuckled nervously.

"I've got eight cars, three trucks, and two motorcycles, Detective," he explained. "I've been busy running one corporation and taking over another. This merger has preoccupied me for months."

"Oh, I understand, sir. Well, I don't understand, but . . . I get it. You've been busy. Would it be possible for me to talk to your wife?"

Jordan was slowly starting to pull this together. Why the hell would the police department want to talk to him about a stolen car? This guy was fishing, and he shouldn't have been here. Jordan was trying to ward off appearing defensive.

"My wife's in Europe, Detective."

The detective paused. "Maybe I could call her? It would be a short conversation, sir. Just get some details from her?"

He was pushing it and Jordan didn't appreciate it. "I don't think so, Detective." Jordan got up from behind his desk and walked over to the door and opened it. "I appreciate the Dallas Police Department's efforts in investigating the theft of my vehicle. I'll follow up with my wife, and we'll look into filing a report, officially. We'll probably need it for the insurance claim."

The detective stood up. "Yes, sir. You will." The man stopped next to Jordan and extended his hand. "Appreciate your time, and we'll keep you posted on what we find."

"Thank you. I appreciate your efforts."

Jordan waited for the man to leave. Moments later, he picked up the phone and dialed Edgar's number.

"You told me you'd taken care of it," he growled into the phone. "What happened to the damn car, Edgar? What the fuck happened to the car?"

Edgar sighed. "It was gone by the time my man got there, Jordan. That's about all I can tell you."

Jordan slammed the phone down and pounded his fist on his desk. He struggled to compose himself so that he could think. He'd told the man that Claire's car had been stolen. It was a decent enough lie. After all, what the hell would a man like Gatewood or his wife be doing at a seedy-ass motel across town? Even to him it didn't make sense. It couldn't.

Chapter 18

"We should call Jordan about this, Olivia." Olivia had informed her doctor that she was leaving the nursing home Jordan had placed her in and was returning to her home. "I don't think it's a good idea," her doctor told her.

"I don't give a damn about any of your damned ideas, Clark, and Jordan has no say in where I choose to live anymore," she retorted. "I'm a grown woman, and I'll live where I choose to live and how I choose to live."

"But Jordan . . ."

"You let me deal with my son," she told him coolly.

"Just promise me you'll continue taking your medication, and that you'll keep a nurse close by."

Olivia smiled politely. "Of course."

She'd been gone too long. Olivia led the entourage of her personal assistant, driver, and nurse through the main lobby of Gatewood Industries, past the front desk, past security, toward the elevators. Businessmen and women cleared a path for her like the waters of the Red Sea had parted for Moses. She needed no introduction. She needed no employee badge to walk into the building she owned. Olivia Gatewood exuded money and power and for all intents and purposes, she was Gatewood Industries, and everyone who laid eyes on her instinctively knew it.

"Wait here," she directed her staff as she approached Jordan's office. "Where is my son?" she asked his assistant, who bolted to her feet at attention as soon as she laid eyes on Olivia.

"H-He's at a meeting," the young woman said nervously.

"I'll wait," Olivia stated, marching into his office.

Ten minutes after she'd sat down, Jordan appeared as if by magic in the doorway.

"Mother? What're you doing here?" He came in and shut the door behind him.

The view from his office window was an impressive one of the city, stretching out for miles. She waited for him to walk over to his desk. Olivia looked at her handsome son, looking every bit as regal as Julian had once looked, so many years ago. Rage flushed warm across her face.

"Edgar says that we can't kill the bitch," she blurted out unemotionally. She walked over and sat down in a chair across from his desk, crossed her legs, and waited for him to take his seat. "So, what do you suggest?"

"Dr. Holmes called. He said that you were moving back to the house."

"Don't change the subject, Jordan. I'm not in the mood," she retorted icily. "Imagine the embarrassment I felt when I saw the headline in that newspaper that Desi Green owned a piece of my corporation."

She knew her son. Olivia could read him like a book.

"Yes, Jordan. She's made a fool of us, and I want to know what you intend to do about it."

He sighed his frustration. "I'm looking into it, Mother."

"Get your ass off your goddamned shoulders, boy! Desi Green has got her greedy-ass hands on my company and I'm not having it! You tell me what you plan on doing about it!"

"What the hell do you expect me to do about it?" He raised his voice.

"You let your guard down, Jordan. You let it down and you let her in!"

"How the hell was I supposed to know she wanted in?" he shot back. "For the last two years, Desi's been pimping books and shoes! Who the hell knew she wanted in on the oil business?"

Olivia sat back and studied her son. "And that right there is the million-dollar question. Isn't it?"

Desi Green had taken the money, written her little book, and ran. As far as Olivia knew, the woman had left Texas altogether. So, what had changed her mind? What was it that not only brought her back to Texas but compelled her to buy into a business she'd never seemed to give a damn about? All of Olivia's questions seemed to reflect back in her son's eyes.

"It's not like you to let something like this get past you, son."

There was something else going on inside that man. Something dark and distant.

"Something else has your mind, Jordan," she said speculatively. "What's really going on?"

He cleared his throat and shifted in his chair. "Nothing I can't handle."

His dismissive attitude pissed her off even more. "Of course you can't handle it," she snapped. "It's got you by the balls so hard that you left the gate wide open for that woman to skip her little black ass into my yard." Olivia gritted her teeth.

"Your yard?" he said, meeting and holding her gaze for the first time since he'd sat down.

"My yard!" she said emphatically. "This is my company, Jordan. It's been mine since—"

"Since you shot your husband, Olivia?" he challenged.

He'd never said that to her before. He'd never said it out loud.

"You watch your mouth!"

"No," he said, leaning toward her. "You watch yours. I run this company—I have been running it since you put him in the ground and I'm not going to let you or anybody else question my ability to not only keep it going but to quadruple the size of it since he died."

"You run it because I say you can," she retorted. "I put you behind that desk, Jordan, and I can snatch you from behind it any damn time I please!"

"And replace me with who?"

She had no answer, because she knew, just like he knew, that there was no one else. But Olivia wouldn't give him the satisfaction of not calling his bluff. "June is waiting in the wings, circling overhead like a vulture."

Jordan suddenly laughed. "Yeah, alright."

The cocky sonofabitch wasn't the least bit threatened, and of course, he had no reason to be.

This time, it was her turn to change the subject, or at least to get it back on track. "What do you plan to do about Desi?" she asked coolly.

Jordan eventually composed himself long enough to answer. "If nothing else, Desi's done me a favor. She brought my money back to my house."

"Edgar said the same thing."

He looked resentful. "Well, Edgar's a smart man. I don't know why she bought into the business, but she's better at selling shoes than oil. Desi doesn't want this. Someone talked her into it and like the mindless robot she is, she did as she was told."

"Who do you think told her to do it?"

His expression changed again. "I have my suspicions, but that's not important. Getting her out of Gatewood Industries is what's important."

"How?"

"I don't know . . . yet. But I am working on it," he assured her.

"I don't care how you do it, Jordan," she said emphatically. "Whatever it takes, you get rid of her. Do you understand me? I can't have my company tainted by that woman. It's not right!"

He stared back at her. "Nothing about our lives is right, Mother."

She sat up straight. "What's that supposed to mean?"

Jordan suddenly looked a bit melancholy. "None of us is guiltless. None of us is innocent. And none of us deserves what we have."

Olivia smirked. "What the hell is wrong with you? What the hell's happened? Just because our hands are soiled doesn't make us any less deserving, Jordan," she explained smugly. "No one can become what we Gatewoods have become without toiling in the dirt. It's what makes us strong. It makes us capable and worthy of our station in life."

He sat there absorbing her words. Olivia could almost see the seed being planted in her son.

Finally, he smiled. "There you go again, Olivia, believing your own hype. The exaggerated image you have of yourself—of all of us, is downright silly sometimes."

She stared unemotionally at him. "You're getting careless with your insults, boy," she warned. "Thoughtlessly hurling them around so randomly."

"Not so thoughtless," he responded coolly. "And not so random."

"I could destroy your black ass with a word, Jordan. My love for you is your salvation."

He held her gaze. "You destroyed my black ass a long time ago, Mother. And your love has been my curse."

Jordan sighed, stood up, walked across the room, and opened the door. "Go home, Mother. Desi's my problem and I'll take care of it."

Chapter 19

"*I didn't know* you were even still in town until I saw the headlines," June Gatewood said to Desi over the phone.

"Can we get together?" June continued. "I have something for you."

Of course, Desi was hesitant. In the nearly two years since they'd met, the two of them had only ever spoken to each other twice before today and both times had left behind some uneasy effects on Desi's life.

"When and where?" Desi reluctantly asked.

"There's a club called Rhinestones in Fort Worth. I can meet you there at say . . . seven?"

"That's fine. I'll see you then," Desi said before hanging up.

June Gatewood had had some kind of agenda when she and Desi first met, nearly two years ago. One that Desi never could get a handle on but had somehow managed to be dragged into. She wouldn't call what the two of them had a connection, but it was certainly something, and for whatever reason, Desi couldn't bring herself to walk away from the woman or that strange agenda of hers.

"The line is out the door and around the corner," the sales clerk at an Atlanta bookstore said happily as she ushered Desi from the back of the store to the front where she'd be signing Beautiful, Dirty, Rich: The Desi Green Story.

Desi still couldn't quite believe that so many people actually gave a damn about her life story, but ever since the book had been released, the damn thing had spread like a wildfire. USA Today *featured it on the front page,* Essence *magazine sent a reporter to interview Desi personally,* Ebony *called her story "propaganda," and the book shot to number five on the* New York Times *bestseller list. Just like that, Desi had become some kind of overnight and reluctant celebrity all because she'd been a victim of circumstances.*

"Who do I make this out to?" she asked the woman standing at the table.

"June," she said softly. "June—June Gatewood."

She looked up at the woman and stared right into the blue-gray eyes of Julian Gatewood. June asked Desi to have a drink with her at a bar around the corner. It was a hard "yes" to come by, but Desi dug deep and reluctantly found it inside herself. June Gatewood had been a child the last time Desi saw her, sitting with her mother and brother behind the prosecution during the trial. She was barely a teenager back then, and she was only there once.

Why Desi agreed to have that drink with the woman was as much a mystery to her then as it was now. She'd braced herself for the worst, but was surprised by what she got instead.

"I've read your book three times," June admitted, sitting across from Desi in the back of the room near the window.

Desi waited, expecting the woman to call her a liar, to throw that drink in her face, or worse—to talk about Desi's momma. Desi's mother and June's father had been lovers for as long as Desi could remember. It was the reason he was dead.

June took a deep breath and surprised the hell out of Desi with what she said next. "I'm so sorry, Desi."

Desi raised her brows in surprise.

June looked almost as if she could read Desi's mind. "I believed every word." *Tears flooded the rims of June's eyes.* "And I'm so sorry you had to . . ." *June took her napkin out from under her drink and dabbed her eyes with it.*

Of all the people in this world—of all the things this woman could've said, the last thing Desi ever expected to come from her or any other Gatewood was sympathy and an apology.

"I miss him," *June said, struggling to compose herself.*

The words slipped out of Desi's mouth before she even realized it. "Me too," *she whispered.*

June looked surprised, and a timid smile crept up on Desi. "He was always so serious." *She cleared her throat.* "Daddy would come home at the end of the day, and we'd all sit at the table, dressed up, and, at mother's insistence, we'd eat quietly, and not bombard him with our childish chatter." *June seemed lost in her memories for a moment.* "He'd still be wearing his suit and tie, and he'd seemed almost too important to look at."

Desi had memories of her own to draw from. "But you did look," *she said warmly.* "Real quick?"

June nodded and grinned. "He'd catch me—real quick—and stick his tongue out at me."

This time, it was Desi's turn to tear up. He used to do that with her.

June stared at Desi, studying her face, like she was memorizing it. "You still look the same," *she said sheepishly.* "You look like your mother, and you really haven't aged a day."

Desi shrugged. "Oh, I've aged." Desi was forty-four, almost forty-five.

"No, girl. You look . . . beautiful," she said shyly.

Desi was taken aback by the compliment, but she kept her guard up. June was Jordan's sister and Olivia's daughter, which meant nothing about her could be trusted.

June must've read Desi's expression.

"I was very close to my father," she volunteered. "Despite what my mother may have said about him or done, I knew he loved me."

Me? Not us? Not her and her brother?

"And I believe what you wrote in your book, Desi," she continued cautiously.

Desi had written a whole lot of shit in her book. Which part was she talking about? The part about the judge who'd been paid off by the Gatewoods to see to it that Ida Green, Desi's mother, never came forward to tell the truth? Or did she believe the part about the jury being bought off to make sure Desi was found guilty of murder?

The color washed from June's tanned face. "I believe my mother shot my father and killed him. . . ." Her voice trailed off. "The saddest part of this whole thing is that I know she'll never pay for that crime."

June was beautiful, as beautiful as her father, but slightly darker in her complexion like her mother. Bone-straight hair, ashen-blond and parted to one side, cascaded past her shoulders. Mr. J's stunning eyes made her look exotic and even otherworldly. Was she black? Was she white? Looking at her, it was hard to pinpoint her ethnicity.

"Sorry I'm late," she said, breathless as she sat down across the table from Desi. Rhinestones overlooked a large lake surrounded by lush, green trees. "Traffic was worse than I thought it would be."

June was tall, five-seven, maybe, with a slender, athletic build. She wore skinny jeans with a pale pink silk blouse tucked into them, belted at the waist, and blue suede flats. Several gold bangles hung around her wrists.

She finally looked at Desi and smiled. "You look gorgeous, as usual," she said, sounding as if she genuinely meant it.

Desi managed to smile back. June had always approached her like the two of them had known each other forever, like they were actually friends. Desi always made sure to keep her guard up. June was a Gatewood. She was Olivia Gatewood's daughter, and Jordan's sister. By default, she and Desi should've been scratching each other's eyes out every time they came within two feet of each other.

"Thank you, June," Desi replied wearily. "So do you."

The waiter came over and took their drink orders. After he left, June took a deep breath.

"So, I guess all that media attention was an unexpected distraction." She laughed.

Desi nodded. "Distraction is right."

"But you shouldn't be surprised, though," she continued. "It was only a matter of time before the media got wind of what was going on."

Desi looked at her. She was on a bus that June was obviously driving, and sitting here, waiting for June to arrive, Desi had realized that she needed to finally take control over what she could of this situation, especially where June was concerned.

"Is that what you were hoping for?" she asked bluntly.

If June was offended by Desi's tone or directness, she didn't show it. "Let's just say, I knew it was bound to happen, Desi. I mean, let's face it—considering the history, this is big news and the whole state of Texas, hell, the whole world is wondering what will happen next."

Did June know that her brother was a murderer? Desi wondered, studying the woman. She was confident that Olivia had killed her father, but did she truly know what her brother was capable of? What was June's motivation in all of this? Desi had to know.

"Why was my buying into Anton so important to you, June? What's all this really about?"

The waiter came back and set their drinks down on the table between them. June never took her eyes off Desi's.

"You know the answer to that, Desi." She paused long enough to take a sip of her wine. "My mother killed my father and she'll never go to prison for it; she'll never have to answer for it."

"This is your way of getting back at your mother?"

"This is my way of killing her," June said harshly. "Gatewood Industries is everything to Olivia."

"So this has nothing to do with Jordan?" Desi asked cautiously, hoping to pull any information she could from June about Jordan and what she may or may not have known about his involvement with Lonnie.

"Jordan's a prop," she said nonchalantly. "Always has been." She shrugged. "I love my brother, but my mother worships him. In some ways, I think he's replaced Daddy in her life. He's her champion, Desi, her knight in shining armor. He's her hero."

Jordan was no hero.

"My father was mine."

Desi was a tool for June. The woman was using her to get back at mommy and to punish big brother for whatever issues the two of them had created for her as a child.

June reached into her purse, pulled out an envelope, and slid it across the table toward Desi.

Desi raised a brow in curiosity.

"It's an invitation." June smiled. "I want you to come to the Investors' Ball next month, Desi."

Desi swallowed. This bitch was taking this shit entirely too far. "If I walk into that damn ball, what's to keep Jordan from having me shot right then and there?"

June laughed. "That's pretty melodramatic. Don't you think?"

"No."

June hesitated, as if she were waiting for Desi to qualify her response, but Desi didn't.

"He'll be pissed, Desi, but he won't have you shot," she said, amused. "You'll make him uncomfortable, and you'll damn near give her a heart attack."

Desi slid the envelope back toward June. "Girl, you're on your own with this one. I'm not playing this role for you. Find another way, or find somebody else to be your damn pawn. I'm not the one."

"You'd rather be Olivia's pawn? Or Jordan's?" June asked, unblinking. "Because that's what you are to them, you know? That's what you've always been, Desi, and still are whether you know it or not."

"Yeah, and now you want to play me too!"

"I want you to step up and play on your own terms!" June looked angry for the first time since Desi had met her. "Damn, Desi." She shook her head in disgust. "You're in this. You've always been in it, ever since my father fell in love with your mother. Do you think I don't know? Do you think I can't see him in you?"

Desi was stunned, and it must've shown on her face.

"You look like your mother, but I see him in you too. He was more than just her lover. Wasn't he?"

Desi didn't answer, but June didn't look as if she needed her to.

"The name Gatewood is damn near royalty in this state, and it's about to become more powerful, more influential than ever. But it's also a curse, especially for you. It's yours whether you want it to be or not. You can't keep sitting back in the rafters watching the rest of us live what it means to be a Gatewood, Desi." June slid the envelope back to Desi. "Let this be your coming-out party, and you use it to slap Olivia and Jordan upside the head with the truth." She folded her arms as she ended her argument.

Desi looked at her. "And where will you be during all of this?" she asked suspiciously.

For all of her cheerleading, Desi still couldn't bring herself to trust that June only had Desi's best interests at heart.

"I'll be standing off to the side, taking it all in, and loving every minute of it."

"While I throw myself to the wolves?"

"While you do whatever it is you want to do, Desi. After all, it is *your* coming out party."

Chapter 20

Jordan sat behind the wheel of his car watching in fascination as Solomon Jones fought off three men. Jones moved like a dancer, throwing kicks like punches and landing punches with enough force to break bones. He wasn't a hard man to find. Jones represented some of the most talented and successful professional athletes across sports lines—football, baseball, and basketball. He even represented a few NASCAR drivers, actors, and hip-hop artists. But Desi Green had made him famous.

To think that Jordan paid good money for these fools to take down Jones and between the three of them, they were getting their asses handed to them by one man. This shit was getting old. He climbed out of his car, walked across the eighth-floor parking garage of the building where Jones worked, and met the man just as momentum spun him around to meet the threat he no doubt felt standing behind him. Jones's mistake came when he recognized

Jordan Gatewood and he hesitated, just for a moment, but long enough for Jordan to bring his right fist from behind him and land it flush against Jones's jaw. Bone gave way to the force and Jones landed on his back.

Jordan glared at each one of those motha fuckas who were supposed to take this man down, knowing full well that when this shit was done, so were they.

"Pick that bastard up!"

Two of the men picked Jones up off the ground and held him while the other man pounded into his gut with fists almost as big as a man's head. Jordan watched as the semiconscious man absorbed blow after blow to his midsection and face. How many times had his hand been forced since that woman had been released from prison? How many times had he been pushed to the edge by something having to do with Desi Green? And how many more people were going to have to pay the price for her salvation?

"I get it, man," Jordan said to Solomon as they continued beating him. "You love her and there's nothing you wouldn't do for her."

Blood sprayed from Solomon's mouth as the big man drove his fists into his ribs, and then crossed a big hook into the side of his face.

"Stop," Jordan commanded him.

He walked over to Solomon, who couldn't even stand up on his own anymore. Jordan stopped a foot away from where they held him.

"She's hell-bent on making me look like a fool," he began to explain, uncertain as to whether or not the man was even aware that Jordan was speaking to him. "Desi got her money. She walked away with twenty million and all she had to do was keep walking. You and I wouldn't be here now if she'd just kept moving."

Solomon surprised Jordan and raised his head. His eyes had

already started to swell shut. Blood filled his mouth and he gasped desperately for breath.

"Lonnie!" he struggled to say. "You . . . killed . . . her, motha fuck . . . !"

Jordan took a step back, stunned by what the man had just said to him.

Jones looked up at one man holding on to him and then the other, and then he turned his attention back to Jordan. "What . . . man!" he gasped. "I'm not . . . a woman?" He forced a smile through swollen lips. "You . . . can't . . . kick my ass . . . with-without . . . help?" Jones spit. "Pussy!"

Jordan stepped toward the man again. If Jones believed that Jordan had killed Lonnie it was only because Desi believed it. Lonnie had talked her into buying that Anton stock knowing that it would lead to Desi's buying into Gatewood Industries. Lonnie had snuck Desi's ass in through the back door. And now, Desi was going to use her position to try and make him pay for what she believed he'd done.

"You're here instead of her for a reason, Jones," Jordan began to explain. "She needs to know what's really at stake here, and it's not money. It's you. It's her. It's me. I don't know you from Adam, and I don't give a shit about your girlfriend. But I will do whatever it takes to take care of my ass and the things that matter most to me."

"You're a bitch, Gatewood."

"If I gave a damn about you, man, I'd give a damn about your opinion of me, but I don't. You take this bloody mess back to Desi," he said, referring to the pile of flesh that was left of Jones. "And you show her how serious I am. You let her know how desperate I can get." He locked his eyes onto Solomon's. "I've been kind to her—so far," he said, making sure the threat didn't go unnoticed by Jones. "I've even been empathetic to some degree, but I will not let her play in my sandbox. If you love her, if you truly care for her, then you give her my message." Jordan adjusted the other man's tie, patted him on the chest, and turned to walk back to his car.

A half an hour later, Jordan sat in the back of a downtown bar finishing off his third cognac. Jordan hadn't been sleeping. He hadn't been eating, but he'd been doing more than his share of drinking. Lonnie's death still weighted heavily on him, and the nagging feeling that he wasn't out of the woods yet. The police still had no suspects and were no closer to solving her murder than they were nearly a month ago when it happened. Not having a suspect in her murder meant that the door was still wide open to build a case against anyone, including him.

His phone vibrated in his pocket. Jordan almost didn't answer it because he was sure that it was Olivia calling again to find out what he'd been doing to get Desi out of Gatewood Industries. But it was Frank. Jordan waved the bartender over and motioned for another drink, before reluctantly taking the call.

"What?" he asked irritably. The last thing he had time for or interest in was Frank Ross's dumb ass.

"I left."

The bartender set Jordan's drink down in front of him. "You left what?"

Frank paused and Jordan knew instinctively that this fool had probably just fucked up in a big way.

"Cotton. I left Cotton."

Jordan tossed back his entire drink before coming up for air. His stomach twisted in disgust. "You left? What the hell did your dumb ass do that for, Frank?"

"I panicked, man," Frank explained. "They questioned me about my card being on file at that motel and I panicked."

They questioned him? That fool jumped bail and pretty much just confessed that he'd had something to do with Lonnie's murder because they'd questioned him? "What did you tell them?" Jordan asked, demanding.

"Nothing, man. But they acted like they didn't believe me."

"Where are you?"

Again, Frank took his time answering.

"Where the hell are you, Frank?"

"With Joel," he responded solemnly.

Joel Tunson. Frank was staying with Joel Tunson, and Jordan suddenly began to feel sick to his stomach.

"What'd you tell Joel?" Jordan asked reluctantly.

Frank was an idiot. Frank was desperate and Frank was scared. "The truth."

The conversation with Frank Ross ended on that note, and Jordan hung up on him. He'd been sitting at this bar, drinking and wondering if things could possibly get any worse, and in that moment, they had done just that.

Chapter 21

Solomon had been adamant about not knowing who had attacked him in the parking garage of his office building.

"Did you get a good look at them?" an officer asked him.

Solomon shook his head. "They got me from behind." He grimaced, slipping into his shirt.

Desi didn't believe him.

He'd spent one night in the hospital and against doctor's orders, he'd insisted on leaving the next day.

"Are you sure you should be leaving, Mr. Jones?" the officer asked, concerned.

Solomon forced a smile. "I'll be fine."

On the drive home he barely said two words to her. It had been like that since she'd gotten to the hospital and found him there, beaten damn near beyond recognition.

"Are you hungry?" she asked as they made their way inside the house from the garage.

"No."

"Thirsty?"

"No!"

Solomon headed out of the kitchen and into the foyer toward the stairs. When Desi tried helping him, he jerked away from her.

"I'm fine, Desi," he snapped, bracing himself against the bannister and carefully taking each step.

She was exhausted. Desi had been operating on adrenaline ever since she got the call from the hospital that there had been an "incident" and that her fiancé had been admitted. Desi collapsed on the sofa in the living room, leaned back, and began to cry. Nothing could've prepared her for that moment at the hospital when she first saw him lying there, struggling to breathe, his face swollen, blood dried on his shirt.

"It . . . looks worse . . . than it . . . is," he struggled to say, reassuring her.

So many feelings rushed over her, but fear stood out the most. Despite what he said or what the doctors said, she was afraid that Solomon wouldn't make it through the night. Desi sat by his bedside the whole night, waiting for him to take each and every breath. She'd just lost Lonnie. Desi had lost everyone she'd ever cared about, everyone she'd ever loved, and she had no idea how she'd cope with losing him too.

"Desi." The sound of his voice caught her attention.

Desi quickly dried her eyes and stood up. "You alright, baby? You should be resting."

Of course he was angry. Solomon was a proud man, a fighter, literally. He was trained in martial arts, some of which had names Desi couldn't even pronounce, and boxing. Those men had to have snuck up on him in order to get the advantage over him like that.

"Sit down, Desi."

Desi tried to lighten the mood. "I will if you will."

Solomon wasn't amused. Desi took a seat.

"I don't think that I believed any of this was real enough until the other night," he began explaining. "Even with Lonnie's death, I couldn't wrap my mind around all of the things you've been trying to tell me."

A knot tightened in Desi's stomach, and all of a sudden, she could sense that her worst fears were actually rising to the surface.

Desi swallowed. "Jordan did this?"

"Jordan's not man enough to take me on by himself. He had three sonofabitches on his payroll do this to me."

Her heart sank into her stomach. Solomon was never supposed to get dragged into her mess, not like this. Her eyes clouded with tears. "I'm so sorry, Solomon," she said shamefully.

"This wasn't about me, Desi," he continued unemotionally. "It was meant to be a message to you to take your toys and go home. He wants you out of his business, out of his life. He wants you gone, and what he did to me was a warning to you."

Jordan took sonofabitch to a whole new level. "Why didn't he come after me?" she blurted out without thinking, but Desi was pissed. "Why would he do this to you? If he wanted to teach me a lesson, then he should've come to me!" She stood up, pointing her finger into her chest.

"He did go after you, Desi!" Solomon snapped irritably. "That sonofabitch went after you when he killed your friend. He went after you when he had those gorillas kick my ass. This was a warning to you—a warning about what could happen if you don't step off and let go of this vendetta you have against him and his family." Solomon grimaced as he walked over to the window and leaned against the ledge. "But then, this is what you wanted. Right?" He paused and studied the look on her face.

"No!" she said angrily. "No, this is not what I wanted, Solomon! I didn't want to get you involved in any of this! That was never my intention!"

"But you are involved in this and I'm involved with you," he explained. "So, how can I not be a part of it?"

Desi had no answers. Solomon was right. She had a knack for letting the people closest to her fight her battles and every last one of them lost, one way or another. He was all that she had left and if she kept on with this foolish vendetta, if she wasn't careful, she would lose him too.

Desi lowered her head and stared at her hands folded in her lap. "I never should've come back here," she murmured. "I never should've bought stock in Anton Oil." Desi dug deep inside herself for the courage to look at him again. "And I am so very sorry for all of the pain and embarrassment you've had to suffer over me." Desi stood up to leave. What else could she do? Staying in Dallas put both of them at risk. Jordan had sent a message and it had gotten through to her, loud and clear. "I can't stay here, Solomon," she murmured. "I can't do this to you. I'll leave in the morning."

"Sit down, Desi," he demanded.

She headed for the stairs.

"No, no, no," he said, shaking his head and forcing himself to stand. "It's not that easy, girl."

Desi ignored him.

His tone definitely caught her attention. "Desi! Desi, don't you even think of walking out on me!"

"What else can I do, Solomon?" She turned to him and yelled back. "If I stay here he'll kill you too, just like he did Lonnie! Look at how far he's willing to go! Look at how far he's gone!"

"You should've thought about that before you bought your way into Gatewood Industries," he said, limping toward her.

"You're right! I should've! I thought I had, but . . ." She was crying. "I'll sell the stock, Solomon! I'll go back to California, and I'll stay as far away from those people as possible! Because I'm not going to let him kill you too!"

"And what about me?" he said, slamming his hand against his chest. "You're just going to walk out on me, run your ass back to California and do what?"

"I don't know!"

"You're not going back to California, Desi." He marched over to her. "I know that this shit is as real for me now as it ever was for you or Lonnie! I know what that motha fucka is capable of and how far he's willing to go! And I know good and damn well that you are not going to walk out on me or turn your back on me like I didn't just take the ass whooping of a lifetime for you!"

He'd never spoken to her like that before. Desi had never seen Solomon as livid as he was now.

"If I don't leave—"

"You're not leaving me, Desi! I swear you're not . . ."

The pain must've been overwhelming. Solomon stumbled over to the sofa and fell back into it, clutching his side. "Shit!" he muttered.

Desi rushed over to him and knelt in front of him. "I should take you back to the hospital."

He reached out to her, grabbed her by the back of the neck and pulled her close to him. "I don't need a hospital!" he said in a low growl. "I need you here with me like I've never needed another human being in my life!" All emotion faded from his face except for his eyes. Solomon stared into hers with an intensity so strong that Desi almost didn't recognize him. "I've loved plenty of women in my day, Desi, but not like this," he said, clenching his teeth. "Not to where I would do anything, absolutely anything to keep them." He swallowed. "Your enemy is my enemy and until that bastard put his hands on me I had no idea how true that was, but he will not get to you and this is the last time his ass will ever get me in this predicament again." He threatened so strongly that it was impossible for her to doubt him.

Desi felt so helpless. Solomon was overcome with pain and bitterness and Desi was a ball of confusion. "I could—we could just walk away, Solomon. We don't have to deal with Jordan," she said, more afraid of Solomon than she'd ever thought possible. It was as if someone had flipped a switch inside him and awakened something as dark as Jordan.

"He wants us to run." He gritted his teeth. "We're not running."

"But Solomon . . ."

"He wants us to hide, but fuck him! No more hiding, Desi, and we're damn sure not going to run!"

"We?" she asked, wondering if he really understood what he was saying.

"I would take a bullet for you," he finally confessed. "I would give my life for you, Desi, all you'd have to do is say the word."

Solomon leaned back and closed his eyes.

Desi didn't know what to say. She knew he loved her, after all, he'd proposed, but this . . . what he was saying now . . .

"There is no turning back for me," he finally composed himself enough to say. "Damnit, girl, if I didn't know it before, I sure as hell know it now." He looked into her eyes.

"I'll sell the stock, Solomon," Desi murmured.

"Sell it or don't." He shrugged. "Hell, I don't care. But whatever you decide to do, I'm here—with you, and this is my fight now too!" Desi leaned in and kissed him. "He's my enemy, Desi. And I promise you—he's going to wish he never knew my fuckin' name."

Chapter 22

His doctor had given him a prescription for painkillers. Solomon had flushed them down the toilet. He didn't need to dull the pain of what Gatewood had done to him. Solomon needed a clear head. He needed to be focused.

Solomon sat across the bedroom and watched Desi as she slept. He had never seen a more beautiful woman. Two days ago he knew he loved her, and he believed that he had loved her enough. Since his encounter with Gatewood, Solomon had blamed Desi for what had happened to him, he'd resented her, and even hated her for dragging him into this chaos. As far as he was concerned, he was a fool for loving her, and a bigger fool for proposing. By the time she showed up at that hospital, he knew something else. He knew that he had crossed a line he never believed existed so far beyond that rational, reasonable place he'd lived his whole life and had moved into a territory without boundaries or rules. That's where she'd taken him. No. That's where he was now willing to follow her.

Solomon made the slow, painful journey to his downstairs office, turned on the lamp on the desk, and sat down behind it. Lying in that hospital bed, Solomon had had time to think. The difference between Gatewood and other men was money. And power. And a blatant disregard and dismissal of the rules. He had no moral compass because he didn't need one. His whole life, Jordan had a pass and he was never held accountable for his actions or trespasses. Solomon was a fighter in the ring where there were rules, and where one wrong move could cost a man the title or his health, his pride. He'd spent his life believing that if a man worked hard, if he was fair and held to his convictions, respected his fellow man and all that shit, that he could be proud of the man he was, that he could be successful and that even if he lost, he'd won.

He hit a button on his cell phone and placed it to his ear. To defeat your opponent you need to know him. To conquer your enemy you need to understand and recognize his weaknesses. On the surface, Gatewood was invincible and untouchable. But no man was infallible, no matter how rich, no matter how strong, and no matter how powerful.

"Hey," he said into the phone. "I apologize for calling so late, but I need your help."

"You know me, man. I sleep with the vampires."

O. P. and Solomon had known each other since they were kids. They'd grown up next door to each other, gone to the same schools, dated the same girls, even dressed alike for a brief period of time in their lives which neither one of them cared to talk about. His real name was Osiris Plato Wells, but for obvious reasons, he preferred to be called O. P., short for Optimus Prime, like the Transformer.

"Whatchu need, bruh?"

Solomon took a deep breath and chose his words carefully. "I need to pit my David against Goliath."

"You've done it before," O. P. said simply.

"Not like this. It's a dirty fight, man. Dirtier than any I've ever been in."

"The kind you bring a gun to."

"The kind you bring a gun to," Solomon agreed.

O. P. was talking metaphorically—sort of, but the point had been made. Solomon needed more than just his fists. He needed to rise to the occasion of Gatewood and be able to stand his ground with the man, on equal footing, to be able to stare him dead in the eyes. For that, he needed an advantage that he didn't already have, something that Desi didn't already know. For that, he needed O. P.

"Give me a name?"

"Jordan Gatewood."

After a brief pause, O. P. spoke up. "Gatewood? As in oil Gatewood?"

"Yes."

Neither one of them said a word for nearly a minute.

"Damn, man. Why don't you ask me to go after Obama?"

Solomon nearly laughed. "There's one thing I already know," he explained. "Some things you don't need to waste your time on because it's all hearsay and his word against everyone else's."

"Like?"

"His real name is Tunson. His father lives in a small town not far from here, but he grew up Gatewood and has nothing to do with the man. As far as he knows, he's never even met him."

"So, he's pretending to be a Gatewood."

"Something like that. There's no real proof, and honestly, I don't even think it would matter if word did get out that he wasn't born a Gatewood. He's made too many people too much money for them to give a damn. Hell, he could be Big Foot and they wouldn't care."

"Is that it?"

"That's it." Solomon sighed. He was tired, and she was upstairs in bed. That's where he needed to be.

"I'll be in touch." O. P. broke the silence, and both men ended the call.

Solomon had known O. P. practically his whole life, and still he had no idea how the man earned his money. But he'd learned long ago that he didn't want or need to know. O. P. lived well. He lived by whatever rules he'd made for his life, and he'd never gotten caught. A certain kind of person paid him good money to do whatever it was that they needed him to do. He had a knack for problem solving—that's what he'd told Solomon one night over beers at a strip club years ago.

"You got a certain class of person out there," he explained, slipping a yard into a blonde's G-string. "They're the worst kind of people. Worse than your gangbangers, your thieves, rapists, even killers."

"What makes them worse?" Solomon asked.

"They're all those things but the difference is, they got the money to buy somebody like me." O. P. looked at Solomon.

Solomon never asked him again what he did for a living.

Chapter 23

June had invited more than five hundred of Gatewood Industries' top investors to this event and it seemed like every last one of them had shown up. Jordan had shaken so many hands that his arm was sore. He'd gotten so many pats on the back that he was sure it was bruised, and he'd smiled so much his face hurt. He wasn't staying long. He hadn't told June that he was leaving early, but then, it was none of her business. She wanted this, she'd insisted on it. Jordan had other things on his mind, like a woman's murder. And Claire, whom he hadn't spoken to in weeks. Desi Green and her kickboxing boyfriend were gnawing at him like ants, as was the woman walking toward him right now, hanging off Edgar Beckman's arm looking like an antique Barbie doll. She was armed and ready with threats. Olivia's salt-and-pepper, shoulder-length hair had been cut short and styled to perfection.

She wore an elegant emerald-green gown, fitted and showing off a still-impressive figure for any woman, let alone one her age.

"Mother," he greeted her, leaning down and kissing her cheek. Jordan made eye contact with Edgar. "Edgar."

The older man nodded.

"Your sister's certainly outdone herself," Olivia touted, scanning the room, drinking in the elegance of the event his sister had obsessed over these last few weeks.

June had rented out Montgomery Hall, a mansion in the heart of downtown Dallas, thirty thousand square feet of history with gleaming walnut floors, thirty-foot ceilings, crystal chandeliers, and woodwork trim polished to look like glass.

"Yes," he agreed. "She has," he said dismally.

The last time he had seen Edgar he'd burst into the man's house and damn near pinned him up on the wall, and the old man still looked pissed. As if she were conjured up by some magic spell, June appeared out of nowhere, wearing a yellow chiffon dress, cut low enough in the front that it was a wonder her navel didn't get cold. June's long hair was pinned up into a haphazard beehive hairdo that women seemed to love these days. In short, his sister was a beautiful mess.

"Mother." June greeted Olivia with a smile and a nod, and when she saw Edgar, her face lit up like he was Santa Claus. "Edgar." She grinned and wrapped her arms around him. "I'm so glad you could come!"

It was no secret that there was no love lost between June and Olivia.

"Everything's lovely, Junie Bee," Olivia said, offering a smile as an olive branch.

"Thank you," June responded coolly, smartly keeping her

emotional distance from the woman, who at any moment could strike like a snake with criticism.

"If I weren't practically a member of the family . . ." Lecherous old Edgar looked at June like she was a meal.

"But you are," Olivia said, dousing whatever wet dream he was in the midst of having over her daughter.

June frowned, and then turned her attention to Jordan. "Lighten up and have another drink, Jordan. Maybe then you could at least look like you're having a good time."

Jordan forced a smile. "I'm having a blast, little sister."

"You should be. We are celebrating you, after all," June added.

There was something about that statement that didn't sit well with him, or maybe it was the look in her eyes that left him wondering.

"I've tried calling that wife of yours a hundred times and she hasn't called me back. She should be here," June continued.

"Yes," Olivia added. "Where is Claire? Why isn't she here?"

For a moment, Jordan and Edgar looked at each other.

"Claire's in Europe, Mother."

"That answers my first question, not my second," Olivia continued. "Why isn't she here with you?"

"Lover's spat, maybe?" June chimed in mischievously.

The two of them were being nosy, and he decided that entertaining them wasn't high on his list of priorities, so Jordan chose not to respond.

"Jordan," Edgar finally spoke up. "Come with me. There's someone I'd like for you to meet."

Edgar Beckman to the rescue, once again. Jordan followed the trail led by Edgar across the room, out of sight and earshot of June and his mother.

"Have you spoken to Claire?" Edgar asked, keeping his voice down.

Jordan shook his head. "Not in a while."

"Shouldn't you speak with your wife?"

"What for?"

The look on Edgar's face was horrific. "You're a fool for asking me a question like that. You need to know what's going on with your wife, Jordan. You need to keep tabs on her so that she doesn't say or do something that's going to blow this whole thing out of the water."

Edgar was angry, and maybe someplace deep inside him, Jordan knew that the man was right, but Claire was a woman constantly in need of bandages to keep her from falling apart and Jordan was all out of them.

"Claire is where she needs to be," Jordan retorted. "She's as far away from me as she can get. In the meantime, I'm the one still here, Edgar, exposed and waiting for that ax to drop on my neck and for the police to show up at my door about Lonnie!"

"And I should feel sorry for you?" Edgar asked bitingly. "Claire didn't create the mess you're in, Jordan. You did. And if by chance the truth does come out, and that ax does fall on your neck, it's nothing but justice, poetic and right as rain."

"Gentlemen, gentlemen!" Don Reedy, owner of the Dallas Mavericks, interrupted a conversation on the verge of turning ugly. He held out his hand for Jordan to shake and placed the other hand on Jordan's shoulder.

Jordan quickly composed himself. "Don. Glad you could make it."

Reedy laughed. "Of course I wouldn't have missed this for the world. Thanks to you I can now afford to retire moderately well."

Reedy nearly fell over at the punch line to his own joke. The man was a billionaire long before the merger with Anton.

"It's good to know you and the wife will have a nice little nest egg to fall back on," Edgar said, playing into the nonsense of this conversation.

"Speaking of wives, I haven't seen Claire here."

"Because she's not here," Jordan offered smoothly. "Claire's out of the country."

"Really? And she couldn't make it back for this event? I hope she's alright."

"She's amazing." Jordan smiled. He was quickly starting to realize that he wasn't drunk enough. "Excuse me, gentlemen." He pushed past them both. "I need a refill."

"Trouble in paradise," Jordan heard Reedy mumble to Edgar.

"Just a bit," Edgar responded.

Weeding his way through the crowd to the other side of the room, Jordan intercepted accolades and pats on the back, wishing like hell that this thing was over. Now was not the time for a party. He needed space. Jordan needed time to gather up all the shit plaguing his thoughts right now and put them into some kind of order. The past several weeks had been nothing short of chaos and calamity, leaving him feeling like a man standing on the edge of a cliff about to be pushed off.

As he passed the huge staircase leading up to the entrance, Jordan happened to glance at the couple standing at the top looking out over the crowd below. The man wore a European-cut tux, his long hair pulled back into a ponytail, and he looked like he weighed all of a buck fifty on a good day. The woman took his breath away and Jordan couldn't help stopping to soak in the sight of her. A fitted exotic-print dress looked as if it had been painted onto soft, beautiful curves. Thick waves of dark hair cascaded down past her shoulders. Full lips pressed together briefly in a moment of what looked like nervous anticipation, and finally, dark, dramatic eyes blinked back a gaze filled with vulnerability that finally and unexpectedly met with his.

The sound of glass shattering shook him loose from the spell of this woman. This woman—Desi Green.

Chapter 24

It wasn't until she opened her eyes yesterday morning that she'd made up her mind to put June's invitation to use. She'd told Solomon that she had a meeting with a new designer in California who she was thinking of hiring for a line of boots she was working on.

"I probably won't be home until late," she told him.

"That's fine." He kissed her and went back to answering e-mails in his office.

After that, all it took was a phone call to Phillip to convince her that she would do better with an escort.

"I can do this alone, Phillip," she'd told him over the phone.

"Then why did you call me?"

"Reassurance, I suppose. Solomon doesn't know anything about this, and I don't want him to know."

"I'm in Miami, but I can be in Dallas this evening, Desi, tux in tow."

He arrived at the hotel where she'd rented a room in a limo. Every reservation she had must've shown on her face. Phillip sat across from her and stared.

"You are exquisite, Desi," he told her.

Desi felt numb, not exquisite. She felt like she was walking into the lion's den about to sacrifice herself to him on purpose.

"I think I understand now why Lonnie was so taken with you." The look of revelation shone in his eyes. "You have every right to be here. You have earned that right."

He looked and sounded as if he truly believed what he was telling her and Desi struggled to believe it too.

"I feel like I'm making a mistake," she whispered.

Phillip lowered his head and gazed over his brows at her. "Tonight is not a mistake. It's a declaration. The Gatewoods want you to run and hide. Do you know why?"

She blinked back tears and shook her head. He sounded ridiculous.

Phillip leaned forward. "Because you frighten them, Desi. You always have."

Now he was mocking her.

"They've done the worst to you," he continued explaining. "They've robbed you of your freedom. They've stolen those you've loved from you. They take and take and still the gods resurrect you and shine a light on you too bright for them to ignore and they don't understand how it could possibly be that you have persevered. Not only persevered, but thrived despite their all-powerful efforts."

Listening to him, she couldn't help thinking of all those she'd loved and lost to the Gatewoods: Mr. J, her mother, and Lonnie.

"If it wasn't for Lonnie, Phillip—"

"Lonnie was motivated by you, Desi. Everything she did for you was because of you," he said in earnest. "Don't you see? As strong as you believe she was, she believed you were just as strong. You were her hero, Desi. From the time she first saw you on the evening news on your way to prison, she looked up to you and used you as her beacon to become all of the wonderful things she was."

Desi had no words. Lonnie had been her hero. Lonnie had kept her alive, from the letters she wrote to her to the war she convinced her to wage for money left to her from her mother's estate by way of Julian Gatewood.

Phillip reached over to her and took hold of her hand. And then he leaned toward her and planted a soft, lingering kiss on her lips. "I envy Solomon," he whispered.

Looking into Jordan's eyes made her stomach churn.

Phillip squeezed her hand. "It's alright," he whispered. "The boogeyman is only scary in the dark."

He had killed her friend, he had attacked Solomon, and walked around like the cock of the roost, free to be everything he believed he was. The sound of the glass breaking caught her attention and Desi followed the source of the sound across the grand ballroom to Olivia, standing with her mouth gaped open and staring at Desi like she'd just seen the resurrection of Ida Green, Desi's mother. In that moment, Desi felt like she was standing in the middle of town in front of the O.K. Corral, about to shoot it out with the bad guys, but she wasn't afraid.

Phillip began to slowly descend the stairs, taking Desi with him. Every wrong thing that had ever happened in Desi's life started with Olivia Gatewood. As she entered the room, the woman couldn't take her eyes off Desi and Desi didn't want her to. Jordan looked like you could knock him over just by blowing on him. None of them ever expected that she'd have the courage to show up here tonight. But now she was glad that she had. Desi was tired of running and cowering from these people. She was tired of them threatening everyone she cared about and doing whatever they could to steal her joy. Phillip had been right. They'd done everything short of taking her life, and maybe it would eventually come to that too, but tonight, Desi was invincible.

"What the fuck are you doing here?" Jordan growled, coming toward her.

Bless his heart. Phillip stepped between Desi and the human bull that was Jordan. Maybe Jordan was stunned by the gesture of the frail-looking Brit, but whatever the case, he stopped short.

Of course, now, they had an audience. "Get your ass out of here, Desi!"

Desi stepped from behind Phillip and walked up to Jordan. Lord, if he put his hands on her . . . Lord . . . let him put his hands on her and she'd sue his ass down to the last nickel in his pocket.

"This is the Investors' Ball, Jordan," she said defiantly. "And I'm an investor or haven't you heard?"

He wanted to hit her. Jordan wanted to ball up his fists and punch her in the face, but Desi had an invisible barrier protecting her or something, because he didn't lift a finger.

She held out her invitation to him. Jordan snatched it from her, stared down at her, and then searched the room for someone else until his eyes locked on his sister. Desi stopped and listened. What was that sound? Distinct. Subtle but definitely familiar. It was the sound of a wall cracking. His wall, the facade surrounding Jordan's powerful demeanor as he realized that he'd been stabbed in the back by family, and all of a sudden, Desi saw something vulnerable in the great Jordan Gatewood.

He glared at her, and dropped her invitation on the floor. "Is this you making a point, Desi? Taking a stance and putting on a brave face in front of all of these people?"

"This is me not running scared from you, Jordan. This is me showing you that you can't make me go away by wishing it, or by . . ." Desi stepped even closer to him. "Your problem is with me," she said, threatening. "Then make it with me and leave everyone else out of it."

"I have to admit, lover boy can take a punch."

"And so could Lonnie, and so can I. That's how you operate, isn't it? Big, bad-ass Jordan's got no problem beating up women, but when it comes to men, he's got to get a football team to help him do it."

She'd struck a nerve.

"We will have this conversation another time, in another place," he said coldly.

"You let me know when and where," she said confidently. "Phillip," she said, looping her arm around the arm of her escort. "I think I'm thirsty."

While waiting for her drink, the sound of a man's voice coming from behind her caught her attention.

"You shouldn't have done this."

Desi turned to him. His face. She'd seen this man before, but she couldn't place where she knew him from.

"Now was not the time." He flushed red.

Desi knew this man. She recognized him from somewhere— some other time in her life, and suddenly it dawned on her. "Mr. . . . Edgar?"

It was him! Desi's knees felt as if they were about to give out.

He looked as stunned to be called that as she had been to say it.

"There are ways to do things, Desi," he struggled to say. "This was not the way to do this."

He had come by the house with Mr. J when Desi was a little

girl. The two men would sit at the table with Desi and Ida eating greens and fried chicken and drinking sweet tea.

"You've humiliated these people," he snapped.

He had been Mr. J's best friend—that's what he'd told her.

"Julian and I have been friends since we were even younger than you, little lady."

"Is he your best friend?" she remembered asking him.

Mr. Edgar nodded. "He's better than my best friend."

A lump swelled in her throat as memories of this man came flooding back to her. He was there when Julian loved Ida and when he loved Desi!

"Do the right thing and leave, Desi," he insisted. "Leave before you make a fool of yourself."

"You were his friend," she said, choking back tears. "You were his friend—that's what you told me!"

Some things needed to be said. This man needed to hear them. He needed to be reminded that he knew all about Ida and Desi.

"He loved her!" she said, clenching her teeth. "He loved us both and you know it!"

"Get the hell out of here," Edgar growled under his breath.

Phillip wrapped his arm around Desi's waist and pulled her away from the older man. "Desi. Not now. We'll talk about him later." He made sure to say it within earshot of Edgar.

"Who the fuck are you?" Edgar shot back.

Phillip stepped to him. "I am the gatherer of secrets, Edgar Beckman," he said in his thick, British accent. "And you, my friend, are bloated with them."

"You bitch!" Olivia Gatewood magically appeared from behind Edgar. "How dare you show your face here! How dare you!" The woman was hysterical.

Edgar gathered her in his arms and tried to console her. Jordan hovered over his sister across the room, bearing down on her like an oversized bear. June made eye contact with Desi and smiled.

"I think you've done what you came here to do," Phillip murmured in her ear. "Shall we leave now?"

Desi looked up at him and smiled. Damn! She'd been here less than five minutes and turned the world of these people upside down. Was that what real power felt like? Desi breathed a sigh of relief. "Yeah," she said. "I'm ready."

Chapter 25

"*Olivia!* Stop it!"

It was Edgar's voice that June heard. But Olivia slapped her again, and again, and again.

"I'll never forgive you for what you did tonight!" Olivia cried as she struck June across the face.

Jordan had stormed out of the party, dragging June along by the arm. Edgar had the task of gathering Olivia. It had all happened so fast, and in a matter of what felt like minutes, the four of them ended up in one of the upstairs parlors in the mansion.

"Enough, Olivia!" Edgar grabbed her by the wrist before she hit June one more time.

June tasted blood in her mouth. "You should've seen the looks on your faces," she finally said, understandably shaken.

Every one of them looked at her like she'd lost her mind, but as far as June was concerned, she was the only sane person in the room.

Jordan had spent the last ten minutes pacing back and forth across the room.

"She brought that woman into our circle, Edgar!" Olivia yelled, and then stopped and looked at her son. "Jordan, do something! Say something!"

"Yeah, big brother," June challenged him. She wanted to hear what he had to say.

"You shut up!" Olivia snapped.

"Do me a favor and lose your mind, Mother," June shot back. "Like you always conveniently manage to do." She turned her attention back to Jordan. "You know what I did," she said, walking over to him. "You know, don't you?"

He stopped and glared back at June. "You talked her into buying into Anton," he said unemotionally. But Jordan wasn't fooling anybody. He was emotional—emotional enough to be dangerous.

June swallowed. "Yes."

"Why, June?" Olivia cried out.

"You pushed to close that deal because you knew what would happen." He stalked around her like a lion. "You planned this."

"I planned it," she murmured. June struggled to maintain her composure. Now was not the time to cave in to these people. It wasn't the time to cry. Now was the time to stand up to both of them.

"I want to know why," Jordan demanded, standing behind her, close enough for her to feel his breath on her shoulder.

"You tell him why!" Olivia was crying.

"Hush, Olivia!" Edgar commanded.

"Why'd you do this, June?" Jordan asked calmly. "Why'd you bring Desi Green into my company? Why'd you bring her to this party? Why'd you bring her back into our lives?"

His tone was chilling, but June had wanted this. She'd wanted to bring them all to this moment, and she had fantasized about this particular moment, when she'd finally be able to say all the things she'd wanted to say for so long.

"This is my father's corporation!" June finally said angrily. June turned to face her brother, and then stared at her mother.

"Your father is dead, June!" Olivia shouted. "Desi Green killed him!"

"No, you killed him, Mother!"

The woman looked appalled.

"June!" Edgar admonished her.

"I saw you get that gun, Olivia! It was the same night that Daddy was killed."

Olivia shook her head. "No! You lie!"

"I know what you did! Desi didn't make those things up in her book and you know it!" June spun around to Jordan. "She killed Daddy, Jordan! She killed our father and you're okay with that? You know she did it! How can you keep pretending that you don't?"

"Shit, June," Jordan said dismally, shaking his head.

"You shot my father and then you framed that teenage girl for murder, Mother," June said, disgusted. "Even as a child I knew what had happened, and for the life of me, I never could understand how you could live with yourself."

Olivia seemed to shrink right before June's eyes. "Since we're on the subject of plans, was that yours, Mother? Were you always planning on taking our father's life and then taking over his company, or did you just get lucky?"

"June," Jordan called out.

"No, Jordan. I need to hear this. I need to hear her admit to me that she never loved Daddy, and that she set him up from the beginning. She never loved him. She never even wanted him. All you wanted was his money, and his company. Isn't that right, Mom?"

"June," Jordan said more urgently. "Stop it!"

She turned to him. "Why should I, Jordan? And why are you always protecting her after what she did to this family? Oh, I forgot. You're her golden boy. She kills our father and puts you in charge, ever the perfect puppet. Isn't that what he is, Mom? Your perfect child, because why? Because you can pull his strings in ways that I never let you pull mine? I lost respect for her the night our father died."

"You need to stop this!" Edgar growled. "Whatever it is you think you saw was wrong, June! Trust me! Your mother loved your father!"

"I trust what I saw Edgar! I trust what I know in my heart! Our mother killed our father!"

"June! He wasn't my goddamn father!" Jordan suddenly blurted out.

"Jordan, no," Olivia cried pitifully. "Don't!"

"Aw hell, Olivia!" Jordan said, disgusted. "This family's coming apart at the seams! And it's about time we moved beyond bullshitting each other!"

June stared at him, stunned. "You mean, metaphorically? I know that the two of you weren't close, but . . ."

"He wasn't my father, June!"

"Not now, Jordan!" she snapped. Now was not the time for her brother to be sarcastic. "Your sense of humor is so fucked up!" This was the worst joke he'd ever told. "This is serious, Jordan," June retorted.

"Jordan, please don't do this," Olivia pleaded, helplessly slumping down into an antique loveseat. "Please."

What the hell? June stared back and forth between her defeated looking mother and her determined looking brother.

Jordan and Julian had never been close, but then again, she'd never been close to Olivia. It didn't mean that the woman wasn't the one who'd given birth to her.

"Julian was not my biological father, June," he repeated more convincingly this time. "He gave me his name," Jordan continued, "and for all intents and purposes, the world believes that I am his son."

There was something sad about his confession and all that was proud and noble about Jordan Gatewood slowly began to fade.

A swell of anger and frustration surged through June as she looked at her mother sobbing quietly.

"She did this," June said venomously. "You did this!" June started toward Olivia, but Jordan grabbed her by the arm.

"You've fucked up, June." He stalked toward her. "You pulled Desi Green into a place she's got no business being, and you've made us all look like fools!"

"I don't give a damn what we look like!"

"I do give a damn!" Jordan's voice must've resonated throughout the building. "I let you come into this company—"

She glared at him. "You didn't let me do anything, Jordan. If what you say is true then I have more of a right to oversee Gatewood Industries than you ever did!"

"You're a fuckin' idiot, June!"

"Fuck—" She started to cuss him out.

"You pack up your shit and your kids and take your ass back to Atlanta," he said dismissively.

"No, really, Jordan." June folded her arms across her chest. "Fuck you! I'm not leaving."

"You sure as hell aren't staying." He poured himself a drink.

Did he really think it would be that easy? "I'm not twelve, Jordan. I go where I please, and this is home for me and my children. Maybe you can pull that big, bad, bully shit with other people, but I'm not the one!"

"Edgar, take Mother home."

"Home?" Olivia asked wearily, doing her best to look confused. "Your name escapes me, sir. Do you work for my father?"

Just like that, Olivia had lapsed into her fragile, helpless, and hapless woman act. Edgar helped the suddenly feeble beauty to her feet, and steadied her as the two of them worked their way to the staircase.

"You need to go with them, June."

He could dismiss Olivia's pathetic ass but June wasn't going to let him off the hook so easily. "How long have you known that Julian wasn't your father?"

He poured himself a drink, loosened his tie, and fell back onto the loveseat, but Jordan was absent with any answers. Despite his best efforts not to, Jordan looked wounded, and despite her best efforts not to care, well, he was still her brother. June went over and sat beside him.

"When we were kids you believed he was your father. I know you did, Jordan. How long have you known the truth?"

Jordan was silent. But an even clearer picture was beginning to come into focus for June. Jordan was as much a pawn in Olivia's schemes as anyone was. He'd been a victim his whole life, used by her.

"Look at what she's done to us, Jordan," June said sympathetically. He had grown up worshipping that woman, and the whole time she'd been lying to him. "I know how much you love her. Believe it or not, I love her too. But Mother's no saint. She killed our . . . Julian. I believe that with my whole heart, and then she set Desi up to take the fall for that. You hate Desi Green for no reason, Jordan. She's not the enemy, and she never has been. Olivia's lied to and manipulated all of us. You have to see that."

Jordan finished his drink in one gulp and then looked at his sister. "I want you to get the hell out of here." His tone stung. "And next week, I want you to get the hell out of Gatewood Industries or I swear I'll have security drag your ass out kicking and screaming, June. It really is up to you how you want to leave."

She could fight him for her father's company, especially if what he said was true. But it would be a long, arduous fight, and expensive, and it would certainly take its toll on June and her children. June had done what she'd set out to do. She'd wanted to wave Desi Green in Olivia's face and pit the woman against her in the ring of Gatewood Industries. She'd pissed Olivia off and showed her that June wasn't the scared little girl she knew and almost loved as much as she loved her son. Anything else that happened between Desi and Olivia now was up to them.

June reluctantly kissed him on the cheek. "One day you're going to realize that your loyalty is misplaced," she said, standing up to leave. "When you do, I'll be here for you, Jordan."

Chapter 26

How long had the bottom actually been crumbling and falling apart underneath him? What was the event that set in motion all of the events leading up to this moment? The sun was just starting to rise. Jordan sat slumped on the side of his bed, staring out the window across the room, watching orange and pink streak across the sky, signaling dawn. He hadn't slept all night. He hadn't slept in many nights. Jordan felt like a man no longer in touch with the world—with his life or what he believed that his life had been. His cell phone lay on the floor at his bare feet. The call had come after he'd gotten home from June's party. It came after Jordan had polished off a few more whiskeys. The call had put an end to everything he had come to know about who he was and what his destiny had always been.

"Señor Gatewood. I am Detective Javier Alamilla." The accent was so thick that Jordan could barely understand him. "Your wife is Mrs. Claire—Claire Gatewood?"

Jordan was drunk. Drunk enough not to think that the call was anything more than a man named Javier calling to tell him something about Claire. Claire had lost her passport. Claire was in the hospital. Claire had been robbed.

"Yes," Jordan answered unemotionally.

She was on the other side of the world where he'd sent her. He hadn't spoken to her in weeks and that was okay because Jordan had nothing to say to his wife. And there was nothing that she had to say to him that he wanted to hear. He didn't love Claire. No matter how hard he tried to, it was never real, never deep enough, never solid enough. A part of his soul had died with Lonnie.

"I regret to inform you, Señor Gatewood, that your wife . . ."

The man's accent was so hard to understand. "Wait—what? What about my wife?"

His wife was pathetic. She was weak and too damned dependent on him. Claire was as far away from him as he could get her, and Jordan did not miss a thing about her.

"Your wife was involved in an accident," the man said.

Did he say that she was involved in an accident or that she *was* an accident? Jordan assumed the latter.

"There's been an accident," he repeated.

Damn! What time was it? Did this idiot even know what time it was?

"An accident? A car accident?"

"She—she cut herself, Señor Gatewood. Your wife cut her wrists and bled to death. It appears that . . . she took her own life."

And just like that, Claire was gone.

Sexy

Chapter 27

The pendulum had swung to her side, and the last thing Desi needed to do was let that momentum shift back over into the Gatewood court. That family was starting to unravel. Desi had seen it with her own eyes the other night at the party. The look on Jordan's face when she walked into that ballroom and the fact that he seemed to understand that he hadn't scared her away was priceless.

She'd been driven to go to that party by forces even she couldn't explain and by doing so she'd put not only her own life on the line but Solomon's as well. Her intent was to send a message to Jordan and Olivia. And the message was for the two of them to bring their fight to her. She could only hope that they got it and that she would be ready for them when they did.

It had been a month since Lonnie was found murdered on the steps of that motel across town. And the police seemed no closer to solving her murder than they were the night it happened. Desi was still staying in her hotel downtown, making Solomon believe that she had flown back to California to take care of some business. She had asked him to pick her up from the airport in the morning. The Dallas Police Department had no leads, but today, she was going to finally give them one.

Detective Bobby Randolph wasn't much taller than she was. Desi had asked to speak to whoever was in charge of the Lonnie Adebayo case and he was it.

"Wow. I uh . . ." He'd led Desi to a room much like the one they'd put her in when she was eighteen and questioned her about Mr. J's murder.

Desi hadn't expected to be flooded with those memories.

"Ms. Green." He sighed heavily. He was a stout man, graying, and he looked tired. "I've read a lot about you," he said nervously. "In the papers."

If she didn't know better, she'd think the man was starstruck, or scared.

Desi cleared her throat. "I was told you were the officer working on the Lonnie Adebayo case?"

Desi hated cops. She didn't trust them, but this one time, she was going to have to try and trust that this one was predisposed to do the right thing.

"Yes." He composed himself and slid into the chair at the table where she sat. "Yes, I am the lead detective on the case," he said almost sheepishly. "You're here to offer some insight into what may have happened?"

This really was the point of no return for Desi. Fear had kept her from coming here and speaking up back when she first found out that Lonnie had been killed. Fear that no one would believe what she had to say, or that Jordan would come after her once he found out that she'd spoken to the police. Desi came here today knowing that she was still afraid, but that perhaps, Jordan was even more afraid than she was.

"I knew her," she finally admitted. "I knew Lonnie." Sudden tears welled in her eyes, but now was not the time to cry. Desi blinked them away. "She was my friend."

Of course he looked stunned. Was he just surprised that the dead woman had a friend, or that Desi had friends? Either way, she was offended.

"May I ask how the two of you came to meet?"

"Does it matter?" Desi asked deadpan.

Her blunt response seemed to make him even more nervous. "It could."

"We met when we were teenagers," she said. "Lonnie used to write to me when I was in prison," Desi explained. "We finally met in person after I was released."

He nodded as if he understood, but it was obvious to Desi that the man had a million and one questions he didn't know how to ask.

"Ms. Adebayo was quite an accomplished woman. She traveled the world, and everyone we spoke to who knew her had nothing but great things to say about her. Do you know what she was doing in Dallas?"

"Yes," Desi responded simply.

He stared at her in anticipation. She had come too far to turn back now. Desi had to say it.

"She was here for a man," she began apprehensively. "Jordan Gatewood." There. She'd said it. Now what this man did with what she told him was the next obstacle.

He cocked a burly brow. "Jordan Gatewood—as in oil Gatewood?"

Desi shrugged. "He's the only one I know."

There it was. Desi spotted it even though he tried quickly to hide it, but that look of disbelief flashed long enough for her to know what he was thinking. The history between Desi and the Gatewoods was no secret. Apparently, he was fully aware of it.

"Lonnie Adebayo knew Mr. Gatewood?"

"They were lovers," Desi volunteered, watching the doubt flood his eyes.

He leaned back in his chair, took a deep breath, and rubbed his chin. "How do you know?"

"She was my friend, Detective."

He didn't believe her. This was what she'd expected. This was why she hadn't come here sooner.

"She told me everything." It was mostly the truth. Lonnie shared what she wanted to share with Desi, but she had shared the fact that she and Jordan had been lovers and that he'd tried to kill her two years ago.

"You don't believe me?" she said, trying to keep the faith.

He didn't deny it. "The lowdown on you and the Gatewoods is pretty much public knowledge, Ms. Green. There's no love lost there."

"None."

"So, can you prove that the two of them had a connection?"

Solomon had warned her that the police would probably not believe her. Desi struggled against picking up her purse and walking out of that place. To say she could feel her frustration building was an understatement.

"Prove it—how? She told me that they were lovers. The fact that she knew the man should be enough to raise a red flag, Detective."

"Do you really expect me to believe this, Ms. Green? I didn't read your book, but my wife did. I know how you feel about the Gatewoods, and if what you wrote in that book is true, I can't say that I blame you."

"But you don't believe me."

"I don't believe you."

"And that's why I didn't come forward in the beginning," she murmured. "The Gatewoods can do whatever they want and get away with it in this town."

He looked insulted. Good.

"But then, that's what money buys you," she said bitingly. "Carte blanche to do whatever you want to people without having to pay a penalty."

"If I felt that your accusation had any meat, Ms. Green . . ."

"It's not an accusation," Desi said coolly. "Jordan was cheating on his wife with Lonnie."

"And she came back here to be with him? To steal him from his wife?" His tone was laced with sarcasm.

"She came back here to ruin him."

That got his attention.

"Two years ago, Jordan tried to kill Lonnie because he found out that she and I were friends. Lonnie helped me do the research for my book. While doing that research she met Jordan at a fund-raiser for an inner-city community center that he sponsored and donated money to build," she explained, digging deep to find tangible things that this man could look for to make her case against Jordan. "She ended up beaten to within an inch of her life in a Dallas hospital, but Lonnie left without telling anyone who'd attacked her."

He looked . . . interested. But was he interested enough to actually check out anything Desi was telling him? Somehow, she suspected that he wouldn't.

"She wanted to make him pay for what he'd done to her."

"And what about you?" he asked, studying her. "Do you want to make him, his family, pay for what they did to you?"

His condescending tone was offensive. The man had made up his mind as soon as Desi had mentioned Jordan's name. Detective Randolph was like every other policeman in this city. He had his hand in Jordan's pocket. Desi picked up her purse and slipped it onto her shoulder. "You should've read my book, Detective." Desi had done all she could do. She stood up to leave. "I was paid twenty million dollars from the Gatewoods for my troubles, so I'm good." She said, realizing she'd wasted her time.

The detective stood up as well. "Thank you for coming in Ms. Green," he said unemotionally. "We appreciate any and all leads on this case."

"But you're not going to do anything with what I've told you. Are you?" Of course he wasn't, because he didn't give a damn about finding Lonnie's killer if it meant that a Gatewood had killed her. He was too busy kissing Jordan's ass.

He smiled politely.

Desi didn't. "Then shame on you."

Desi had done all she could. And it still wasn't enough.

Chapter 28

Every mouth shut, every pair of eyes in every head in the room locked onto that woman and stared at her from the time she walked out of the interrogation room with Bobby until the front doors of the precinct closed behind her. Nothing could've prepared any of them for seeing that woman in person. Desi Green's hair was as breathtaking as a lion's mane and just as full. She glided across the room in five-inch stilettos like she'd been born in them and they were just a natural extension of her legs. And speaking of legs—that form-fitting skirt she wore hugged every inch of her curves, fitting like a glove and showing off some of the prettiest legs Bobby Randolph had ever seen.

"Damn," he heard Anderson mutter from across the room as she disappeared. "That was Desi Green? She don't look like any ex-con I've ever seen."

"Yeah well, most ex-cons don't come out of prison to a thirty-something-million-dollar inheritance," one of the office aides said.

"I heard it was twenty," Anderson offered.

"Twenty—thirty—whatever it was, it was a hell of a lot of money," the aide finished off, rolling her eyes.

Bobby finally took a breath, the first one he could remember taking since he had laid eyes on the woman and sat down at his desk.

"What she want, Bobby?" someone asked. "She know something about that Adebayo woman?"

He shook his head. "Nah . . . She just—Nothing."

As fascinating as their conversation had been, Desi Green really hadn't given him anything he could bank on. She had a thing against the Gatewoods. He got that. And maybe, she was bitter enough to try and set one of them up for murder, the way she claimed that they had set her up. She came to him with a lot of hearsay, probably lies, and one big-ass coincidence. This was the second time Gatewood's name had come up in his investigation. The first being when they discovered the license plate registered to him in the back of a stolen car.

"Really?" Iris sat down at her desk across from his. "Desdimona Green graces us with her appearance, asks specifically for the detective heading up the Adebayo murder case, and you're gonna sit there and tell me she gave you nothing?"

Bobby just looked at Iris.

Iris looked at Bobby.

He stood up, stuffed his cell phone in his pocket, and left. Iris got up and followed him out the door and to the car. Once inside, he turned to her.

"Don't you tell a soul what I'm about to say to you."

She shrugged. "I won't."

"Because it's bullshit, Iris. It's the kind of shit that if it got out, it could create a goddamned circus in this city."

"What did she tell you, Bobby?"

He faced forward, stared out at the parking lot, took a deep breath, and rubbed his temple. "Nothing I can use," he said dismally.

"Then why the hell does it matter if I tell anybody?"

The Adebayo case was the biggest case he'd ever caught because the woman was almost a celebrity and everybody, including the mayor, was coming down hard on him to find out who'd killed her.

"Bobby?" Iris sighed. "Come on, man. What did she tell you?"

Iris was his partner. If he couldn't trust her, then he couldn't trust anybody. "It's ridiculous."

"Fine. What is it?"

"She said she knew Yolanda Adebayo and that they were friends," he began explaining.

"Really?" Iris took hold of that information and pondered it for a moment. "Convicted murderer, Pulitzer-nominated author," Iris shrugged. "Well, what's so ridiculous about that?"

"Nothing," he said. "But there's more."

Iris waited, but when he didn't respond, she gave him that nudge he needed. "I'm listening."

"She said that the woman, Adebayo, was having an affair with Jordan Gatewood." He looked at Iris, who raised her brows in surprise. "That he'd actually put her in the hospital a few years back and that she had come here to get revenge for what he'd done to her."

"And you don't believe it?"

He looked at Iris. "You do?"

She shrugged again. "It's been a month since the murders, Bobby. I just don't think we can afford to turn our noses up at any lead no matter how crazy it sounds."

"We also don't need to be wasting time chasing rainbows either."

"But what if what she told you is true? What if he did know the woman? I mean, think about it. We already know that his car was somewhere in the area of the murders, Bobby. We found the man's license plate, for crying out loud, and I don't give a damn how rich you are or how many cars you have, if someone steals your eighty-thousand-dollar Mercedes you're going to report it stolen. He didn't do that and I have to admit, I got heartburn over that."

Bobby had heartburn over it too. Gatewood's excuse for not reporting the car stolen was weak, but hell, he was who he was and Bobby let it slide because of that.

"These people are rich, Bobby, they're not angels. And they're not angels because they're rich," Iris argued.

"Desi Green's no angel either," he countered, still trying to make his case. "She did time for murdering one of them, Iris."

"She claims they set her up."

"She went to prison."

"Did you read the book?" Iris asked.

"No! I didn't read the damn book!"

"Well, I did and after reading it, I have to admit, Bobby, her claim that those people set her up for killing Julian Gatewood wasn't all that far-fetched."

"Lord," he said, exasperated.

"Taking the Lord's name in vain isn't going to make your point," Iris retorted. "All I'm saying is that we don't have the luxury of not chasing any and every lead that comes our way no matter how bad a taste it leaves in your mouth. It's been a month and we got nothing, Bobby. We got less than nothing except for one common denominator that's come up a few times now and that's Gatewood."

She was right. Hell, no matter how many different ways he tried to wiggle his way out of this one, he just couldn't do it.

"And what about the other two victims found at that motel, Iris? Why the hell would he kill them, which wouldn't make a damn bit of sense considering the fact that they were shot with a different gun?" The more he argued, the more he began to believe what Desi Green had told him.

"What if it's a revenge thing for Ms. Green?" he asked, bringing his final argument to the table.

"She's pissed at the Gatewoods. I get that. But men like Gatewood don't skulk around dirty motels waiting in the shadows to kill people," he concluded.

"No, but they do hire people to do it."

That damned Iris! The two of them stared each other down. He hated her for saying it, but damnit if it didn't make sense.

"Why now?" Iris probed. "And why this murder? People get killed in this city every day, so why would she pick this one? Desi Green's been lying dormant since she wrote that book a few years back and she's got money. She could be resting on her laurels now and living her life, but she came here today to talk about this particular murder."

"That's my point," he retorted, coming to his senses. "Why didn't she come forward in the beginning?"

Iris shrugged again. "She probably thought you wouldn't believe her."

Bobby froze.

"Because you don't."

He didn't want to. It was bad enough that he didn't have any leads on the murders at that motel, particularly Lonnie Adebayo's murder, which seemed to be the only one anybody gave a damn about. But to add Gatewood into this investigation was only going to make it worse. The man was a god in this city, and the brass wasn't going to take it well at all if they knew that Bobby was looking at him as a suspect.

"I'll be honest, Bobby," Iris continued. "I have a feeling there might be something to what she told you today."

"Why?"

Iris pulled out her cell phone, punched in something on her touch screen, and then held it out for him to see. "Check it out."

He pulled it close. It was the headline on the *Dallas Morning News* Web site.

Claire Gatewood, Wife of Jordan Gatewood, Found Dead in Lisbon, Spain

"News broke this afternoon," Iris explained. "They're calling it an apparent suicide."

Bobby was speechless. Nearly a month ago he'd asked Gatewood about his wife and now the woman was dead? Suicide. Gatewood had refused Bobby's request to question her about the stolen vehicle and now, conveniently, she was gone.

"You might not want to do it, Bobby, but I don't think we have much choice in the matter."

The nuances were subtle, so subtle that on their own, they wouldn't mean a whole lot, but as far apart as the dots were, Bobby could see that it was still possible to start to connect them.

"It's all we got, Bobby," Iris reasoned. "And my gut tells me that it's something."

He nodded slowly. "Yeah, Iris. My gut is telling me that it might just be something too."

Chapter 29

"*Where were you*, Jordan?" Claire's mother cried, approaching him after the memorial service. "She needed you! She loved you! Why weren't you with her?"

"Edna." Claire's father gathered the woman in his arms and led her away. "Let's go, Edna."

Jordan slipped on his Ray-Bans, walked down the steps of the cathedral, and headed toward his car. Less than a week after her death, Claire's body had been flown home and she'd been cremated. Jordan had lived in a bubble during that time, secluded in his house. What had surprised him the most was how hard he was taking his wife's death. Claire had been a fixture in his life for so long that not having her a phone call or plane ride away left a void in him he didn't expect.

———

He drove for hours before he finally went home.

"I know I'm probably the last person you want to see, Jordan, but . . ."

June was there when he walked in. Jordan took off his shades and dropped his keys on the bar before pouring himself a drink.

"I'm so sorry about Claire," she continued sincerely. "Is there anything I can do—anything you need?"

Jordan loosened his tie and walked past his sister as if she weren't even in the room.

"I love you," she said, following behind him but keeping her distance. "I know you may not believe that, but I do."

As if it mattered.

He opened the door leading out to the patio and stepped outside. Jordan stared out at the pristine pool and the perfectly manicured gardens. Claire had wanted that damn pool. He tried to remember the last time he'd actually seen her in it and drew a blank.

"Jordan? Son?"

The sound of Olivia's voice grated on his nerves. She came rushing outside to him and wrapped both arms around him. "I tried to catch up to you after the service." She squeezed. "You left so fast."

If Olivia was here, Edgar couldn't have been far behind.

"How're you holding up, son?" Jordan heard him ask.

Olivia released her grip on him, cradled his face between her hands, and stared with concern into his eyes. "It's going to be alright," she said reassuringly. "We'll all help you to get through this, son. You know that. Don't you?"

Jordan knew no such thing. His face must've expressed his thoughts openly because Olivia stepped back like she was looking into the face of a monster. *Wasn't she?*

"You need to rest, son," she murmured more to herself than to him.

"Maybe we should give him some space, Mother," June spoke up.

Olivia shot her a look as if she'd just now noticed that June was there.

"I'm sure Jordan's tired," June concluded.

"Jordan," Olivia said, not taking her eyes off of June. "Who is this woman?"

It was a peculiar statement, especially under the circumstances, that it even managed to get his attention.

"Don't start," June said dismally.

"Who are you? And what are you doing at my son's house?" Olivia looked confused as she looked up at Jordan. "Who is she? Do you know her?"

He shook his head and almost laughed at the absurdity of it all.

"You're being ridiculous, Mother, and so very transparent," June said irritably.

"Julian!" She motioned toward Edgar. "Get this woman out of here! She has no business being here! Make her leave!"

Most of the time, Olivia's acts of senility were pretty convincing. This wasn't one of those times. Was it any wonder that Jordan was the man he was? He studied her beautiful face, looked deep into her lying eyes, and suddenly understood how manipulative, cunning, and evil this woman truly was. And she had made him. He was his mother's son. Not his father's, because she'd seen to it that he'd never really had one. Keep your enemies close. Was she his enemy? Or, was he hers? He backed away from her. Jordan wanted no part of this woman.

"Son?" Edgar asked. "Are you alright?"

"Did you take care of us, Edgar?" Jordan suddenly blurted out. He hadn't meant to say it out loud, but it had slipped, a question from his heart, for himself and for Claire. No. Claire was gone. And all that was left was Jordan.

"Yes," Edgar said.

"What are you talking about?" Olivia asked, looking between the two men.

Jordan glared at her and he wanted her gone. "Shut the hell up, Olivia!" He growled, turned, and went back inside.

"Jordan! Jordan, don't talk to me like—Jordan!"

His world was spiraling out of control and Jordan was in a free fall. Nothing was set in stone anymore, not even Claire, the woman he'd believed would be there forever, whether he loved her or not, whether he wanted her or not. The women in his life were dropping like flies, except for the two he loathed the most.

"Jordan." June reached out to him as he passed by her. He stopped and dared her to put her hands on him.

June recoiled.

He needed to get away from these people. Jordan headed up the stairs, taking them two at a time. The slope was slippery. His footing uncertain. The faith he'd once had in his life was quickly eroding away, taking with it his wife, Lonnie, his business, his sanity. Who was he really?

"What did you want to be when you grew up, Jordan?" Lonnie's questions echoed in his mind as he closed the bedroom door behind him.

He wanted to be Jordan Gatewood! *The* Jordan Gatewood! King of the mountain! On top of the world! He wanted Lonnie! He wanted Claire! He wanted Gatewood Industries to be one of the largest oil companies in the world! He wanted not to be responsible for the deaths of two women. He wanted Desi Green to vanish! He wanted . . . He wanted . . . To not be afraid that the world would find out that he was a fraud!

———

Jordan hadn't even realized that he'd fallen asleep until the sound of the phone ringing woke him up. The sun had set and the room was dark. He lay across the bed still wearing the suit he'd worn to Claire's memorial service.

"Yes," he answered groggily, rubbing the sleep from his eyes.

"Mr. Gatewood?"

"Yes," he said again, irritably.

"Sir, I'm sorry to bother you. I really am."

"Who is this?"

"Sir, it's Detective Randolph from the Dallas Police Department. We spoke a while back about your car that had been stolen? We talked about the plates we'd found in the back of a stolen vehicle."

Jordan sat up. His heart drummed in his chest so loudly that he wouldn't have been surprised if the man on the phone could hear it.

"What can I do for you, Detective?" he asked, forcing a steady rhythm in his voice.

"Sir, let me say that I am sorry for your loss. I know that this isn't the best time for me to be calling, but—"

"Why are you calling?"

The man sighed. "Well, Mr. Gatewood, I was hoping to set up a time to ask you a few more questions."

"About the car?" Jordan probed.

"That and some other things," the man said hesitantly.

"What other things?" Jordan asked forcefully.

"Well, sir . . . I'd really rather not address them over the phone."

"Then we won't address them at all," Jordan told him.

"Do you know a woman named Yolanda Adebayo, Mr. Gatewood?" the detective suddenly asked.

Jordan paused. Fear gripped him in the gut and twisted like a knot until he couldn't breathe.

"Mr. Gatewood." The detective's voice reminded Jordan to respond.

"I may have met her once or twice," he said cautiously.

"You do know she was murdered about a month ago."

Jordan almost didn't hear the man for the sound of his world crashing down around him. "Yes."

He knew. Somehow, this man knew.

"I'd like to discuss the nature of your relationship with Ms. Adebayo in person, sir. It's a formality and we're just following up on any and all leads. You understand."

Randolph wanted to make his inquiry seem trite, a minor technicality that the two of them needed to reconcile just to tie up loose ends. Yes, he understood.

"Mr. Gatewood? Sir, are you there?"

"Yes. Yes, I understand." He swallowed. Jordan's mind began to race. The gears shifted into automatic. "Call my office tomorrow and my assistant will set up a time, Detective."

"Yes, sir, I'll do that. And thank you, Mr. Gatewood. Once again, sir, I am sorry for your—"

Jordan hung up the phone before the man could finish.

His palms were sweating. Jordan sat on the bed, struggling to catch his breath. The man knew that Jordan was somehow involved in Lonnie's death. He had been careful not to say it, but he'd said so much more by avoiding saying it. He knew that Jordan was acquainted with Lonnie. Maybe he even knew how he was acquainted with Lonnie. That and the fact that there was evidence that Jordan's—Claire's—car had been at the scene of the crime was enough to put Jordan in a panic.

Claire was dead. Even if he confessed that Claire was the one who'd shot Lonnie, it was his word against . . . no one's.

There were some things that came second nature to Jordan. Some reactions that were lightning fast and instinctive. These things didn't require much effort on his part. He just knew what needed to be done and he did it.

Jordan dialed a number on his phone. The man he called, Alex Richards, was an attorney, one of the best criminal attorneys in the country. It was late, but he didn't give a damn. Alex eventually answered. "Alex. It's Jordan."

Jordan had hired Alex to work on another criminal case. He'd hired Alex to represent Frank Ross, who was accused of killing a cop in Cotton, Texas. Frank had been connected to the motel where Lonnie had been killed, got skittish when they brought him in for questioning, and ran. Frank was an idiot, and an idiot was just what Jordan needed.

"I'm going to give you the address of where Frank Ross is staying," Jordan continued unemotionally. "Call the Cotton Police Department and give them that address. Have them pick Frank up."

Jordan hung up.

Chapter 30

It had been a week since Desi had confronted the Gatewoods at the Investors' Ball, and in that week, they'd buried Claire Gatewood.

"Reporters are dogging us like you wouldn't believe," Leslie, Desi's assistant in California, told her over the phone.

It was late, but Leslie and Desi had been playing phone tag for days before Desi finally caught up with the woman. Solomon was downstairs in his office working and Desi lay in bed.

"Ever since they found out that you now own stock in Gatewood Industries, they're all wondering if you're going to jump ship from the fashion world and become some kind of an oil baroness," Leslie said sarcastically.

Desi smiled.

"You're not—are you?" Leslie asked, concerned. "I mean—you're not giving up Konvictions for some stinky old oil. Are you, Desi?"

"Of course not," Desi reassured her. "Oil is just going to be my side gig," she joked.

The truth, though, was that she had never planned to invest in the oil business, had no business in the oil business, and was pretty sure that she wasn't going to be in it for long. June had talked her into this craziness at a time when Desi's voice of reason had left for vacation, but the venture had made her even more money than she already had. Desi's investment in Anton tripled in value when it changed over to Gatewood stock, literally overnight, and all of a sudden she had more money than she could possibly spend in her lifetime.

"Saks finally sent over the purchase orders we've been waiting months for."

"Good," Desi said, genuinely happy. She'd been crossing her fingers and toes and eyes, hoping that the Saks buyer hadn't changed his mind. This was a huge victory for Konvictions and it was also a reminder of just how important her business still was to her even though she'd been mostly hands-off for far too long. "That's great news, Leslie."

"It would be greater news if you were here and we were at a bar clinking wineglasses together celebrating," she said, not bothering to hide her disappointment.

How many times had the two of them done just that, over every little thing: a balanced budget, an ad in a magazine, selling out at a boutique.

"I've never been to Texas," Leslie offered. "But I mean, if you're going to run Konvictions from there, or if you were thinking about it . . . I mean, so, yeah. I guess I could move."

Desi laughed. "I'll keep that in mind, girl."

"Cowboys are sexy," she added for good measure.

"Go to bed," Desi teased. "It's past your bedtime."

"Night, Mom." Leslie giggled before hanging up.

It was midnight already and Solomon was still downstairs. Ever since the attack, Desi had been walking on eggshells around him and Solomon had been unusually quiet, but also quietly affectionate. Whenever Desi tried starting a conversation, the best she could get out of him were one-word answers or short sentences in response. But every now and then he'd lean over and kiss her, or touch her back as he passed by her. At night, he slept close, draping his arm over her the way he always had. Of course, her nature was to fly away, to leave and give him the space she believed he needed to process what had happened to him, and to consider his feelings for her in all of this. Before she'd come along, Solomon's life had been pretty stable. He had his career, his house, his daughter—who had made it pretty clear that she hated Desi. She was eighteen now, and she refused to visit him if Desi was close by. He said it didn't bother him, but Desi knew better. Solomon loathed drama, but his life had been filled with it since he'd met Desi. Meanwhile, she tiptoed around the house waiting for that ball to drop and for him to tell her that he couldn't do this anymore.

A text message suddenly appeared on her phone. It was a picture, and Desi surmised that it had to have been Leslie messing around until she opened it and recognized the image of herself, wearing the dress she'd worn to the ball, with her arm looped around Phillip's. She glanced at the sender's phone number. It was Solomon's. As big a city as Dallas was, it sometimes wasn't big enough. Desi had hoped that he wouldn't find out that she'd gone to that ball. Obviously, he had.

Solomon was leaning inside the doorway of his office, waiting for her, when she got downstairs, wearing jeans sagging low on his hips and a white beater, with his hand stuffed into his pockets.

Desi walked over and stopped in front of him and cleared her throat. "You look kinda pissed," she said quietly.

He stood nearly a head taller than Desi. "I am kinda pissed."

"How long have you known?" she asked.

"Oh, I probably got that picture texted to me within a few minutes of you arriving at that event," he explained, looking down at her. "I've been waiting all week for you to tell me, yourself, that you were there."

"I didn't tell you because I was hoping you wouldn't need to know."

"You lied to me, Desi."

She looked up at him. "If I'd have told you that I was planning on going you'd have tried to talk me out of it, or you would've insisted on going and you weren't in any shape for that."

"You're right," he admitted, "on both accounts. But that doesn't change the fact that you still lied to me."

She opened her mouth to protest, but Solomon interrupted.

"How are we going to make this work, the way it's supposed to work, if we're not truthful with each other?" Solomon wasn't yelling. He wasn't arguing or belittling. He was reasoning and rationalizing and sounding too damn much like a lawyer.

"I had to go, Solomon." She was starting to argue.

"Why?" he asked quickly.

Desi was standing too close to him, close enough to feel the warmth of his breath on her face, and so she started to back away, but Solomon reached around her waist and pulled her back.

"Why'd you have to go?"

"For so many reasons," she said, feeling herself start to get emotional, and pissing herself off because of it.

"Tell me."

He was so beautiful and he was so wounded. He was probably in pain now and it was because of her.

"I needed for him to know," she began, fighting back tears, "for all of them to know that I'm not afraid of them, and that I'm through running from them." Desi swallowed and raised her hand and pressed it against the side of his face. "It's between me and him, Solomon. I reminded him that this—whatever this is between me and Jordan—is just between us." She shook her head, hoping that he understood what she was saying. "Nobody else."

Of course he had his pride, and Solomon's ego was more bruised and broken than his ribs. Of course he wanted to pound on Jordan and take back his dignity. But Jordan wasn't a fair fighter, and Desi had let Lonnie step in and take her place in a fight that should've been hers. She was not going to make that mistake with him.

The look on his face was beyond grave and so close to being angry.

"So you think that by going there that night, you flexed a little muscle?"

"Little muscle?" she repeated, feeling almost offended.

"You think Gatewood was intimidated enough to just let this whole thing go?"

Now Desi was offended. "You weren't there, Solomon. I didn't just intimidate Jordan. I shocked the hell out of him and his mother," she said defensively. "And yes," she continued, forgetting the fact that Solomon was not the enemy. "He got the message that this shit is between me and him and nobody else!"

She wanted him to understand. Tears flooded her eyes and Desi leaned in close, put her hand on the back of his neck, and pulled his head closer to hers. "I can't lose you," she whispered in his ear. "You're all I have left, Solomon."

There was no truer statement and in that moment, Desi felt it more deeply than she had expected. She felt it in her heart, in her stomach. Desi knew people, she had what could be referred to as friends, but Solomon was more than that. He was her family, the only family she had left, and if anything happened to him—she would vanish.

He looked into her eyes. "Where do you think I'm going, baby?"

When she was younger, before the Gatewoods, before prison, before hopelessness, she was like most teenage girls and dreamed of falling in love with a man made just for her. Until he came along, that's all it was—a dream.

Solomon took hold of her hand, lowered it, and pulled it around his waist. "Believe it or not, this isn't the first time I've had my ass kicked." He smiled. "A skinny kid, growing up in my 'hood, with a big-ass mouth and an even bigger attitude, I got jumped on the regular."

This time, she did laugh.

"It became routine. You know?" he explained matter-of-factly. "I had a standing appointment with ass whoopings back in the day, so this is nothing, baby."

"It's not nothing," she said, wiping away tears. "He could've killed you."

"He didn't. He probably should've, but . . ."

"Don't say that, Solomon."

"I'm still here, Desi, and I don't plan on that changing anytime soon, so I don't need for you to go and fight my battles for me."

"But it was never your battle, baby. This happened to you because of me. It's my fight, and all I'm saying is that I can handle it, so you don't have to. I was raised in a cell block, damnit," she said, attempting to lighten the situation. "I know how to fight."

Solomon put his hand under her chin and raised her lips to his. "I know," he said, pressing his lips against hers.

She loved the taste of him, the feel of his body pressed against hers, and of being held by him. He hadn't said it, but she knew that Solomon wasn't even thinking of backing down or walking away from this beef he now had with Jordan. Desi couldn't stop him, but she could keep her part in this away from him. And she would.

"Where'd you get that dress?" he asked, breaking the seal of their kiss.

Desi smiled. "You like it?"

"You looked beyond beautiful in that dress."

Desi raised her eyebrows. "Beyond beautiful? Wow."

"I'm jealous that I didn't get to see you in it live and in person."

"Well, I still have the dress, Solomon."

"Here?"

She nodded. "It's upstairs in the closet."

He took hold of her hand and pulled her behind him. "Show me."

Chapter 31

Woody had offered to hide the car Frank had been driving in his garage. The two men stood in the driveway and waited while the door closed.

"You see the news this morning?" Woody asked.

Woody was a heavyset man, well over six feet tall like the rest of them, but he had to weigh close to three hundred pounds. He was a minister, aiding and abetting a wanted fugitive. Frank wondered if there was some kind of commandment against that but didn't think he should ask.

Frank nodded. "I saw it," he said dismally.

"Police have issued a statewide manhunt for suspected killer Franklin Ross. Ross is out on bail, awaiting trial for the killing of a Cotton, Texas, police officer. His ex-partner, Colette Fisher, is scheduled to stand trial next month. Ross, who had been under surveillance, allegedly assaulted a police officer and fled town."

A picture of Frank's face filled the screen. "Police have released this image of Frank Ross. The public is directed to contact local police departments if you suspect you've seen this man or know of his whereabouts."

Frank followed Woody inside his house. His wife, Regina, was in the kitchen cooking. He had two kids. A son, Woodrow, Jr., was in the army and stationed in Korea. His daughter, Lisa, was a sophomore at a local community college studying nursing. She lived with her boyfriend in a town called Maynard.

The two men passed through the kitchen and went outside to the backyard where Woody had a deck underneath a big shade tree. They sat there for several minutes, not saying anything at all to each other, which was fine with Frank. Talking, especially now, was overrated. His mind was clogged with too many thoughts. He had done some dumb shit in his life, and now he was paying for it. Frank had a lot to sort out. Woody seemed to know that without Frank having to say it.

It wasn't until Frank saw Malcolm walking across the lawn toward them that he started to get that sick feeling in his stomach. Woody was a patient, nonjudgmental man. Malcolm was an asshole. He went over to the cooler and got himself a beer without acknowledging either man. Of all of them, Malcolm reminded Frank the most of Jordan. He was leaner than Jordan, but they wore that same hardened expression in their eyes, unforgiving and just plain mean.

Malcolm took a seat next to Woody, and finished half of his beer before finally opening his mouth to say something.

He looked Frank dead in the eyes. "So, what you planning on doing?"

Frank took offense at the tone and the attitude. "Who the fuck are you?" he blurted out. "My goddamned daddy?"

Frank half expected Malcolm to leap across the deck and take a swing at him, but he didn't. Malcolm leaned forward. "I'm one of the men whose ass you're putting on the line by coming here," he shot back. "So, if I'm going to get my ass hauled off to prison for harboring your dumb ass, I'd like to know what to expect."

Frank almost believed that Woody liked him enough to step up for him, but obviously he was wrong. The big man just sat there, nodding. And Frank had no idea how to answer Malcolm's question. He needed to leave, but the whole damn state of Texas was looking for him. His only other option would be to turn himself in, but he had a feeling that that expensive lawyer Gatewood had hired for him wouldn't be so accessible this time.

"Pop said he told you to stay away from Gatewood," Malcolm continued. "Shoulda listened."

Frank was still shocked that the two of them knew about Jordan. He didn't know why, but he just figured that if they knew about it, maybe they'd have tried to . . . Then again, maybe they never had the same motivations as Frank. He had needed money to try and get him and Colette out of town, hell, out of the country. Lonnie Adebayo talked a good enough talk to convince him that Gatewood was the answer with the money and the means to hook Frank up, with the right motivation. She made it sound too easy, and too good to be true. It was neither.

Curiosity got the best of him and Frank had to ask. "Either one of y'all ever meet him?"

Woody shook his head. "Never interested in meeting him. He ain't nothing to us." He looked at Frank. "Just like we ain't nothing to him, and that's fine. No loss. Not for any of us."

He said it like he meant it. He talked about Jordan like he was just somebody out there who he'd heard about and not someone he shared a father with.

"Teddy's a bitch, man. Not that I blame him, hell. If I'd been dropped into all that money, I'd be a bitch too."

"Teddy?" Frank asked, confused.

"Theodore Tunson." Malcolm emphasized the word *Tunson*. "Jordan is his slave name." He and Woody looked at each other and laughed.

"Pops named him Theodore," Woody explained. "After Theodore Roosevelt? I'm named after Woodrow Wilson."

Frank looked at Malcolm.

Malcolm shrugged. "Hell, Pops just liked the name Malcolm."

He felt foolish but another question came to mind. "So, since y'all knew about Gatewood, did you know about me?"

Malcolm and Woody looked at each other. Woody nodded. "We knew."

That's all he said. Frank thought it was pretty fucked up that Woody left it at that.

"Now his feelings is hurt," Malcolm said sarcastically.

Frank just looked at him. Malcolm met his gaze with an unapologetic stare of his own.

"You still haven't answered my question," Malcolm said. "Maybe they'll track you to us and maybe they won't. Maybe you can stay here for the rest of your life and grow old or maybe not. But you got to do something, man."

"What would you suggest?" Frank asked resentfully.

Malcolm sighed and finished what was left of his beer. "Truthfully, I think you ought to turn yourself in." He shrugged. "Take your punishment like a man."

"You shot a man, Frank," Woody chimed in. "You got that woman killed too. Whether you meant to do it or not, it happened. Where you gonna run to? For how long? How far?"

Shit! Were they really telling him this? Frank hadn't exactly expected to be welcomed with open arms by these fools, but he sure as hell didn't expect them to tell him this!

"Oh, is that what the two of you would do if you were me? Walk into the nearest police station and let them send your ass to prison knowing good and damned well you wouldn't last a month in that joint? I'm a cop! They'd kill my ass in prison!"

Woody looked away and shook his head. Malcolm didn't blink. "Seems like you're the one doing all the killing, Frank," he said coolly. "But I guess that's okay?"

Frank felt his blood pressure start to rise. His heart raced in his chest. "I didn't mean for any of that to happen! Man!" He wasn't going to argue with these fools. Joel lived a few miles away and Frank could use the walk.

That cop pulled a gun first. I was just defending myself. It was him or me. That's how I saw it." They acted as if he was speaking a foreign language, but it didn't matter. This was the first time that Frank had ever met his brothers and if it was going to be the last then they had to understand that he wasn't the man the news stories made him out to be. Frank was better than that. "I didn't know he'd kill her," he said earnestly. "He told me to make the call to get her to that motel. Said I owed him."

Hearing himself say all of this, Frank couldn't help feeling like a fool. It just didn't sound right. Not even to him.

"I thought he was going to talk to her. They had a thing," he tried to explain. His brothers and his father all just stared at him. They didn't believe him. Hell, could he blame them? He got up and left the two of them sitting there.

He took his time walking back to his father's house. Frank had given himself a headache wondering what he could do, what he needed to do to get himself out of this mess, but every idea led to another dead end. Frank was trapped in a situation with no way out. He'd painted himself into a corner, and as far as he could tell, there was no escape.

Joel was standing on the front porch of the house when Frank arrived. Beside him stood two police officers.

"Frank Ross?" one said, coming up behind him holding a gun to his head.

All Frank could do was nod. He looked at Joel while they handcuffed him. The old man nodded too, and then disappeared inside the house.

Chapter 32

Four days ago, Claire was laid to rest, and now, Jordan was sitting in his living room being questioned by a detective about his relationship with Lonnie. Jordan hadn't been to the office since he got the news of Claire's death. He wasn't taking calls from his mother, June, or even Edgar.

The older, overweight man sat across from Jordan. "I apologize for intruding at a time like this, Mr. Gatewood."

He'd said that before, when Jordan answered the door and saw him standing on the other side of it.

"And I'm so very sorry for your loss."

His loss. Had he lost Claire? Or had he thrown her away? Either way, did it matter?

"What can I do for you, Detective?" Jordan asked unemotionally.

Of course, he knew why the man was there. And he knew that by the time this meeting was over, Jordan would either remain the untouchable force that he was and had always been, or he'd be led away in handcuffs. No. Not handcuffs. Even this fool wasn't foolish enough to put handcuffs on a Gatewood. But Jordan's freedom, his reputation, could be in jeopardy by the time this interrogation ended.

"Well, sir. If you remember, several weeks ago we spoke about your stolen automobile and the license plate we found from it on another vehicle."

"I remember."

"You said that the vehicle had been taken and that you had failed to report it stolen?"

Failed? Yes. Jordan had failed in so many ways.

"The vehicle had been stolen from a parking lot of a motel off the 635 where several murders had taken place," he explained. "You may have seen something about it on the news. Three people were killed at that motel, including one Yolanda Adebayo." He looked up from the notepad he was reading and waited for Jordan to say or do something. When he didn't, the detective continued. "We have reason to believe that you may have been acquainted with Ms. Adebayo, Mr. Gatewood."

He had loved her. Jordan wanted to say that. He needed for someone real to know that he had indeed loved Lonnie, more than he should've. Loss. This was new to him, compounded by Claire taking her own life. He'd lost both of these women.

"We met some years ago, I believe."

His memory opened up for just a moment back to the instant he first saw her, pointing that camera at him, snapping picture after picture.

"At a fund-raiser."

Why was his heart so broken? Jordan had been perplexed by

this for the last week. He hadn't loved Claire the way he'd loved Lonnie. He hadn't wanted her. But maybe in some strange way, his own twisted way, he needed her.

"I want to be your constant," she'd told him after he'd proposed to her. *"I want to be the one person you can always depend on, the one who'll be there for you when nobody else is."*

Claire had kept her promise so much longer than she should've. Claire had shot Lonnie. She'd killed her, and the man sitting in Jordan's living room probably suspected that Jordan had been the one who'd shot her.

"You were . . . friends?" the man asked carefully, too carefully.

We were lovers, man. We were enemies. We were kindred spirits. Hell, she owned me!

"I barely knew her," he heard himself say.

It was a lie that flowed like water down a falls—second nature, and automatic. Jordan was surprised to hear those words come out of his mouth, but he understood immediately what was happening. Even in his grief and confusion, a sensor kicked in, forcing him to step up and save his own ass.

"Rumor has it that you were more than just acquaintances," the detective probed, more confidently this time, as if he knew more than he wanted to say at the moment.

"Whose rumor?" Jordan challenged, his mind reeling with ideas of who could know something like this. Who would go to the police and who had put this man on his trail in the first damn . . . "Desi," he said without thinking.

The expression on the man's face confirmed what Jordan suspected. The bitch had gone to the police and told them everything.

"She put you up to this," he muttered introspectively, almost smiling. Damn! That woman had finally grown a spine.

"Were you at that motel that night, Mr. Gatewood?" The detective looked him directly in the eye this time and held Jordan's gaze with all the courage he could muster.

"You do know the history between my family and Ms. Green, don't you, Detective?"

"Everybody in the state of Texas knows that history well, Mr. Gatewood."

Jordan saw an opening. It wasn't much of one, but it was there, and being who he was, it really was all he needed to get this man out of his living room.

"Then you know that she'd do anything to humiliate and make a mockery of my family," Jordan shot back.

"You and Ms. Adebayo weren't lovers?"

Jordan didn't like the look in the other man's eyes.

"We weren't lovers."

"And you weren't responsible for an assault on Ms. Adebayo"— he flipped through that notepad of his—"a little over two years ago that put her in the hospital?" He looked up at Jordan.

He was challenging Jordan. Daring him to say or do the wrong thing, to flinch or blink in a way that indicated he wasn't telling the truth. That's not how this game was supposed to be played and Jordan was starting to resent ever letting this man set foot in his damn house!

"I have no idea what you're talking about," Jordan responded, gathering everything about him that made him the man he was into a tight ball and squeezing it to his chest.

He couldn't afford to fall apart. Not here. Not today. Desi had made the worst mistake of her life talking to this man. She'd crossed the line again. And not only was Jordan angrier than he'd ever been at that woman, but he was afraid for her too. Afraid of what he was capable of doing to her because he'd seen that dark side of himself he'd just as soon shut his eyes to, and he knew just how far he could go if pushed.

"Even if Desi Green was the one who'd told me these things, and I'm not saying that she was . . ." The detective stared at him strangely. "It would be your word against hers. And knowing the history between you two, I'm sure that Ms. Green would be in no danger of reprisal of any kind."

It was a warning.

"There's no need for this thing to escalate unnecessarily," he finished, closing his notebook and slipping it into the inside pocket of his jacket. "No messy lawsuits or—anything." The man chuckled.

But Jordan had been warned to stay away from Desi and not to break her neck.

"Desi Green is a thorn in my side that I've learned to live with, Detective Randolph. But you would do well to take anything she has to say about me with a grain of salt." Now it was Jordan's turn to send a message. "And to choose your battles wisely, man." The detective stared at him. "It's just advice. Take it," he said, and shrugged. "Or leave it."

The detective nodded and then stood up to leave.

Survival of the fittest was a part of Jordan's DNA. It's what made him the successful businessman that he was. It was that attitude that had put him on top of the food chain and kept him there. Detective Randolph walked out of Jordan's house with doubts. Jordan closed the door behind him and then slumped against it and took a deep breath, relieved that he'd managed to hold it together long enough to convince Randolph that he may not be an innocent man, but he wasn't guilty enough to arrest either.

Chapter 33

"Lord have mercy!" Edgar Beckman stood up when he saw Desi approaching the table. Staring wide-eyed at her, he murmured, "You look so much like your mother."

It dawned on her in that moment that, other than Olivia Gatewood, he was the only person alive who could make that statement and mean it. But she wasn't stupid. It wasn't necessarily a compliment.

Desi sat down across from him. She wasn't totally surprised when he'd called, but the sound of his voice had caught her off guard. He'd gotten her number from June and asked Desi to meet him at this bar off Mockingbird Lane in Hyland Park Village. Moments after she'd sat down, a waitress appeared at their table.

"Are you ready to order now, sir?" the young woman asked.

He motioned to Desi to go first.

"I'll have a Chardonnay, please."

"We have several brands to choose from," the waitress explained. "Sonoma-Cutrer, Orogeny, Grgich Hills," she said, listing them.

"Orogeny," Desi told her.

Edgar looked curiously at her. "And I'll take a Chimay Red, please."

He hadn't taken his eyes off Desi since she'd sat down, but she was finding it hard to hold eye contact with him. She was a child when she knew Mr. Edgar. It was hard for her to see him in any other light, even after all the years that had passed. But Edgar was a connection to her past, that missing link reminding her that she hadn't made up those events from her life. Desi had been that little girl, and Ida had been the mother she'd loved and who'd loved her. And Mr. J, Julian, had played as intricate a role in her life as she'd believed.

He seemed to have been reading her mind, because all of a sudden, Edgar looked as if the past had snatched him back in time too.

"I don't believe that I've had a home-cooked meal as good as Ida's Sunday dinners since Julian passed," he said warmly.

Desi nearly smiled. "Me either," she murmured.

His choice of words was interesting: ". . . since Julian passed." Not "since Julian was killed" or "since the night you killed Julian." He made it sound as if the man had died from old age in his sleep.

"He was happy," Edgar offered. "That's a confession I've never made to anyone else in my life, Desi, but it's the truth. Julian lived for those times he got to spend with you and your mother."

What he'd just said—that was everything to Desi. When Desi was on trial for Julian's murder, the prosecutor went out of his way to make their relationship seem like something meaningless and dirty. Ida was Julian's plaything, his side chick and little more than a distraction. "We loved him, Edgar. We loved him so much."

He shrugged. "It was mutual. Julian was a different kind of

man when he was with you and Ida, which I never would've believed if I hadn't seen it for myself. He was a man who had it all, Desi, a beautiful wife, a successful business, children who adored him. I asked him once, What could a woman like Ida Green ever have to offer you that you don't already have?" Sadness filled his eyes as he spoke of Julian. "He laughed and told me how sorry he felt for me." Edgar swallowed.

The waitress came back with their drinks and set them down on the table. Edgar took a desperate sip of his beer.

"There is no greater love, no purer love than soul love, Desi." Edgar looked at Desi and smiled. "That's what he told me. Julian couldn't put his feelings for your mother into words because no such words exist. He had married the wrong woman and he was stuck with her."

It was as shocking a confession as Desi had ever heard, and the last person she'd expected to hear it from was Edgar Beckman, who stuck to Olivia Gatewood like glue.

"Eventually, I understood exactly what he meant." The look in Edgar's eyes sent a chill up her spine.

"Why did you really buy oil stock, Desi?"

The kindness in his face dissipated, and Desi was suddenly sitting across from an enemy. Edgar was never Desi's friend. He was never Ida's friend either. All he'd ever been was a parasite attaching himself to any Gatewood who would have him.

"My accountant told me that I would need to diversify my portfolio," she said with a straight face. It wasn't a lie. But of course, Edgar wasn't buying it.

"June could very well have gotten you arrested again, girl," he said menacingly. "Insider trading is a crime. But even more surprising is that you'd actually be so simple as to let another person talk you into investing millions into something you didn't even want."

"I'm so simple that I'm worth three times what I was before I bought into Anton."

"But it isn't about the money. Is it?" Some of that good-ol'-boy Texas charm was starting to seep from Edgar like sweat. "You don't want that stock, Desi. You just want to piss people off. You want to strut around them, proud and defiant, showing your ass and making sure that they remember you're still breathing. Isn't that the truth?"

Was that all he wanted? If Edgar wanted the truth, then she'd surely give it to him.

"Julian Gatewood was my father, Edgar," she confessed. If she expected the man to gasp, clutch his chest in shock or horror, she was disappointed. Edger Beckman didn't so much as blink at her announcement.

"Of course he was," he said indifferently. "Hell, I was there with him the night Ida gave birth to your little black ass, girl." He laughed.

And just like that, Edgar Beckman stole her thunder and Desi ended up being the one who was shocked.

"Julian was there and I had never seen a man so proud as when he held you, his daughter, in his arms, crying and laughing at the same time."

"You gotta be fuckin' kidding me?" she murmured more to herself than to him.

Edgar's placid smile was nauseating.

"Julian was my friend but he was a fool over all the wrong things." He stared at her. "Ida was out of his league, but what can I say? The man had a thing for slumming."

Without thinking, Desi threw the contents of her drink in his face. Edgar picked up his napkin from the table and began drying his face, as if getting a drink thrown at him was commonplace.

"You sonofabitch!" she cursed.

"Yes, my dear." He dabbed at his face and shirt. "I am that and more," he boasted.

The waitress rushed over with more napkins, glancing nervously at Desi. Edgar shooed her away.

"At least I'm blood, Edgar!" Desi argued. "Which is more than I can say for Jordan! If anyone has a right to the Gatewood name, it's me!"

He could not argue that! She dared him to even try.

"Every time he looks in the mirror there's a bastard staring back at him!" she continued. "And you've got your head so far up his ass . . ." Desi paused. "Or is it buried in Olivia's ass?"

Finally! Desi struck a noticeable nerve as Edgar's face flushed red.

"Sentiment is what's keeping me in this chair, Desi," he said evenly. "Despite what little respect I have for you, it's Julian's memory that's kept you alive."

"Is that what you think his memory is doing for me?" she asked tearfully. In that moment, Desi felt the spirit of Julian moving through the room and wrapping itself around her. She was his daughter. She was a Gatewood by birth and she was entitled.

"His memory made me strong when the whole world was against me. His memory kept me alive in that prison. His memory made me a rich woman, Edgar. And his memory led me back to Gatewood Industries where I belong," she said proudly. "And when it's all said and done, it'll be Julian's memory holding me up when Jordan's in prison and Olivia's dead and buried. Because I'll still be here. I'll still be standing."

She'd never felt like this before, but it felt good. It felt right, and Desi would remember it and draw her strength from him from now on.

"Now, get your ass back to Jordan and Olivia and tell them that

I've got karma in my damn corner," she said confidently. "And karma never loses."

Edgar finished what was left of his beer, then put money down on the table to pay for their drinks. "Save your soul, Desi." He looked at her. "Sell your Gatewood stock, take your money, and leave. You have no business in oil, and you've invested your money for all the wrong reasons. I commend you, though." He smiled at her and stood up to leave. "You are your father's daughter, and for that, Olivia Gatewood will always despise you."

Desi sat at that table long after Edgar had left. He was right. Buying into Anton, and eventually Gatewood Industries, was never about making a smart investment. Desi had gotten lucky, but she wanted no part of the business. She'd been a fly in the Gatewood soup, and in the beginning, that had been enough motivation. They knew that she was still here, out here, and despite everything they'd put her through, she was still standing, and that counted. It mattered. She mattered, and now they knew it. They'd tried to erase Desi and failed.

Chapter 34

"Sit down, Junie." Olivia used the same tone with June now that she had when June was eight.

So much had happened since the night of the Investors' Ball that this was the first time the two of them had had a chance to be alone in the last week. It had started with a phone call.

"June. I need you to come by the house tomorrow at six." Olivia hung up without waiting for a response.

So, how come June was kicking down the door to forty and feeling like she was about to get a spanking? She sat down in Olivia's lavish living room, on the sofa she'd ordered custom-made from France back when June was a little girl. Olivia wore her signature hand-sewn, silk housedress. This one was baby blue with a gold roped belt cinched at her waist. The short hair complimented her fine features and made her look even more regal than she already was.

"How are my grandchildren?" she asked cordially as she sat down in Julian's favorite Italian leather chair. Olivia hated those chairs. The only reason she'd kept them was because he'd insisted. June wondered why her mother had never gotten rid of them after her father's death.

"They're fine," June responded.

"I'd like to see them more now that I'm home." It wasn't a request.

Olivia hadn't asked her here to talk about the kids. This was to be the big showdown. The one that had been brewing ever since June was twelve and they told her that her father was dead. The image of her mother getting that gun and dropping it on the floor the night he was shot took root inside June and had been germinating ever since.

"I think it's past time that you and I had this conversation. Don't you?" her mother asked. "You think you know the facts, June."

Her mother was so cold, so calculating. June realized sitting across from her that Olivia was nothing more than smoke and mirrors, a figment of her own imagination, and while June and Jordan were growing up, they believed the lie that was Olivia Gatewood.

"Why didn't you just divorce Daddy, Mother?" June expected the words to sting Olivia, but they seemed to have no effect on the woman. "Men cheat." She shrugged. "Men cheat and the women they cheat on leave them."

Olivia didn't blink or fidget. She showed no emotion whatsoever, which June found chilling. Who was this woman who had given birth to her and raised her? And where was her soul?

"You think you're so smart," Olivia finally said. "So intelligent and so very, very right, but you have no idea what it's been like for me."

"I don't care," June blurted out, appalled that her mother's feelings should even matter. Olivia Gatewood was the sun and everyone else were smaller, insignificant planets orbiting around her. She wondered if Julian had seen it too. Was that why he had an affair? She was better than everyone else. And as far back as June could remember, Olivia had always made that point crystal clear. "An eighteen-year-old girl went to prison for something you did, and you let that happen. My father is dead because you weren't woman enough to leave him, and you really think that I should give a damn about what it's been like for you?"

"You believe Desi Green over me?" she asked, wounded.

"I believe what I saw, and the night my father was killed I saw you with a gun. You don't think I heard the arguments? The begging and the pleading? I heard all of that, Mother. Despite the airs you and Daddy put on in public, I knew the truth."

"I begged him to leave that woman! I begged him to let me love him the way I knew he needed me to! I pleaded with him to be true to our family!"

"But you weren't true to it!" June blurted out. "Daddy's not even Jordan's father, so you weren't any better than he was!"

"I had Jordan before I came to your father!" Olivia's eyes filled with angry tears. "He was my son! My boy!" Olivia's pinched expression held back those tears. "Julian came to me, June!" she said smugly. "He saw me and he wanted me and he came after me, damnit! I was married to another man—had another man's child—and he wouldn't take no for an answer! But I made it clear to him that if he wanted me, he had to accept my son as well! A package deal! That was it!"

June was stunned. Jesus! If it was true then just how diabolical was this woman? "You left your husband for Daddy?"

"I wanted a better life for me and for my son! Joel Tunson had nothing! Nothing to offer us, not a goddamned thing!" Her face flushed a dangerous shade of red. "Julian offered me the world on a silver platter, so yes! Yes, I took it! And I've never regretted what I did! I've never apologized and I never will." She raised her chin in proud defiance.

June had spent her adult life believing that she knew who her mother really was, but she had no idea. Olivia was a stranger to her, wearing her mother's clothes and pretending. Was Olivia even capable of love?

"You have betrayed your brother and me, June," Olivia said sternly. "You brought the enemy into our mix and for that, I can never forgive you."

June was appalled. "I don't want your forgiveness. My methods might not be the best, but my intentions are fuckin' justified!"

"Don't you cuss at your mother!"

"You killed Daddy! I loved him! I needed him and you took him from me and then you had the gall to pin your crime on a child!" she shouted, disgusted just thinking about it.

"She was eighteen!" Olivia shot back.

"Desi was still in high school, Mother! And you made sure she went to prison for what you did!"

"Why do you care?" Olivia yelled. "Why do you give a damn about Desi Green? She's no kin to you! She's nothing to you!"

"Why . . . her?" June yelled back. "If you wanted to set somebody up, why Desi? Why not her mother? If you wanted someone to take the fall for you, then why not set up Julian's lover for his murder?"

"Because I wanted Ida Green to suffer!" Olivia said, gritting her teeth.

Olivia Gatewood was evil. And June knew that she wasn't some dumb kid with an overactive imagination and mommy resentment issues back then. Olivia was evil. She'd shot and killed a man she supposedly loved and put a young girl in prison for his murder. And she'd done it all, she said, to punish Ida Green. Somehow, to June, that didn't seem to be enough of a reason for ruining so many lives.

"The look on that woman's face when they put handcuffs on that girl was my retribution," she said smugly. "After all she'd put me through, fucking my man, and trying to take him from me—hmpf!" She rolled her eyes. "I took something from her. I took him and I took that child and I might as well have cut out that woman's heart because she died that day!"

Shock. Disbelief. June was numb.

"You had no business bringing her back into our lives," Olivia said defiantly. "Desi got her money." She nodded. "After she got out of prison. I let her have her money, June, and she needed to disappear."

"Daddy left her that money. It was never yours to give," she replied softly.

"He left that money to that bitch Ida!" Her eyes clouded over again. "Twenty million dollars out of my house—and he gave it to that whore! That's how Desi got her money, June! It didn't come from your father, it came from her mother!"

Olivia was delusional, and she was capable of anything.

"You could've left him," June said, feeling so overwhelmingly brokenhearted by it all.

Olivia leaned forward and stared hard into her daughter's eyes. "He wasn't Jordan's father." She spoke carefully. "That was evident every day of that boy's life. If I'd have left Julian, Jordan would've gotten nothing."

June cocked her head to one side. "He'd have paid alimony, Mother, child support. He'd have taken care of us."

"He'd have taken care of you, Junie. But Jordan was nothing to him, and my son deserved better."

The pieces of the puzzle all started to come together to June. When Julian died, Olivia had handed over the keys to the kingdom to young Jordan Gatewood. The boy hadn't even so much as graduated college and all of a sudden he was head of a multimillion-dollar oil company.

June struggled to catch her breath.

Olivia leaned back, crossed one leg over the other, and wiped away her tears. "I really do expect to see my grandchildren more often, Junie," she stated simply. "Maybe you can bring them by this weekend, and I'll take them shopping."

Chapter 35

"Hiding isn't going to bring back Claire—or Lonnie—Jordan," Edgar Beckman told him.

He'd come over uninvited when news broke of Jordan's alleged relationship with Lonnie. The story that he knew her broke almost days after Randolph had paid him a visit. Lonnie had known a lot of people, rich, famous, and infamous. But he was the most notable person she'd known in Dallas, and that was enough of a coincidence to make headlines. Jordan hadn't been into the office since he'd gotten the news of Claire's death. Lately, it seemed like every time he so much as took a piss it made the news.

"I just buried my wife, Edgar," he said irritably, standing on the edge of the patio, looking out over the expanse of his property. "I think that's a pretty good excuse to be absent."

"You've got me mixed up with somebody else if you think I'm going to fall for that bullshit," Edgar snapped. "You didn't give a damn about Claire when she was alive. Why the hell would you give a damn about her now?"

Jordan didn't bother to dignify that comment with a response. Edgar didn't know shit about what Jordan felt for Claire. And it wasn't any of his business.

"You need to come forward and make a statement, Jordan," Edgar continued.

"My attorney made my statement for me."

"They need to hear it from you."

"Who is they?" Jordan asked, agitated, turning to Edgar.

Edgar's frustration surfaced. "I didn't inconvenience myself to cover up the fact that you were at the scene of that crime so that you could have the police sniffing around your crotch like dogs," he said gravely. "I covered your ass, Jordan, but you've got to help me to keep it covered. Right now you're the only connection they have to that woman and they're getting a lot of pressure to try and put together some kind of story of who killed her and why."

"I didn't kill her."

"No, but the person who did is dead. If it comes down to you and your dead wife," Edgar began to conclude, "well, you don't stand a chance, son."

It wouldn't go that far. Jordan had to believe that no one would ever be able to make more than an incidental connection between Jordan and Lonnie. He had to believe that the Dallas Police Department knew better than to pursue this nonsense any further than necessary. Jordan Gatewood was innocent of pulling the trigger of the gun that had killed Lonnie and they had nothing to prove that he had.

"How did that detective connect the dots?" Edgar asked.

"How do you think?" Jordan responded dismally. He turned to face Edgar. "Desi."

Edgar looked stunned. "She told them," he said introspectively. "And they believed her?"

"Enough to question me about it."

"She must've been pretty convincing," he said, sounding almost impressed.

"What the hell? You part of her fan club now, Edgar?"

"Momentum seems to be swinging in her direction, son," Edgar said coolly. "Somehow, she's playing your game, with your rules, and looking pretty good. Even you've got to see that."

"You rooting for the other team now, Edgar?" Jordan challenged him. "I mean, hell." Jordan shrugged. "You practically raised her. Right? You and your buddy, Julian? Shit, I wouldn't be surprised if you were Desi's biological daddy."

Edgar's smile faded. "Julian's her daddy, son," he said bluntly.

Jordan waited for the punch line, but the longer he waited, the more he realized that there wasn't one.

"Surprise," he said dryly and sarcastically.

"You're lying," Jordan challenged.

"I am a liar who has told many lies, but this is not one of them." Edgar gloated. "I was there with him the night that little girl was born. I was there when he held her in his arms for the first time. And I'm convinced that the only reason that girl's still standing after everything she's been through is because she's got Gatewood blood running through her veins." Edgar smiled. "You, on the other hand, have been hella-lucky."

The call came late, but Jordan had been expecting it. "Where is she?" he asked, waited, and then hung up.

His whole life, he couldn't recall ever being in a darker place. Jordan had never felt so uncertain or overwhelmed. It was unfamiliar territory for a man like him, and moment by moment, he found himself clinging desperately to rational thought. But there was nothing rational about coming here—except to see her, to look at her from a new perspective. Desi Green—Desi Gatewood. It was too damned fucked up to be wrong.

Jordan had had a man on Desi since he discovered that she was the one who'd told the cops about his relationship with Lonnie. His man had called and told Jordan that she was here. Cervantes was a private, by-invitation-only, upscale nightclub in the heart of downtown Dallas. Desi was there with her man, Solomon Jones.

Jones sat on a bar stool while Desi stood between his legs and braced herself against him. Desi wore her long, thick hair in a braid hanging over one shoulder. The hem of her dark-orange dress ended just below her knees, exposing beautiful, shapely, toned calves, accentuated by red-bottomed gold stiletto pumps. She nuzzled up to Jones, whispering in his ear, tossing her head back and laughing at the things he said, and then grazed her full lips against his. When in the world did Desi Green become such a beautiful woman?

Jones kept her close, and Jordan understood why. Every man in the room had his eyes on her. Jones grazed his fingers possessively across her exposed skin, following the trail down to the curve of her back that spread into her behind and hips—Jordan imagined himself squeezing her ass. A particular song came on and Desi stepped back from Jones and began to dance in front of him—for him. Her erect nipples pressed against the fabric of that dress. Jones licked his lips. So did Jordan. Jordan tugged at his belt and subtly adjusted his pants. His dick was starting to swell. What the hell was wrong with him? It was Desi, for crying out loud! When was the last time he'd been with a woman? Lonnie. When was the last time he'd craved one like this? Lonnie. But Desi wasn't Lonnie.

She was Julian Gatewood's flesh and blood. She was Jordan's enemy, but right here and now, he couldn't recall why.

Jordan swallowed and collected himself. What was he doing here? It wasn't right and it didn't make sense. Nothing made sense anymore. Jordan seethed in jealousy and envy as he watched Desi fall into Jones's arms, gaze into his eyes, and press her lips against his. Jones motioned to the bartender for another round of drinks and handed a fresh glass of wine to Desi. She mouthed the words, "Thank you, baby," turned her back to him, and rested against his chest while she bobbed her head to the music. *Desi Green looks just like her mother, Ida,* he'd heard time and time again. If that was true, if she really did resemble her mother as much as they claimed she did, then Jordan understood Julian's obsession with the woman.

Jordan noticed Jones pull his phone from his pocket. He looked as if he was checking for a call or maybe a text, before sliding it back into his pocket. Jones looked out into the crowd and immediately made and held eye contact with Jordan. Seconds later, another brother brushed passed Jordan, bumping into him. Jordan stared at the back of the man as he passed, and then saw the man turn back and look at him. Jordan quickly analyzed what had just happened, and all of a sudden, he knew, as he looked back at Jones, still looking at Jordan and kissing the top of Desi's shoulder, Jordan acknowledged the encounter to Jones. The sonofabitch had just sent Jordan a message. While Jordan was busy keeping an eye on Desi, Jones was busy keeping an eye on Jordan.

Jordan finished the beer he was drinking and left.

Chapter 36

This trip to Texas was supposed to have been just that—a trip. Desi still had a house in California with her name on it. She had a condo in Manhattan that she loved, but Dallas held the one thing that she loved more than even her freedom. It had Solomon, and he was doing a damn good job at keeping her in this city.

They both needed this, maybe for different reasons, but getting out tonight was the break from real life that would swallow them whole if they let it. Desi was celebrating a personal victory. She'd told that detective about Jordan's affair with Lonnie and he'd actually thought enough of what she'd told him to look into it. And then some cosmic force had made sure to publicly confirm that the two of them had known each other. Nothing had come to light tying him to her murder, but it was a start. Desi had struck the match to light the fire, and whatever happened next was as much a mystery to her as anybody. Maybe, Lonnie would be pleased.

The wine was good, the music was good, he was so damn fine, and she was happy. She closed her eyes, buried her nose in the crook of his neck and inhaled. "Mmmmmm," she moaned, getting high off of his pheromones. "I love the way you smell."

"Really? Well as long as you love it, I'll do my damndest to smell like this all the time," he said coolly, making the kind of eye contact that reached down into her soul.

Desi laughed. She was working on her third glass of wine and starting to feel the walls come down. She'd always found it strange that even with him, she'd managed to put up barriers and only allowed pieces of herself to be peeled away a layer at a time. Solomon knew this, and he understood, but his patience never seemed to wear thin and she was in awe of this man, and in awe of how much he wanted her—loved her—even, needed her.

"Thank you," she said, looking into his eyes.

Desi swayed in his arms to the luscious beat of the music.

He looked down at her. "For what?"

A strong surge of confessions was building in her. Desi felt a tidal wave of emotion starting to rise up inside her and she wanted to tell him everything she'd ever felt but was afraid to tell him before. Obviously, she was on her way to being good and drunk.

"For . . ." Hell! Where should she start? She wanted to thank him for everything, absolutely every kind and wonderful and romantic thing he'd ever said or done for her. So, she might as well start at the beginning. "Not turning me away that first day I came into your office. Remember that? I needed someone to look over that contract for me for the book, and when I went to you, you could've turned me away, Solomon."

He smiled. "But baby. I did turn you away."

"Yeah, but not for long, Solomon," she reminded him. "You were nice to me—eventually—and I really appreciated that."

"Well, you're welcome." He looked confused.

Why did he look so confused? Desi decided that it didn't matter, because she had a long list to get through before the night was over.

"And thank you for asking me out, Solomon," she continued, taking another sip of wine. "I definitely didn't expect that."

"I don't think that I ever really asked you out."

"You did," she insisted.

"Where'd we go?"

Desi thought for a moment. "You had to have asked me out, Solomon. I mean, we didn't just go from meeting each other to you asking me to marry you. Somewhere in there, you had to have asked me out on a date."

He laughed. "Nah, I don't think so."

Solomon didn't sound like he was as buzzed as Desi. But that was fine. Someone had to be the designated driver.

"First time I saw you I thought you were fine but so did you, and I wasn't going to give you the satisfaction of knowing that you were right."

"You think that I thought you were fine?" he asked, surprised.

She nodded. "You still do."

"But you think I'm fine too." He said, probing.

"You know I do. I just said it."

"Good. Then we're on the same page."

"And, thank you for putting up with my drama."

"It's a challenge," he replied dryly.

"I know I'm not as open with my feelings as you'd like," she continued. Her thoughts were rolling in faster than she could express them all of a sudden. But Desi had a lot to say to him, and she felt like she needed to say it all tonight.

"Uh-huh," he replied.

"But you understand why, though. Right?" Desi looked at him, hoping that he could feel her sincerity and the genuine depth of her appreciation.

"Not really. Why don't you explain it to me."

But then that song came on—that one she'd always loved. "Ooh!" Desi stepped back from him, and for a moment she forgot that he wasn't dancing with her, but the music felt so good, soul good, and it felt like it was coming up from the floor and making her feet move. "I love this song."

Desi missed his touch, and so she stepped back into his arms again and pressed her body against his chest and searched to recover her original train of thought. "Being in prison for twenty-five years does things to you, though, Solomon," she continued. "When you come out, you're different, guarded, and suspicious of people, because bitches in prison can't be trusted."

"I trusted you when I met you. And I certainly didn't think of you as a bitch."

"But I was out of prison," she slurred. "I'm telling you when I was in, you would've been a fool to trust me."

"Why?"

She promised herself she'd never tell him about the kind of person she'd been in prison. But he was going to be her husband. It was a sin against God and marriage to keep secrets from your husband.

"I was scared all the time," she finally said contemplatively. "Imagine being scared, constantly, for twenty-five years, all day, every day. Fear makes you desperate in ways you can't even imagine."

Images of things she'd said and done flashed in her mind.

Images she'd just as soon bury away when this conversation was over.

"I did my best to fly under the radar," she continued. "Keeping away from other inmates, the guards." She shrugged. "But sometimes, it was impossible."

"So, what would you do when it was impossible?" he asked carefully.

"I used people," she confessed. "Lied to them, told them things that weren't true, made them believe that I was someone I really wasn't, just so they'd look out for me," she said, ashamed.

Solomon was quiet for a moment, no doubt trying to piece together and fill in the blanks of this cryptic confession she'd just made. Desi wished she could take it all back and simply bask in the glow of his company.

"It sounds to me like you were just trying to survive, Desi," he surmised. "You were young, naïve, and I can only imagine what it must've been like for you in that place. But I wouldn't hold anything you said or did while you were there against you, and you shouldn't be so hard on yourself."

She loved him even more for saying that, but it wasn't so simple.

"By the time I was released, Solomon, I didn't even know who I was. I didn't trust me either. It was harder being on the outside because I had come to believe my own lies. And I couldn't keep doing what I was doing to people because people on the outside weren't as desperate as people on the inside. All I had was me, and I didn't even know what that meant."

Did he understand? Could he really grasp what she was telling him?

He sort of nodded. Another glass of wine seemed to come out of nowhere.

"So, I'm careful with other people and with myself because I'm not always sure that I'm being the real Desi."

God, she hoped he was getting this! Solomon needed to really focus so that he could understand what she was talking about so that he could know just how much he meant to her, even though she'd probably never said it out loud, but she'd felt it! It had just never come out of her mouth—probably.

He was smiling. What did that mean? Did it mean that he understood what she was talking about? Or did it mean that he thought she was stupid?

"Don't look at me like that," she said defensively, afraid that he really might think she was stupid.

"Please don't ask me to stop looking at you," he said lovingly. "I love looking at you." Solomon kissed her.

Desi blushed. "I'm trying to tell you that I love you, Solomon. I love you more than you know that I love you."

He raised his brow. "You just told me all that to say that you love me?"

She laughed. "Yeah. I guess I did. I trust you and I want you to trust me."

"I do."

"I need you and I want you to need me."

"I do."

"I can't live without you and I don't want you to be able to live without me."

He smiled. "I can't."

Desi spun around and pressed her back to him. His heart beat in rhythm to hers and Desi leaned back into his arms. He kissed her shoulder and squeezed her tight. When she was a girl she used to dream of a man like him. Alone in her prison cell, sometimes he came to life in her dreams. But he was real now. Wasn't he? She prayed that she wasn't still dreaming.

"I want to make love to you before you pass out, Desi," he whispered in her ear.

Desi smiled, stood up, and took one last sip from her glass. She took hold of his hand. "Then let's go."

Chapter 37

She straddled his lap. Solomon cupped her breasts and feasted on her nipples like fruit. Making love to Desi was a ritual never to be rushed and Solomon wasn't in a hurry to end this. Desi raised his face to hers and stared into his eyes as she froze the motion of her hips.

The walls of her pussy pulsed against his shaft, making it almost impossible for Solomon to control himself. He grabbed her by the waist and raised her up off of him. "Not . . . yet," he commanded.

She groaned her displeasure. "Don't . . . do that, Solomon!"

He smiled because she wanted him as much as he wanted her. His cock throbbed in protest between their bellies. But somebody had to take control of the situation.

"There's no rush, baby," he moaned, kissing her neck and shoulders.

Desi writhed and twisted like a snake in his lap, and sighed. "I want you so bad," she whispered, sweeping her tongue into his mouth.

She'd torn open his shirt and ripped off the buttons.

"You got me, Desi," he murmured sensually. "I'm yours and you know it."

She looked into his eyes and nodded. "I know," she said, breathless. "I know."

His dick would explode if he didn't put it inside her. Desi seemed to read his mind. She raised herself up on her knees, then slid slowly down his shaft. Desi's sweet pussy was intoxicating, and Solomon knew that he wouldn't last nearly as long as he wished he could.

"Slow," he whispered, holding on to her hips.

The position he was in made it hard for him to move, but Solomon knew that tonight, she was in control, and tonight, she was the one putting her mark on him. Desi worked to pull the most magnificent orgasm out of him. She worked to build the fire of her own climax. In a perfect world, the two of them would come together, but the world wasn't perfect, and Solomon knew when he'd been bested.

The devastatingly delicious roll of her hips in his lap left him helpless. The massaging of her inner walls around his cock made him weak. He was literally putty in this woman's hands, and loved every minute of it.

Solomon rested his head against the backseat, and held on while Desi worked her magic. "That's it, baby," he muttered, gazing into her lovely, dark eyes. He'd nursed two beers for most of the night, but right now, he was drunk on her. "That's it." She brushed her lips against his. "Hold on, baby," she said seductively. Desi smiled. "I got this."

An hour later they were home and in bed. Desi slept with her head resting on his chest and her arm draped across him. She had been magnificent tonight and he had what amounted to no less than an obsession. Solomon kissed her head. He'd do anything for her and he'd do anything to keep her safe.

Gatewood hadn't shown his ass tonight, but Solomon knew that it was only a matter of time before he would. But he wasn't the only one who knew how to play this game. Solomon didn't prefer it, but he knew the rules. Rule number one, and the only rule that mattered, was that there were no rules.

The man was more volatile now than ever and it was clear tonight that he had placed a bull's-eye on Desi's back. He'd gotten the jump on Solomon once, but that was the last time he'd get that lucky.

Chapter 38

Jordan held on to a fistful of red curls, watching as his date worked hard to help him sustain his erection with her lovely mouth. It wasn't her fault, and he was more disgusted with himself than ever.

"It's okay," he said gently, coaxing her to back away. "Tasha." He put his hand under her chin, breaking the hold she had on him, and looked into her beautiful green eyes. "It's okay, darlin'."

She bit down on her bottom lip and batted those lovely eyes at him. "I don't have to stop," she said softly.

Jordan smiled warmly and then stood up, tied his robe closed, and stepped over her. Yes. She had to stop. He left her in the bedroom and went downstairs to the kitchen to get a beer from the refrigerator. What the hell had his life come to when he couldn't get it up for a blow job? he thought miserably, gulping down the cold beverage. Jordan's thoughts drifted back to a phone conversation he'd had earlier with one of his attorneys.

"I just got a call from a judge that a warrant request has been issued for your personal phone records," he explained.

Jordan raked his hand across his head. He hadn't shaved or had a haircut in weeks. He hadn't set foot in the office since before Claire died. Jordan was drowning in a kind of funk he couldn't seem to pull himself out of, and the last thing he needed was this.

He squeezed his eyes shut. Jordan didn't need to ask who'd submitted the request for the warrant. What worried him more was why? Was Randolph pushing forward with this investigation of Jordan simply because of what Desi had told him? Or was there something else?

"Frank Ross," he eventually said to his attorney, his mind settling on the one solid move he had on the board. "Where is he?"

"They've arrested him and taken him back to Cotton," the man explained.

Jordan opened his eyes. "Have they charged him?"

"He's being held for jumping bail and assaulting a police officer, but as far as I know, that's it."

Frank Ross wasn't an innocent man. Jordan reminded himself of that. He had killed someone, not Lonnie, but someone. There were people in this world, some people, who served a different kind of purpose, and Frank Ross was one of those people. He'd made the mistake of putting himself in Jordan's line of fire, and now it would cost him, it would cost him dearly.

"You tell that judge to deny that warrant request," he demanded.

"I'll see what I can do." The man sounded uncertain.

"No! You don't see what you can do, damnit!" he insisted. "You just do it!" Jordan ended the call.

Before he realized it, Jordan had polished off the bottle and was reaching for another one when the doorbell rang. He couldn't remember if the housekeeper was back or not, but he sure as hell didn't feel like answering the damn thing.

"Mr. Gatewood." Jordan heard his housekeeper's voice behind him. "Your sister is here."

Jordan glanced at the clock on the wall across the room. It was going on five o'clock, and one of the last people in the world he wanted to see was June. Jordan leaned back against the massive marble center island, lowered his head, and sighed.

"I've tried calling," she said, coming into the kitchen.

"I don't think I answered," he responded distantly.

"Which is why I'm here."

He turned his head slowly to her. "Tell me why you're here, June."

He'd learned in short order that June was the one that he needed to keep his eyes on. She was the one most capable of drawing him in, believing that she had his back, when in fact, she never did. June was the best kind of liar. She was like him.

She stood there in skinny jeans, sneakers, and a plain tee shirt, wearing a ball cap and a ponytail, looking every bit of sixteen again.

"I haven't seen you since the funeral." She shrugged. "Everybody at the office is worried about you, Jordan," she explained tenderly. "Including me, especially after finding out—finding out that Julian wasn't your father. I had no idea, Jordan. And I know how hard it must've been for you to find out the truth."

Now that was funny. "Remember who you're talking to, Junie." He laughed. "I can do the backstroke through bullshit with the best of them."

"It's not bullshit," she said softly. "This is a tough time for you. I just . . . Despite everything, Jordan, I do love you."

Jordan pushed away from the counter and walked toward his sister. "Good, Junie," he said, nodding. "I'm glad you love me, baby, because," he stopped next to her, "I'd sure hate to see what you'd do to me if you didn't." Jordan left the room.

June followed, and as they made their way into the formal living room, Little Miss Ginger Sunshine was making her way down the winding staircase looking every bit the goddess that he'd paid for. June paused and watched the other woman descend. Jordan studied the look on his sister's pretty face with amusement.

"Who is this?" June asked him, looking past the young beauty.

The shapely, porcelain-skinned Tasha sauntered over to Jordan and stopped mere inches away from him. She looked up at him with those vivid green eyes of hers—weapons, both of them—and whispered, "I don't have to leave," loud enough for June to hear. "I can stay."

Jordan pulled five hundred dollars from his pocket, slipped it into her delicate little hand, and tenderly kissed the top of her head. "No," he murmured, looking across the room at June. "You can't." He took hold of her hand, led her to the front door, and held it open for her to leave.

"Is this how you've been spending your time since your wife's funeral, Jordan?" June asked, folding her arms across her chest. "Fucking and drinking?"

It was none of her goddamned business. "Why are you here, June?" The booming sound of his voice surprised even him, as June took a step back. "What the fuck do you want?"

The anger came from nowhere, but it filled him with such a rage that he felt as if he would explode. Jordan had desperately needed to nut, and he'd just let the only person remotely capable of making it happen walk out the door. But there was more, so much more!

"I told you!" she shouted back. "I'm worried about you, Jordan! You're not yourself!"

Jordan turned his back to her and walked away. "You have no idea," he muttered under his breath.

"I know you hate me for what I did." June's voice cracked. She followed him into the other room. "But it's done, Jordan! And you can be angry with me, but you can't hate me forever!"

He stopped and glared at her.

"Do you want me to say I'm sorry?" She looked to be on the verge of tears. "Will it help? I'd say it if I thought it would help, but I know you, and I know that it won't so why waste my breath?"

"You knew," he said coolly. Clarity had been coming lately in bits and pieces, making it hard for him to focus on everything happening to him. But this moment brought such clarity that it nearly blinded him. "You knew that she was his daughter."

June's expression went blank. "What are you talking about?"

Her feigned ignorance was nauseating. "You knew and that's why you did it! You talked Desi into buying that stock because you knew, June! Don't fuckin' keep lying to me!"

"I suspected, Jordan," she finally admitted. June shrank right in front of his eyes. "I guessed that maybe she was, I mean, look at her. Yes. She looks like her mother, but there are parts of him in her too."

"So, what? You did what you did to us out of some kind of loyalty to her? You've got a long-lost sister now, come into the fold, and you felt the need to reach out and bring her into the family business?"

God! He was still pissed. All of a sudden, it was as if June didn't know why she'd betrayed him. "I was so sick of being on the outside." She'd begun to whine.

Jordan hated to hear her whine.

"It was you and Mother and then there was me," she droned on.

"You were the favorite—her favorite! You were the golden boy and I was just . . ." June shrugged. "You can do no wrong in that woman's eyes and I could never do anything right," she said, defeated.

Jordan cocked a brow in awe. "Excuse me, but how old are you again?" he asked, unapologetically sarcastic. "You did this to teach me a lesson? You wanted to piss off Mommy?" Jordan's face contorted in confusion. "What are you, June? Fuckin' nine?"

"She killed my father!" she shouted angrily. "That's why I did it, Jordan! The bitch shot my father, and blamed it on Desi, and yes! I wanted to punish her, even if it meant punishing you too, because she shot him! She shot him, killed him, took his corporation and never looked back and yes! I thoroughly hate the bitch!"

There it was. Jordan stared back at his sister, satisfied that he'd finally seen the beast rear its ugly head. It was the Gatewood in her, and that shit was fuckin' hideous, and real, and deadly. Julian might not have been his biological father, but he'd inherited that shit by proxy, or maybe, and much more likely, they'd inherited it from their mother.

"Desi Green is Julian's daughter by blood, Junie," he quietly explained. Jordan smirked. "She has as much right to the Gatewood empire as you." Jordan felt sick and he felt dangerous. "Technically, the two of you could pool your resources and ruin me."

The expression on June's face was priceless. She swallowed visibly. "I wouldn't do that to you," she said unconvincingly. "I would never let Desi do that to you."

Poor baby June. She'd unwittingly become the victim of her own circumstances and so had he.

"And I thought that Olivia was the one I needed to worry about snatching Gatewood Industries out from under me," he said, staring into her eyes.

June eventually found her voice. "Olivia is the one you have to worry about, Jordan," she said tearfully. "She always has been."

"I don't think so, June."

"After all she's done to you and you still think she walks on water."

"I used to think you did," he said.

"I'm not perfect," she admitted. "I've lied to you, Jordan, but I've never killed anyone. And I've never framed a teenage girl for murder. Do you see how manipulative she can be?" June was crying. "All she's ever done was use people to get what she wants. And she's been using you your whole life, I guarantee it. Desi's not your enemy, Jordan. She never was."

June didn't wait for him to respond. She left quietly. Jordan just stood there.

Chapter 39

"June Gatewood was never your friend," Edgar Beckman said, sawing into his filet mignon. "She's a spoiled child with mommy issues and she's pulled you into her temper tantrum, Desi. That's all."

He'd called Desi, asking to see her. Reluctantly she agreed to meet him at a steak house he loved on the outskirts of Fort Worth.

"Bottom line," he said, shoving a slice of steak into his mouth. "She's still a Gatewood, and I personally wouldn't trust the lot of them."

"You're talking out of both sides of your mouth, Edgar," Desi said calmly, not caring one way or another if she offended him.

Edgar was the Gatewood errand boy who'd sell his soul for those people.

"Lonnie met Edgar Beckman before she died," Phillip told Desi when he called from Europe and she told him that she had known Edgar since she was a little girl.

"How did she know him?" Desi asked anxiously.

Phillip's weighted pause pretty much answered that question for him. "I did some digging and discovered that he had a long history with the family and that he had been friends and business colleagues with the elder Gatewood before his death," he explained. "I suggested to Lonnie that there might be some leverage against Jordan from Beckman. She did her investigative reporter thing and discovered that the man had some terrible secrets, namely a young wife who'd gone missing and has never been heard from or seen in decades." He paused. "He's not really uncle material, Desi. Not the kind of uncle you probably remember."

Edgar looked at Desi and laughed. "Money had bought you a spine, I see," he said maliciously. Edgar leaned over the side of the table and looked at Desi's lap. "Got some balls up under that dress of yours too now?"

"Why'd you ask to see me, Edgar?" Desi's patience was growing thin.

"Aw, c'mon now, darlin'. You can't crash the party and not expect to dance, now, can you?" He eyed her cautiously. "They're going to force you to sell, Desi," he stated matter-of-factly.

Desi was caught off guard by what he'd just said.

Edgar seemed to revel in her surprise. "I'll bet June didn't tell you that. Did she?" He didn't bother waiting for a response. "Of course not, because the bitch lied to you, and she betrayed her mother and her brother. Like I said, momma issues." He frowned.

"Could have something to do with her mother killing her father, your so-called best friend."

He shot an angry look at her.

"How could you even call yourself his friend, Edgar, knowing what she did? You're still sniffing around that woman's skirt like the pussy is Grade A USDA Prime. What's that about?"

"A nasty mouth on a woman is not attractive, Desi." He frowned.

"I'm an ex-felon, Edgar." Desi smirked. "I got a lot more nastiness where that came from."

"You think this is funny?" He clenched his jaw. "That this is some kind of game, Desi?" Edgar dropped his knife and fork down on top of his plate, wiped his mouth, and threw his napkin on the table.

"What do you want?" she asked again, under her breath, leaning in toward him.

"Sell it to me," he suddenly demanded.

Desi sat up straight. "What?"

"All of it!" he said gruffly, suddenly breaking out in a sweat. Edgar picked up his napkin and dabbed his brow and neck with it. "Name your price—right here—right now!"

"Are you drunk?" Desi asked, dismayed.

Edgar balanced his elbows on the table. "Let me explain how this works, you twit!" he spat. "You bought your stock under Anton Oil," he said introspectively. "Technically, Gatewood Industries can retire those shares. If the majority of shareholders agree to take the Anton part of the company privately, then they could force you to sell at a designated price. In a perfect world they could give you the opportunity to trade those shares for corresponding stock in GII, but I'm willing to bet my last dollar that the Gatewoods would swallow their own piss before they let that happen." Edgar finally leaned back, crossed one leg over the other, and stared at Desi. "You choose. I can pay you what you want now, or you take a loss when the Gatewoods finish butt-fucking you once again, Desi."

Desi stared, fascinated, at this man who was the epitome of everything dysfunctional with all of the Gatewoods. "Did Julian know what kind of man you really are, Edgar?" she asked without thinking.

June had betrayed her mother and Jordan. Edgar was willing to buy GII stock out from under them. Olivia had killed her husband. And Jordan . . . ?

The color washed from his face when she asked the question. "I remember the two of you sitting in our living room after dinner, telling stories about the two of you growing up together, and playing the blues too loud on Momma's old record player. Mr. J taught me how to dance, while you tapped your foot and every now and then, you'd take my hand and spin me around just like he did."

Was this that same man? Or had Desi just made him up in her mind?

"It's one thing to be naïve as a child, Desi," he said grimly. "But you're a grown woman now, and you should know that people are seldom who we believe them to be."

"He believed you cared about me and my mother, Edgar," she explained. "I don't think he'd have allowed you to be around us if he didn't believe that."

Edgar looked so thoughtful all of a sudden, and burdened. "My friend is dead," he said, clearing his throat. "I see no reason to revisit his memory now."

"But you stick to his wife, like a fly to shit," Desi said offensively. "Were you sleeping with her?"

Edgar toyed with the corner of his napkin. "No," he said hoarsely. "But I sure as hell hoped that one day I could." He looked up at Desi and half-smiled. "I loved him, but I have always loved her more."

Desi sat back and sighed. "That explains it," she said. "I guess you didn't mind him being dead if it meant the possibility that she would come running to you."

Edgar noticeably swallowed. "Love can drive a man to do some insane things," he confessed.

"You can call it what you want, Edgar, but I call it fucked up."

He looked offended. "If he didn't love her, he shouldn't have married her."

"If she didn't want him, she should've filed for divorce."

"That's not her style," he said smugly.

Desi picked up her purse to leave. "That bitch has no style."

She stood up and left that old fool sitting there.

Chapter 40

Round One

"Why'd you run, Frank?"

"My old man was sick. I knew y'all wouldn't let me leave."

"Why'd you really run, Frank?"

"I wasn't running, man. I told you. My father was ill, and I had to go see about him."

"This is the last time I'm asking, and this time, I expect you'll tell me the truth."

This fool knew why he'd run. He had to know. He just wanted to hear Frank say it. He wanted the truth. Frank gave it up.

"You bring me in asking about that woman they found dead at that motel in Dallas. You got my credit card info and you sound like you want to put her murder off on me. I'm no killer, man. That's why I ran."

Round Two

"How many times do I have to tell you that I don't know nobody named Yolanda Adebayo?"

"But you've met her?"

"No. To the best of my knowledge, I've never met a woman by that name."

"She was a beautiful woman, Frank. If you met her you surely wouldn't have forgotten her."

They slid a photograph of Lonnie across the table to him. She was smiling and holding an expensive camera in her hand. Her hair was different, though. It was short, down-the-scalp short.

"That's her, isn't it? That's the woman they found dead in Dallas."

"So, you do know her?"

"Man! Weren't you listening? I've never met that woman before in my life!"

Round Three

"Your number was in her phone, Frank. Now, if you didn't know this woman, never seen her before in your life, then tell me how your number got into her phone?"

Frank looked at the detective. *"I want my lawyer."*

A week had passed since he'd made the call to his attorney. Finally the man decided to grace Frank with his presence. Frank had been held without bail or even the option of posting bail. Fortunately for him, they'd left him in county and hadn't sent him to a state facility. Frank's attorney, Alex Richards, sat at one end of the gray conference table in the private consultation room, wearing a storm-gray suit, crisp white shirt that probably cost more than the average cop made in a pay period, and a blue silk tie. The man smelled of money, and in his best years, Frank couldn't have afforded this man's services on his own.

He took a seat on the other side of the table next to Richards, who sat composed, rigid even, with his hands on the table, his fingers laced together. Jordan had hired the attorney to represent Frank on the other murder charges he was facing for killing another cop, off duty. His partner, Collette, had confessed to her part in the killing of the two officers, and also to the murder of a known drug dealer. She'd implicated Frank in the murder of one of the cops, but just when Frank felt the bottom fall out from under him, Jordan Gatewood came to the rescue and sent the Lone Ranger here to save him.

Richards's pinched expression looked like it hurt. He stared at Frank, watching every move he made as if he were taking it all into his memory. When Frank realized that Richards wasn't going to say anything, he knew that he had to.

"I uh . . ." He paused. "Looks like I made a mess of things," he admitted. "I got spooked when they brought me in for questioning in another murder, and . . . yeah. I took off, man, and I'm sorry for that."

Frank sat quietly, waiting for the other man to say something. Richards continued staring at Frank, looking absolutely pissed.

"My old man called the cops on me," Frank continued. "I don't think they'd have found me if he hadn't. . . . " His voice trailed off.

Damn! Frank had panicked. He knew better than to panic. He knew better than to run, but it had all gotten to be too much and running was all he knew to do.

"I know I messed up, man." Frank kept talking. "But I didn't have anything to do with that woman's death, man, and they think

I did, but I didn't. I just . . . I'm dead if I go to prison." He sounded so pitiful that he made himself sick. "I'm an ex-cop, and they'll kill me in prison."

Finally, Richards took a deep breath, lay both hands flat on the table, and leaned closer to Frank. "I want you to listen carefully to what I'm about to tell you, Ross." The man didn't blink. "You will keep your mouth shut," he commanded. "No matter what they ask you, or what they wave in front of your face, you say absolutely nothing. Is that understood?"

Frank nodded. "Of course. Yeah. I got that, man. No problem."

"This is very important," he said gravely.

"I know how important it is," Frank shot back. "But—do you think that you can get me out of this? They haven't charged me yet, but I know it's coming, and I didn't do it. But they're going to try and pin it on me—somehow they're going to think that I had something to do with it."

"Let them."

Frank wasn't quite sure he'd heard this man right, and even if he did, he wasn't sure that he understood what Richards meant by that.

"Let them?" he asked, seeking clarification. "What does that mean?"

"Are you deaf?" he asked sarcastically.

"No, but . . . What do you mean, let them? I didn't do anything."

This was some kind of a newfangled lawyer thing that this dude was trying to pull. Richards was one of the best criminal lawyers in the country. Frank had done his homework on the dude. So, maybe he was coming at this thing from another angle—one that didn't make sense to Frank—but shit! The dude had to have known what he was doing. He just needed to let Frank in on it.

"Explain this to me so that I can understand it, Alex," Frank asked humbly. "I trust you, but I need to get where you're coming from with this."

Richards lowered his head to Frank's, so close that the two of them were almost touching. He cleared his throat. "You are a maggot, motha fucka. Something to be squashed under my shoe."

Frank started to jerk away from this dude, but before he realized it, Alex Richards grabbed him by the back of the neck and held him there.

"You fucked up, Frank," he said in a low growl. "You ran like a bitch and drew far too much attention to yourself and now you have to suffer the consequences."

What the hell? "I told you—"

"It wasn't your father who turned you in," Richards said menacingly. "But the deed has been done and here you are and here you'll stay."

Frank's heart raced in his chest. What the hell was this fool saying? Whose side was he the fuck on anyway?

"Men like you are sacrificial lambs, Frank. Men like you don't matter. Men like you get butt fucked and won't tell a soul about it because it's your lot in life. In the grand scheme of things you mean absolutely nothing to the universe so you will not be missed."

Frank was fucked! Now he knew it in a way he'd never known it before. Frank was being set up! "Get your goddamned hand off me!" he said, struggling to get free.

Richards dug his fingers into the back of Frank's neck almost to the spine, and Frank grunted.

"Do as I say and you'll at least have your life, Frank. Do as I say and you may live out your days in peace with three square meals a day, a warm cot, and a boyfriend named Boo. But fuck up!" Richards shoved Frank's head down on the table and leaned over him to whisper in his ear. "Fuck up and you will wish for death, but it will never come," he threatened. "Implicate the wrong person, say one wrong word, and trust that you will pay dearly for your transgression."

Richards finally released his grip on Frank. He stood up, straightened his suit, picked up his briefcase, and knocked to be let out of the room.

This was a nightmare and Frank was going to be forced to live it.

Revenge

Chapter 41

"*Mr. Gatewood,* this is Detective Randolph."

Jordan listened to the man announce himself over the phone like he was the leader of the free world.

"Yes," Jordan said, rubbing sleep from his eyes.

What the hell time was it? He turned over to look at the clock. It was 9:05. The sun was up so it was 9:05 a.m.

"Sir, I'd like to talk to you some more about the relationship you had with Ms. Adebayo."

Jordan sighed, frustrated. "I told you. I didn't have a relationship with Ms. Adebayo."

The lie rolled off his tongue like water. But there was no denying the inflection in the man's voice when he'd called what Jordan had with Lonnie a "relationship." And there was no denying that sick feeling Jordan suddenly felt in his stomach. Where was this coming from? A man like him didn't sweat the bullshit, and the fact that this man insisted on pursuing Jordan about any connection to Lonnie's murder he believed may have been there was bullshit. Jordan hadn't killed Lonnie. That was a fact. But the person who had killed her was dead now too.

"Well, we have reason to believe differently, Mr. Gatewood," Randolph explained confidently. "We'd like for you to come in today, sir, to discuss the issue."

Randolph chose his words carefully. Even hungover, Jordan could tell that the man knew something more than what he wanted to say over the phone.

"You can come to my home . . ."

"No." Randolph brazenly interrupted him. "Sir, we'd like for you to come into the precinct."

Jordan's annoyance kicked in. "A man like me doesn't come into precincts, Detective," he shot back defensively. "I'm sure you understand," Jordan challenged.

"I do, Mr. Gatewood. However, I am conducting a murder investigation and I'm sure you understand the pressure I'm under to find this woman's killer. I don't have time to drive all the way out to your ranch to conduct this interview."

Detective Bobby Randolph had obviously found some balls somewhere since the last time Jordan had seen him. Right then and there, Jordan made up his mind to castrate this motha fucka.

"I'll see you here at eleven," Randolph said simply.

Jordan paused for a moment before answering. "I'm bringing my attorney." It was the best he could do at the moment.

"Yes, sir," Randolph said before abruptly ending the call.

The one emotion Jordan could never remember falling victim to was anxiety. He couldn't remember ever feeling unprepared. He had never felt fear or apprehension and now it seemed that he was drowning in all of those things at once with no clue about how to salvage his life. Lonnie's murder and Claire's suicide both circled back to him and he felt responsible. Jordan felt convicted for the demise of both women and he couldn't shake the feeling.

His whole life had been nothing short of a shadow of what he'd grown up believing it was. Jordan was not a Gatewood by blood and the man he'd grown up believing was his father was the furthest thing from it. He'd hated a woman for nearly thirty years for taking something away from him that was never his in the first place. No, Desi Green had not killed Julian, but she was certainly making them all pay for their trespasses against her and had proved to be smarter than the average bear. She'd openly made a mockery of the Gatewood clan, and especially of him. Olivia and Edgar had both known that she was Julian's daughter, and they'd both known that Jordan was that man's child by proxy.

He'd worshipped his mother, who had orchestrated his whole world and designed it to her specifications. And more often than not, he found himself wondering just how much of her was true, and how much of her was the lie she'd manufactured. Even his own sister had crafted some twisted idea of revenge against him, and Jordan could only imagine what her true motives were, which had yet to be fully played out. June was a Gatewood, after all. And none of them could be trusted.

The hush that fell over the entire precinct when he walked in with one of his attorney's trailing behind him was deafening. Randolph led them through the maze of corridors and desks toward a small room at the back of the building. He closed the door behind them and motioned for the two men to be seated.

"Thank you again for coming in, Mr. Gatewood," he said, but there was no real apology in his voice.

Randolph wouldn't have called him to come in if he hadn't discovered something. He wouldn't be acting like the goddamned cock of the roost if he hadn't found something that he felt could incriminate Jordan somehow.

"I'm Patrick Broussard." Jordan's attorney introduced himself. "Mr. Gatewood's attorney."

Randolph nodded and shook the man's hand, then proceeded to open a file on the table in front of him and began flipping slowly through pages, taking his sweet-ass time.

"You said before that you only knew Ms. Adebayo casually." Randolph looked up at Jordan as he reminded him.

"Yes," Jordan's attorney answered for him.

Randolph looked displeasingly at Broussard, then back to Jordan. "Is this how this is going to go?" he asked, annoyed.

"Yes," Broussard said again.

Randolph shot a disapproving look at Jordan. "We did a check of Ms. Adebayo's phone records," he proceeded to say.

Randolph had tried to warrant Jordan's records but Jordan made sure that that didn't happen. Jordan stared unblinking at the man and made it a point not to swallow that lump that had just swelled in his throat.

"Imagine my surprise when a number belonging to you turned up," the detective said coolly.

"As Mr. Gatewood mentioned earlier," Broussard chimed in, "he and Ms. Adebayo were casual acquaintances."

"Maybe more than casual," Bobby said to Jordan.

"So, my number turned up in her phone, Detective," Jordan said coolly. "What of it?"

"Mind telling me what you and your casual acquaintance had to talk about?" Randolph probed.

"I don't remember."

"She was a beautiful woman, Mr. Gatewood."

"And I'm a married . . . I was a married man," Jordan retorted coolly.

Randoph shrugged. "Most times, that's not an issue."

Jordan had to pull his emotions back. His defensiveness was beginning to show and he needed to stay cool.

"For me, it was an issue," he said calmly. "I loved my wife."

Randolph studied him too long, but Jordan held on tightly to his composure, and it was a good thing he did. Slowly he began to notice the subtle changes in the other man's demeanor. That's all he had? Evidence of a phone call or two between Lonnie and him? Jordan had always had a knack for knowing when the advantage had slipped in his favor and he'd always been an expert at taking advantage of it.

"You called me in here for this?" he asked sternly, not bothering to hide his annoyance.

The detective struggled to maintain his own composure. "I'm following all leads, and so far, you're the best one I have."

Broussard cleared his throat and started to chime in. "If that's all, Detective . . ."

Jordan wasn't finished. "What did you expect me to say when you dropped that little bombshell on me, Randolph?" Jordan demanded to know.

Who the hell did this fool think he was dealing with? Jordan wasn't some thug off the street and he wasn't some weak-ass pussy who was going to be bullied into spilling his guts to some squat-ass cop.

Randolph's own frustration began to surface. "I expected you to tell me the truth," he shot back. "I don't believe that your relationship with Ms. Adebayo was casual, Mr. Gatewood. I believe that you knew her—intimately—and that you had something to do with her murder."

Randolph looked almost as if he wished he could take back what he'd just said, but his pride wouldn't let him. The man was obviously at his wit's end. Jordan had followed the news. The Dallas Police Department was getting pressure to solve those murders, particularly Lonnie's since she was the most high profile of the three, and Randolph was pissing in the wind with this interrogation, more than anything.

"I did not kill Lonnie Adebayo," Jordan said carefully, emphatically.

His attorney stood up first. Jordan followed his lead, and both men left the detective alone in that room to lick his wounds.

Chapter 42

"*His car was at* the scene of that crime," Bobby Randolph explained, sitting across from Desi in the living room. Solomon was at the office. "His number was in her phone and he admitted that he knew Lonnie—casually—but other than that I got nothing," he said earnestly.

Desi was feeling hopeful, but she had to keep that hope in check. The Gatewoods were good at getting away with murder, and she had to remember that. "So, how come I feel like you almost believe me?" she asked.

His eyes locked onto hers. "Because I've got his car at the scene and his number in her phone. Plus, my gut aches, and I've learned to pay attention when my gut aches because usually it's trying to tell me something."

"But you don't have enough."

He shook his head. "Not to arrest the most powerful man in

Texas for murder, Desi, no. I don't have enough. Can you give me anything else? Something tangible that I can bank on? Something proving that the two of them had an affair?"

She had Lonnie's word and that's it. Desi thought about Phillip, but then, all he had was Lonnie too. "I don't have pictures or anything if that's what you're looking for, Detective," she said with a hint of sarcasm. He was the investigator. Desi had planted the seed and given him the link to Jordan. It was his job to put it together.

"I've got nothing, then, Desi," he said, raking his hand over his head. "Circumstantial shit, but that's it. And I can't do nothing with that."

"So, Jordan walks?"

It was happening again. These people were about to get away with another murder and there was nothing anybody could do about it.

"The man can afford the best criminal lawyers in the world and they'd shred this case in front of a jury. I've got nothing on him."

"What about the gun that killed her?" she asked angrily. "Haven't you figured out what kind of gun it is and checked to see if he has a gun like that registered to him?"

He looked at her like she was crazy. "The gun that killed Lonnie was a .45 caliber Colt revolver," he stated.

"Is one registered to Jordan?" she asked excitedly.

"Of course," he said matter-of-factly. "He's got several that we know about, but that same type of weapon is registered to half the state of Texas."

Desi had watched enough crime dramas to know something. "Then test his guns."

"I'd have to get a warrant to do that."

She looked at him like he was crazy. "So get a warrant."

The man looked absolutely defeated. "Based on what?"

"On the evidence you have already?"

Detective Randolph surprised the hell out of her and laughed. "Yeah."

"Oh, come on!" she said, nearly shrieking. "You're not really going to just give up?"

"I couldn't even get a warrant for the man's phone records, Desi. No judge in this town is going to issue me one to get my hands on his guns."

And that was it. That was the power of the untouchable force behind the Gatewood name. These people bought and sold judges like used cars. Desi had seen firsthand just how far and wide their influence had reached and she had no business being surprised now by this revelation. It was the Gatewoods that drew the line of justice in the sand and anyone who crossed that line had hell to pay if they did. Desi could feel her heart quietly breaking knowing that the man who'd killed her friend would never see the inside of a jail and that if the police department absolutely had to prosecute someone for the crime, it would be the wrong person.

"Short of a confession, there's nothing I can do."

"What if I got him to confess?"

Desi had said it before she'd even realized it and immediately regretted it when she did. What the hell was she thinking? Why would Jordan confess to killing Lonnie to her?

He looked as shocked to hear it as Desi had looked to hear herself saying it.

"Forget you heard me say that," she said, still stunned.

Foolishness had taken over where common sense and self-preservation had left off.

"I don't think I can," he said, seemingly mesmerized by the idea.

Desi felt the familiar emotion of retreat rise to the surface. "It would never work. He's not going to talk to me and I sure as hell don't want to be in the same room with him. Forget I said it, because it's not happening." She vehemently shook her head.

"Let me think on this for a minute," he said anxiously.

"You can think all you want. I'm not doing it."

He just looked at her. Desi could tell that the idea was rolling over in his head, and she didn't like it. There was no way she was going to come face-to-face with Jordan, alone, and risk having him do the one thing to her he'd been wanting to do since she first saw him in that courtroom at Julian's murder trial.

"You would be protected," he eventually said.

Desi glared at him. "You have no idea who you're talking about," she argued. "I know what he's capable of and I'm not willing to put myself on the line like that."

"Not even for Lonnie?" he challenged.

Desi cringed. "That's not fair."

"It could work, Desi," he explained desperately.

"How do you figure that it could work? Why would he confess to me?"

"In the heat of an argument, a man's likely to say anything."

"Do you hear yourself?" She frowned. "I didn't mean to say that. Jordan and I can't be in the same room together, Detective. It won't work. Trust me. I never should've said anything."

The man looked as if she'd kicked him in the stomach, like all of the wind had been knocked out of him. This was undoubtedly the biggest murder case in his career and he was not equipped for it. Bobby Randolph would fail in his investigation and Lonnie would never get justice.

———————

Lonnie would've done it for her. Long after the detective had left, it was that thought that haunted Desi. Brave, fearless, and gutsy, Lonnie wouldn't have hesitated to step up to the plate to take on Jordan if it meant possibly getting him to admit to killing Desi. So, how far was Desi willing to go for her friend? Could she even get Jordan to meet with her? Wouldn't he suspect something if she suggested a meeting? He was a smart man, an angry man, defensive and guarded.

The sound of the phone ringing interrupted her contemplation. Desi immediately recognized June's number.

"Did I catch you at a bad time?" June asked.

"No," Desi lied. But it was better than saying, "Yes. I'm actually sitting here contemplating how to set your brother up to get him to admit to killing my friend."

"Well, you're not going to believe this, but my mother asked me to call you," June confessed. "She wants to talk."

She was right. Desi didn't believe it. "Is this your idea of a joke, June?"

"I knew you wouldn't believe it. No, Desi. It's not a joke. She wants to talk."

"Talk? Like what? Over tea and crumpets kinda talk?"

June sighed. "I told her I'd ask. I don't expect you to say yes."

"Good," Desi said unemotionally.

"I don't think you have anything to worry about, Desi. I mean, it's not like she can set you up for killing Julian again. Been there. Done that."

"What the hell does she want, June?"

"She wants you to take your stock shares and go."

"Yeah. I'll bet."

For years Desi had imagined what it would be like to have an opportunity to talk one-on-one with Olivia and now that moment was being handed to her and she was going to turn it down?

"If I agree to meet with her, it'll have to be someplace public," Desi eventually answered.

June laughed. "Olivia would die before she was caught dead talking to you in public, Desi. Don't tell me you're afraid of a senior citizen," June quipped.

"Aren't you?" Desi said condescendingly. "She's got no soul, June. And I personally think she's possessed."

"If I can get her to meet on neutral ground, will you agree to it?" June asked thoughtfully.

Desi thought about it. She didn't trust June any more than she trusted any of the Gatewoods. "You find a place we can both agree on, and I'll meet with your mother."

She'd done this to herself. Desi had come back to Dallas to personally take on the Gatewoods and now it seemed that they were closing in on her. She could do what she always did—run—or she could hunker down and stand her ground.

Chapter 43

Bobby knew that his ass was on the line as soon as his lieutenant called him into his office.

"Close the door, Bobby," the man demanded.

Bobby closed the door and then stood across from his boss's desk like a soldier.

For the first time since Bobby had been summoned, the lieutenant looked up at him. "Sit down."

Lieutenant Carl Rice had come over to Bobby's house for barbecues. Bobby had been to Carl's house to watch football. They were friends.

"What the fuck is your problem, Bobby?" Carl growled at him. "You drag Jordan Gatewood into my precinct for questioning in a murder investigation?"

"I'm following some leads in the murder investigation I'm

working," Bobby tried to explain. "You know I wouldn't have called a man like that in here if I didn't have a reason to."

"Just what is it that you think you have, Bobby?"

Carl's attitude spoke volumes. He was acting as defensively as Gatewood.

"A car registered to Gatewood had been in the parking lot at that motel around the time of the murders."

"A car he told you had been stolen," Carl argued.

"Then how come he didn't report it stolen?"

"What else?" Carl asked impatiently.

Bobby thought about telling him about the conversation he'd had with Desi when she told him that Jordan and Adebayo had had an affair, but he had a strong feeling that that wasn't going to fly.

"His personal phone number showed up in Adebayo's phone records."

"And Desi Green's visit here had nothing to do with you looking at Gatewood for this?"

Bobby wasn't completely surprised that Carl knew he'd spoken to Desi, but he'd hoped it wouldn't come up.

"I didn't rely on that, Carl."

"I think you did," the other man challenged him. "Desi Green's got a vendetta to ruin the Gatewoods. Everybody knows that."

"I don't think—"

"That's the problem, Bobby! You didn't think! You listened to that woman's lies and you started sniffing behind them like a blood-hound! Do you really believe that a man like Gatewood would be caught dead in a dump like that motel? Do you think he's got nothing better to do than shoot a few random people outside of Dallas?"

"I believe that he was there, and that he did shoot Adebayo! The other two were killed by somebody else! Ballistics proved that! But Gatewood killed Adebayo! I'd bet my career on it!"

"You'd lose," Carl sneered. "The commissioner called me into his office this morning and he ripped me a new asshole. Gatewood's office contacted the governor's office, who in turn called the mayor in and demanded that he pass on a message to the DPD."

Bobby grit his teeth. The governor? The damn governor?

"You will cease your investigation of Gatewood, Bobby!"

Bobby couldn't believe what he was hearing. "Oh, hell no, Carl!"

"Oh, hell yes, Detective!"

"He's the best lead I have, Carl! If I could just get a warrant for his guns . . ."

"Have you lost your goddamned mind?" Carl bolted to his feet.

"I'm trying to solve a murder case!" Bobby stood up too. "That's my job, Carl! That's what I'm hired to do! Not to kiss the ass of some punk-ass, spoiled motha fucka who has to go crying to the fuckin' governor's office when he can't get his way!"

"Then you get your shit and get your ass out of my precinct, Bobby!"

Bobby stumbled backward. Was he serious?

"I don't need you working for me if you can't follow orders," Carl continued. "Do as I say or get your shit and go. Those are your options—your only options."

Bobby couldn't believe it. Three people had been murdered, Carl had been riding Bobby's ass like a mule to find the killer, and now he was willing to fire him over pursuing the one lead he had?

"So, I got to let it go? Three people are murdered and because of one man, you want me to just let it go?"

Carl looked uncomfortable all of a sudden, convicted by this stance he felt forced to take. Carl slid a folder across his desk to Bobby. "The Cotton Police Department has arrested a man named Frank Ross," he began to explain. "Ross is believed to have killed a cop and was out on parole awaiting trial. His phone number showed up on Adebayo's phone records too, Bobby, but you were so focused on Gatewood that you missed it."

"I didn't miss it, Carl," Bobby protested. "I checked it out and Ross was in Cotton, Texas, the night of the murders."

"He knew the Adebayo woman."

Bobby understood this, but Ross wasn't in Dallas the night she was killed.

"Do you see how Desi Green has swayed your judgement, Bobby?" Carl reasoned. "Because of her, all you can see is Gatewood and you're blind to any other possibility."

Bobby stood there with his mouth hanging open. How could Ross have killed those people if he wasn't even in town? Or, maybe he was, and maybe Carl was right. Maybe he had let his judgement be swayed by Desi and coincidence, and . . .

"I want you to work with the Cotton PD on this, and try to pull together a case against Ross," Carl explained. "He's in jail for parole violation. It seems that he left town the day after he was questioned about Lonnie. Why would he run if he was innocent?"

Bobby went back to his desk and slowly began to leaf through the file on Frank Ross.

"The boss get all bent out of shape over you questioning Gate-wood?" his partner asked reluctantly.

Bobby felt like everybody in the room was staring at him. "He's bent out of shape," he said simply. "Do me a favor." He looked up at her.

"Sure."

"Call the Cotton, Texas, Police Department and let them know we'd like to talk to Frank Ross."

"The credit card guy?" she asked, remembering that they'd found Ross's card information on file with the motel early in the investigation.

Frank nodded. "Can you get away tomorrow?"

She shrugged. "You drive?"

"I'll drive."

Chapter 44

Jordan stood across the room watching his mother's lips move, wondering if he could count the number of lies she told in each sentence.

"Grieving is universal, Jordan. Losing Claire was devastating to all of us."

Jordan used to mistake her smug expression for beauty. His mother had always been the most elegant thing in his life and there were moments when she would take his breath away. Lie number one was the "devastating to all of us" part. Olivia could always take Claire or leave her. The truth was that Claire was as insignificant to her as she had been to Jordan.

"But Gatewood Industries is a corporation in transition and you're needed there now more than ever before. Her death was tragic, but drinking yourself to death isn't going to bring her back."

"There are more reasons for drinking myself to death than losing Claire, Mother," he stated simply.

She looked caught off guard by his admission. "What else could it be?"

He didn't bother to respond. Olivia's world was so much smaller than his. She lived a sheltered life, in a bubble protected from every bad thing in the world.

"A more pressing matter is, of course, the issue of Desi Green," she continued. "I told you to do something about that woman and you haven't."

"You want me to kill her?" he asked deadpan.

Olivia didn't even blink at the suggestion. "I want you to do what is necessary to get her out of our lives" she said coolly.

Jordan stared at her for a moment and then laughed. To say that he had never flat-out had people killed would've been a lie. But only when there was no chance that it could ever be traced back to him, and only to make a point.

"Anything happens to Desi, who do you think they're going to look to blame?"

"They can blame all they want, Jordan," his mother responded. "But what can they do about it? Or haven't you been paying attention?"

"The untouchable Gatewoods." He smirked. "We're fuckin' invincible."

Jordan raised his glass in a toast to his mother and shoved a potato chip in his mouth.

"I'm tired of her," Olivia said dryly. "And I'm getting extremely tired of you, son."

"What happened to Alzheimer's, Olivia?" he asked sarcastically and unapologetically. "Got any of that in that purse of yours you can snort?"

She looked offended. "You are brazen these days. Aren't you?"

"I think I'm drunk, but I can't be sure. But, getting back to the subject, you were saying something about me taking out Desi Green?"

"This isn't a joke, Jordan," she said gravely. "She's making money off of us, and she's making a mockery out of us, and I've asked you before to do something about it."

"Once upon a time, Olivia, I gave a damn. But that was a long time ago," he said flippantly. "Desi sounds like she's more a thorn in your side these days than she is in mine."

"She killed your father, Jordan!"

"No, you killed him. And oh, by the way, he wasn't my father, and he made sure that I never felt like he was. But he was hers." He stared calmly at his mother, whose face flushed a crimson hue. "You knew that, though, even back then. Isn't that true, O-liv-i-a."

"What the hell is wrong with you?" Olivia's pinched expression showed her disapproval.

"They think I killed a woman," he suddenly blurted out, relishing in his mother's shocked expression. "For real this time." He smiled and winked. "Or hadn't you heard?"

"What woman?"

"Don't worry, Ma," he said sarcastically. "I got it covered."

"What woman, Jordan!" she snapped.

"Lonnie Adebayo," he blurted out.

Jordan saw no reason to keep this from Olivia. Hell! She'd asked who and he'd just told her. Let her fragile ass try and swallow that. His mother searched her often selective memories. "The reporter woman they found at that cheap motel?"

"Yeah." He sighed. "Her."

"The police think that you killed that woman?" she asked, astonished.

He nodded. "They do indeed."

"Why would they think that?" she asked carefully.

He walked over to Olivia, bent at the waist leaning over her, and he whispered, "Because I was fucking her."

Jordan straightened up, walked across the room, and fell back on the sofa across from his mother.

"She was your mistress?" she murmured.

He shrugged. "She was . . . something," he said introspectively, nodding and thinking of the two of them together.

She had been his mistress. She had been his enemy, his vice, his regret, his love, his demon, his obsession. Lonnie had been his everything—both good and bad, right and wrong. It had been an upside-down, inside-out kind of relationship, destructive, passionate, everything good and bad.

"Well?" she asked. "Did you kill her?"

He just looked at her.

"I can call the governor. He'll put a stop to any investigation that—"

"I called him."

"Then that should've taken care of it."

"I've taken care of it."

Olivia leaned forward. "Then get your ass back to work and finish building my corporation. There's too much work to do for you to be sitting in this house mourning a woman you obviously didn't give a damn about. Or are you even mourning Claire at all?"

"I'm mourning . . . my life, Olivia," he muttered.

"Your life is damn good, Jordan, and it's because of me that it is."

"My life is a fuckin' mess."

She sat up, straightened her back, and raised her chin. "Don't you dare," she said, threatening. "You don't have the luxury of self-pity, Jordan. If it weren't for me, you'd be working in some factory somewhere in some dirty little town in the middle of nowhere, with a fat wife and a house full of dumb-ass children that wouldn't amount to anything more than you."

He found the analogy amusing. "If that's what you think, then why the hell did you marry Tunson?"

"Because I was stupid enough to get pregnant by him."

Jordan raised his brows in surprise. "Wow," he said unemotionally. "Don't hold back, Mother. Tell me how you really feel."

She did her best to look apologetic. "Don't try and twist the meaning behind what I say, Jordan. I wanted more for myself and my child. I wanted more than that man could offer, and when the opportunity presented itself, I took it."

"Did you know back then that one day you'd put a bullet in that opportunity?" Did she know that Gatewood was living on borrowed time?

Again, he'd offended her. "I loved him," she murmured.

"To death," he concluded.

"Do you really believe he'd have left you as his successor if I hadn't done what I did?"

That was it. The question that Jordan had never had the courage to ask himself because he feared that he already knew the answer.

Angry tears flooded the woman's eyes. "That motha fucka was going to change his will," she said, gritting her teeth. "It was bad enough that he was fuckin' that bitch, but he was going to change his will, Jordan! He was going to leave us with what amounted to little more than change and the rest would've gone to Ida, June, and—"

"Desi," he finished for her.

"The twenty million she got was nothing compared to what she could've gotten if I hadn't done what I did."

Jordan thought about the big picture. Even from the grave, Julian

Gatewood had worked his magic. It was cosmic, and almost scary, how ultimately Desi Green had survived everything that had happened to her, to the point that she had made a fortune off Gatewood Industries—Julian's will be done? What else could it have been?

"Twenty million and rights to his name," he said, staring back at his mother.

Olivia blinked away tears. "Tread lightly, son," she warned. "Gatewood Industries isn't going to wait on you forever."

"Who else could run it as well as I can?" he challenged.

"June," his mother stated simply.

Jordan was shocked she'd even mentioned June's name without gagging on it. He burst out laughing. "You trust June? After the coup she pulled?"

"She had the balls to pull it. She wants to be at the helm of her father's company," Olivia said smugly. "I didn't think she was capable, until now."

"So, you're going to fire me and hand over the reins to Benedict Arnold?"

"June's no idiot." Olivia almost looked convinced. "She proved that with this little scheme of hers and she executed it in such a way that neither one of us saw it coming."

Jordan shrugged. "Well, when you put it that way." He raised his glass in the air. "Cheers to the backstabber!"

Olivia picked up her purse to leave. "Get your act together, son." Olivia stood up to leave. "I love you with all my heart, but you are as disposable as a dirty diaper."

Conviction had been festering like a plague inside Jordan since the night Lonnie was killed, or maybe, even before that. All the wrong things suddenly felt wrong, and gnawed at him like termites chewing on wood. After Olivia left, Jordan searched long and hard for a valid reason to despise Desi and he came up empty. She'd been a victim, as much a victim of his mother's schemes as any of them. But another part of him couldn't let go of this place he'd been planted into, this Gatewood world, where he was king and everyone else was less than. Frank Ross was less than—because Jordan had decided to throw him to the wolves to save his own ass. It was messy, messy business being Jordan Gatewood. But as long as he lived, that would always be the case.

"Amanda," he said over the phone to his assistant.

"Yes, sir, Mr. Gatewood," she responded excitedly. "How are you?"

"I'm . . . better. I'll be in the office tomorrow. Schedule a meeting with all VPs and department heads for first thing in the morning."

"Yes, sir."

Jordan hung up, leaned back, and took a breath. Olivia was right. On him, self-pity looked like shit. GII was the only part of his world that was real and tangible anymore. Everything else was a figment of his imagination.

Chapter 45

June had called Desi and asked to meet her for coffee. Reluctantly, Desi agreed. June looked tired. She wore no makeup, her hair was pulled up into a disheveled bun, her jeans looked to be two sizes too big, and the yellow tee two sizes too small.

"Neither one of them talk to me anymore," she said dismally, sitting across from Desi, tracing her finger around the lip of her cup.

Desi was dumbfounded. "You expected them to after what you did?"

June's light eyes weren't blue like Julian's. Right now, they were more hazel. When Desi had first met her, they looked more green.

"I get emotional," she volunteered, shrugging.

Desi felt herself start to get annoyed all of a sudden. June was coming across as some confused teenager who couldn't understand why her parents were mad at her for taking the car without permission.

"What's that got to do with anything?" Desi asked, perturbed.

June sighed, leaned back, and crossed one slender leg over the other. "It means that I may not have thought this whole thing through."

Desi cocked a brow. "This whole thing. What whole thing are you talking about?"

"I was angry at my mother, Desi," she explained, exasperated. "Jealous of my brother—I just wanted . . ."

Desi couldn't believe the change in this woman. June had gone from this confident, intelligent, decisive woman to this—this silly wisp of a girl in the blink of an eye.

"No . . . no . . . no . . ." Desi shook her head in denial. "You are not going to start tripping out now, June. Not after you talked me into buying into this mess."

"I'm sorry."

Desi was pissed. "Sorry? What are you sorry for, June?" she asked unsympathetically. "You came to me about this business proposition of yours and now you're sorry. What am I missing here?"

June was Olivia's daughter. She was Jordan's sister. Had she been lying to Desi all this time? Had she set her up?

Desi studied this woman, and then realized that June looked like she was high or something.

"What's going on, June?"

June shrugged again. Her eyes filled with tears, and suddenly she was crying. "I don't know what I was thinking," she murmured helplessly. "I hate my mother, but I don't hate Jordan. He's my big brother, Desi, and he's always looked out for me—always."

Desi couldn't believe what she was hearing. June was suddenly feeling guilty over Jordan?

"He hasn't been back to work since Claire's death." She sniffed. "I had no idea he'd take her death so hard, but Desi—it's killing him."

Was she looking at . . . Desi turned to see who the hell June was looking at that she expected should feel sorry for Jordan.

"You feel sorry for him?" Desi asked carefully.

June nodded. "What I did to him—with you, and then with Claire's death . . ." June shook her head. "I've never seen him like this, Desi. And knowing that I'm partly to blame is killing me."

Desi was stunned. "You have got to be kidding me."

"I don't expect for you to understand."

"Good," Desi told her.

"I meant to piss him off. I didn't mean to destroy him."

Watching the woman, it became painfully clear to Desi that June was an idiot.

"My mother deserves to be punished for what she did to my father, but Jordan—he's like me," she said pitifully. "He's just a pawn on her chessboard to be played however she chooses. The difference between me and my brother is that I know this, and he doesn't. He believes that she loves him and I know that she only loves herself." June swallowed. "He needs someone now, and I can't be there for him because he doesn't trust me and I don't blame him."

"Just shut up," Desi said, suddenly disgusted.

June looked stunned.

"Shut the fuck up, June. I know you didn't call me out here to talk about poor, pitiful, helpless Jordan. I know you don't believe that I could possibly give a damn about his hurt feelings or heartache."

Of course June looked offended. "I guess I expected too much."

"Way too much," Desi agreed. "Your brother is a bastard. I wouldn't care if that sonofabitch lost his legs, arms, his best friend, or his dog—there is nothing in this world that would ever make me feel sorry for his ass."

June glared back at her.

"He's evil." Desi leaned toward her and said, "He's mean, and he's capable of absolutely anything and everything."

"He's still my brother, Desi," June said, defending him. "And he was never any of those things to me."

"Good for you, June. But I know what he can do to people. Jordan destroys people. I've seen him do it. You think he cared so much about that wife of his? You have no idea." Desi shook her head. "I read in the paper that she killed herself. I wonder why?"

"Don't you dare go there, Desi! He and Claire loved each other. Did they have problems? Sure. Most married couples have problems. But don't sit there and imply that he's the reason Claire committed suicide."

"Who the hell said it was an implication?" Desi argued. June was falling to pieces right in front of Desi's eyes and it was making her sick to her stomach. That brother of hers was no hero, and he was definitely not a victim.

"He's a murderer," Desi said suddenly, watching all emotion fade from June's eyes. "He killed someone close to me, June. Maybe you read about it in the paper? Yolanda Adebayo, the reporter they found shot at that motel?" she told her. "Lonnie was my friend. She was Jordan's lover. And he killed her."

The color washed from June's face. "That's a fuckin' lie!"

"No," Desi said calmly. "The lie is believing that he could give a damn about anybody but himself." Desi reached inside her purse and pulled a five-dollar bill out and laid it on the table. "You lose my number, June. Don't call me again. I mean it."

June stared her down. "Don't worry. I think I'm through with you."

Desi stood up and left that idiot sitting there.

———

Desi was still fuming ten minutes after she'd left June behind in that coffee shop. Of course June's motives to use Desi to get back at her mother and to somehow teach Jordan a lesson set off red flags from the beginning but Desi had been pulled in by just how much money could be made by her involvement, not to mention, it was the perfect way to get under that old woman's skin. Until now, Desi hadn't even admitted that truth to herself, but knowing that Julian Gatewood was her biological father, there could be no bigger insult to Olivia Gatewood than for Desi to buy shares in the company he started and that she murdered him for.

But just how committed was Desi to keeping her money in Gatewood Industries? She had invested millions to become a significant shareholder, and it was only a matter of time before Jordan played his hand to force her out. He was grieving right now, mourning the death of a wife he tolerated, and trying to cover his ass in Lonnie's murder. But when he snapped out of it . . . When he finally did get his act together and got back into that office he'd come back to his senses.

By the time Desi realized that the oncoming car had crossed over into her lane and was headed straight for her, it was already too late. The terrible sound of crunching metal was deafening. Tires screeched, and the smell of rubber burning scorched her nostrils. Desi's head slammed into the deployed air bag that felt as if it had exploded in her face. She spun at dizzying speeds, flipping over and over again, until the spinning stopped and Desi lay breathless, her heart racing, her head pounding, blinking her eyes rapidly to try and get her perspective in control. She was . . . upside down . . . the car was upside down . . . Shattered glass fell into her mouth when she opened it to cry out. The pain in her neck was excruciating as she turned her head in time to see someone walking toward her . . . black shoes . . . jeans . . .

"Help me!" she tried to cry out, but couldn't. Desi coughed. Her vision blurred behind tear-filled eyes. "Help . . ." she managed to say, but she didn't know if he'd heard her.

He raised his hand toward her . . . She reached for him, stretching her fingers hoping to feel his touch. "Please," she mouthed desperately.

A gun! He had a gun pointed at her! Desi's eyes widened with fear! What was this? What was happening? And then . . . She heard the sound of a gunshot as her eyes closed, and suddenly there was nothing.

"Desi? Desi, what is it, baby?"

Her mother sat up in bed and turned on the light on the bedside table next to her.

Desi was small. She was so very—so very small, and afraid.

"I had a bad dream," she said, shaking in her bare feet.

Her mother smiled and reached out her hand. Desi smiled and quickly padded across the room to get scooped up into her mother's arms and hugged.

"Another one?" Her mother smiled. "How come you only seem to have bad dreams on Wednesdays?"

Desi didn't know what she meant. She had no idea that it was Wednesday. She just knew that she was afraid, more afraid than ever, and that she didn't want to go back to her room.

"Can I sleep in here?" she asked, staring wide-eyed at her mother.

Her mother frowned. "Now, I don't know about that."

"Lay her down, Ida." His voice came from the other side of the bed. "Let her sleep."

Desi scrambled over into the middle of the bed and crawled under the covers. Her mother turned off the light and stretched out next to her.

"Stop all that wiggling, little girl," he fussed, half asleep with his back to her.

Desi stopped moving because he told her to. And then he turned over and draped his strong arm across her and rested his hand on her mother's hip.

"There's a monster in my room," Desi whispered, thinking that only he could hear her.

"He can stay the night," he told her. "But I'll get him outta there in the morning."

"Promise?" she whispered.

"On my life."

"Desi?"

Her eyes fluttered at the sound of his voice.

"Hey, baby." He stroked back her hair and kissed her softly on the lips.

"S-Solomon," she murmured, forcing her eyes open.

"I'm here," he said, squeezing her hand.

Desi swallowed. "Something . . . the car crashed and . . . ?"

He nodded his handsome head. "I know," he whispered. "But you're okay."

"I had a bad dream." Maybe that was it. Maybe Desi had just been dreaming.

"Something happ— Something bad happened," she struggled to say.

Desi wasn't sure where she was. She wasn't home. She wasn't in her bed. Where was she?

"I had a bad dream," she repeated almost incoherently.

"Shh," he whispered. "It's alright, baby."

She believed him—that it was alright. It was alright because he said it was.

"Promise?" she asked.

He kissed her again. "On my life."

Chapter 46

"*They're saying* I'm the one that killed her," Frank said wearily over the phone to his father, Joel. "They know I was here in Cotton when she died. So, how can I be in both places at once? But," he sighed, "they charged me with murder, and because of the other murder," he swallowed, "I'm fucked."

Frank had been sick to his stomach ever since that attorney had made it clear to him what was going down.

"I've been a fool, Joel—Pop. I believed that somehow it would all work out," he said, choosing his words carefully. The phones in this place were tapped, and Frank had to be careful not to incriminate himself in the cop murder, and not to implicate Gatewood in Lonnie's.

"What did that lawyer of yours tell you?" Joel asked in that lazy drawl of his.

"He told me to keep my mouth shut. I'm keeping my mouth shut, man."

An ex-cop in prison for murder was a death sentence. He hadn't trusted Gatewood, but he'd wanted to believe that maybe there was something to the whole relation thing. He was Frank's half brother. The two of them barely knew each other, but still, they shared Joel Tunson's blood. Frank had been foolish enough to think that that should've counted for something.

"That's not bad advice, son," Joel said dismally.

"The mistake I made was running," Frank admitted.

"Your mistakes go back further than that."

Joel was right. Frank had shot another cop and, self-defense or not, it was his word against—what? Who? Had he never shot the man, he wouldn't have needed Gatewood or his fancy lawyer. His ass might've been dead, shot by the other man first, but hell, at least he'd have died a cop by a bullet. There would have been some honor in that. In prison, if he didn't get the death penalty, he'd be killed by other means at the hands of men he'd probably helped put there.

"You're right," he said, sighing again. "My life ain't amounted to shit, and I can't blame nobody but myself."

He paused to think over the span of his life, thinking of how little he'd made of it. Even becoming a police officer hadn't been about anything noble. It had been a job, an opportunity, and he'd fucked it up by being too greedy, pussy-whipped, and dumb.

"I guess I'd better get off this phone," he said with resolve. Frank might not ever talk to this man again, and he had to come to terms with the turn in the road his life had finally taken. "I uh . . . I wish we could've gotten to know each other better, man," he told his father. "Wish I could've been a better son."

It took a while for the old man to finally say something. "You through?"

Frank nearly smiled. "Yeah. I'm through."

"When you get off the phone with me, I want you to call that attorney of yours," Joel explained patiently. "And fire his ass."

Frank laughed. "Wish I could."

"Don't wish nothing. Just do it," Joel demanded.

"He's not gonna let me do that," Frank said reluctantly.

"He ain't gotta let you do shit, Frank. Just fire him."

"You don't get it, Pop," he argued. "It's not as easy as me firing him. We made an agreement, and if I don't stick to it . . ."

If he didn't stick to it, Gatewood would have that fancy-ass lawyer lay Frank out and filet his ass.

"Don't worry about it," Joel said gruffly. "Call me in a few days, son. You hear me?"

"I hear you, but why?"

"Just call me," he commanded. "Give me till Wednesday—no, Thursday. You understand?"

Frank nodded. "Yessir."

Joel hung up abruptly, leaving Frank to wonder what the old man was up to.

Chapter 47

"*I don't care* how you do it, Jordan, but I want Desi Green gone! I want her out of our lives once and for all! Do you understand me?"

Olivia had woken him up from a dead sleep with a frantic call about being dragged back to Blink, Texas, by Desi.

"Why the hell did you agree to go to Blink, Texas, Mother?"

"To reason with her," she sobbed. "To make her understand that she and her money have no place in this company. She wouldn't talk to me anyplace else. She insisted in going back to that house . . ."

"What made you think that she gave a damn about anything you had to say to her?" he asked, frustrated. "It was a revenge move of some kind, a farce to rub what happened there in your face."

"It doesn't matter. You get rid of her, Jordan! I have never been foolish enough to believe that you were a saint. The oil business is dirty business and only the dirty thrive in it."

"Is that supposed to be a compliment?"

"It's supposed to be a fact of life. Julian was hard, he was mean, but nowhere near as hard or mean as you are, son." She paused. "I'm tired of this girl. Tell me you understand."

Jordan sighed. "Completely."

That old familiar fire was beginning to burn inside Jordan again. He'd spent a full day at the office, putting plans in place to force Desi Green out of his company. Olivia had been up in arms over nothing. Jordan always knew that he could force Desi to sell whether she wanted to or not, and sell at a price determined by the board.

He sat alone in the executive steam room of Gatewood Industries long after the last person had left for the night. Jordan closed his eyes and breathed in lethal doses of the soothing scent of eucalyptus to clear his head. During these last few months since Lonnie's death, Jordan had felt like he had been caught up in a cyclone, his life out of focus and out of control. In reality, Jordan had started to spin out of control even before Lonnie died. The threat of his demise began when she showed up again, after two years, out of the blue and back in his life.

Their relationship had ended violently and abruptly, and Jordan had never reconciled those feelings he'd always had for that woman. On the one hand he hated her, and at one time had even wanted her dead. On the other, he could never quite get the taste of Lonnie out of his mouth, or the memories of her out of his thoughts. She had been the most delicious, intriguing, and intoxicating woman he'd ever met. The night she died, he realized just how deep his addiction for her ran, and he knew that as long as the two of them walked the earth, he would never stop loving her. When Claire shot Lonnie, Jordan swore that he felt that bullet pierce his heart at the same time it went through hers.

Olivia had been right, though. Jordan was still among the living and he had a corporation to run and falling apart was not an option. He had to admit that it felt good being back in the office today. Jordan had been feeling like a derailed train for too damn long, and today, he was back on track and doing what he had been born to do. Jordan was back in control. Randolph hadn't contacted Jordan since he'd had him come to the precinct for that ridiculous questioning.

Jordan had called on the favor of a few loyal and dedicated friends, and had them put a muzzle on that dog. The attention had turned to brother Frank now. Enough circumstantial evidence, along with suspicion of murdering a Cotton, Texas, police officer was enough to practically convict the man without the frustration and cost of even having a trial, but Frank would bide his time in jail until it came to that, and he knew to keep his mouth shut.

Lonnie's death, and then Claire's suicide, had pushed him to the brink of a kind of darkness he'd never known before. And if he'd given it one more second of his time and attention, Jordan knew he'd have crossed that point of no return and would've self-destructed under the weight of guilt and helplessness that he had no business feeling.

Half an hour later, Jordan was freshly showered and walking toward the locker where he'd hung his clothes. All of a sudden, he was airborne!

Jordan's right leg had been swept out from under him, a man's hand grabbed him around his neck from behind, and he landed so hard on his back against the concrete floor that it knocked all the wind out of him.

Solomon Jones seemed to appear out of thin air like a magic trick, shoved his knee into Jordan's diaphragm, and grabbed him by the throat with one hand and squeezed.

Jordan fought like hell to catch his breath, clutching at the other man's hand, pounding his forearms against Jones's arm. He felt like he was about to pass out.

"Your man didn't kill her, Gatewood," Jones growled low and deep.

His dark eyes bore holes into Jordan, and for the first time in his life, Jordan worried that he might just die.

"He came close," Jones continued. "But not close enough!"

What the hell was this fool talking about? Jordan mouthed the word, "What?"

"You sneaky motha fucka," Jones snarled. "I could rip out your throat if I wanted to," he threatened, leaning down close to Jordan. The look in his eyes gave warning of how badly he wanted to rip out Jordan's throat. The other man's fingers dug deeper into the skin around Jordan's Adam's apple.

Jordan grabbed Solomon by the wrist with both hands. This bastard was strong as hell! If he wanted Jordan dead, it wouldn't take much to make it happen.

The man knew half a dozen styles of martial arts and yes, he could absolutely kill Jordan if he wanted to. Jordan prayed silently to his god that Jones really didn't want to.

Jones gradually loosened his grip, slowly stood up, and backed away, leaving Jordan in a heap on the floor, coughing and gagging and fighting to catch his breath.

"What the hell do you want?" Jordan finally asked.

Solomon Jones stared down his nose at Jordan.

"Until now, we've been playing this game by your rules, in your arena," Jones explained calmly.

Maybe it was the extended lack of oxygen or the very real fear that he had come within inches of dying, but Jordan felt a spark of amusement rise in him. "It's never been any other way with any opponent."

"Until now." Jones's confidence was almost inspiring. The man stood there, as cool as a block of ice, with his hands in the pockets of his European-cut suit, wallowing in his own hype.

"Believe what you want, man," Jordan said dismissively.

"You came close, man," Jones continued cryptically. "Too damn close, but it's the last time."

Jordan had no idea what he was talking about.

"Your man didn't kill her. You didn't kill me. And the rules of engagement have changed because of it."

Your man didn't kill her. It was a statement that made no sense to Jordan whatsoever, but Jones implied that it should have. Jones had reason to believe that someone had tried to have Desi killed. And he believed that that person was Jordan. Jordan saw no reason, at least at this time, to explain to Jones that he had had nothing to do with whoever had tried to take out Desi.

"The planets will align again when Desi gets her greasy little hands out of my corporation."

If Jones was offended by the insult to his woman, he didn't show it.

"To hell with the planets, man," he shot back.

Jordan laughed. "Who the hell are you supposed to be?" He'd entertained this fool as long as he could without giving in to this joke standing in front of him. Solomon Jones was an entertainment lawyer. He was nobody in the grand scheme of Jordan's life. He was a fool in love with another fool and not even in the same league as Jordan.

"I'm the man who knows your deepest secret, Jordan," he said.

Jordan just looked at him.

"I know where you were the night Adebayo was killed," he

explained coolly. "I know who you called to clean up behind your desperate ass. I know who showed up, who erased any evidence that you were there, and who made sure that no one there that night had the courage to describe you or your wife to the police."

An icy chill washed over him. "What the hell are you talking about?" Jordan asked bitterly.

That smug look on Jones's face was too confident for him to be making this up.

"Motha fuckas like you think that you can just get away with this because of who you are," Jones explained.

"What is it that you know, Jones?"

"I know that you killed Lonnie," he said evenly. "I know that right after you did, you made a phone call. I know that Edgar Beckman gets a hard-on at the mention of your name, and I know the name of the man he called that night to come and clean up after your slobbering ass."

Jordan froze. No! He couldn't know all that. How could he fuckin' know?

"You're going to stay away from her," Jones warned. "Or I swear, the same sonofabitch who killed those other two people will be coming for you next."

"I want her out of my company!" Jordan growled.

"She'll leave when she's good and damn ready, man!" He shrugged. "Or she might decide to stay the course. That's up to her. But you will not fuck with her or her money, man. You will not speak to her, look at her, or lay a finger on her, or I swear I'll bust your world wide with a word. Just pretend she's another shareholder."

Jordan froze.

The moment of silence between the two men hung heavy in the

air. Jordan waited for Jones to say something, but instead, the man turned and headed out of the locker room. Before disappearing, however, he did say one more thing.

"There's a package waiting for you outside your door at your ranch, Jordan." He turned and glanced over his shoulder. "Special delivery?"

Chapter 48

Desi had a concussion, whiplash, and a sprained wrist. She remembered leaving June at the café, a car driving toward her, and a man pointing a gun at her, but the details of everything else were vague at best. They kept her overnight at the hospital, but thankfully now, she was home. Home—not at Solomon's house, but at their house, and more than ever, this place was her home now.

Desi was stretched out on the chaise near the pool when Solomon came outside with a tall, dark gentleman trailing behind him.

"Baby, I want you to meet someone."

Solomon's friend stood several inches taller than he did. The other man wore a pair of expensive faded jeans with a black V-neck tee shirt tucked in and belted, and shades. He was the darkest man she'd ever laid eyes on, with skin so smooth it looked like he'd been dipped in oil. He held out his hand to Desi.

"O. P.," Solomon continued with the introduction. "This is

Desi. Desi, this his O. P. He and I grew up together and I'd have to say that he is one of my closest friends."

The big man bent at the waist, gently held her hand between his two sizable palms, and smiled. Lord have mercy! Why'd he do that? Desi's heart fluttered like the wings of a bird. Before he left, she'd have to make it a point to get the name of his dentist.

"Pleasure," he said, with a voice that reminded her of Barry White.

"O. P.?" she asked. "As in Mayberry, Opie?"

He let go of her hand and straightened up to that massive height of his again. "Not quite," he said with a hint of menace in his tone.

The two men sat down across from her.

"He saved your life, Desi," Solomon said, fighting back a tide of emotion as he looked at her, and glanced quickly at his friend. "Let me rephrase." He cleared his throat. "He saved my life."

Desi looked over at the man who suddenly became noticeably uncomfortable.

"Nah, man," he said sheepishly. "I just happened to be in the right place at the right time. That's all."

"After I was . . . attacked," Solomon explained, using the word reluctantly. "I needed to make sure that you were safe, baby, so I asked O. P. to keep an eye on you."

Desi stared back and forth between the two men, and finally stopped at O. P. "You've been following me?"

He had quickly regained his supercool-mac-daddy composure. "Sometimes."

She expected him to elaborate, but he didn't seem interested in doing so.

"The man who crashed into your car did it on purpose," Solomon continued. "And when he saw that you were alive, he got out of his car and came at you with a gun."

"I heard him shoot," Desi said in disbelief. She had distinctively heard a gun firing.

"I shot first," O. P. said.

Desi stared at him, stunned. "You killed him?"

He didn't respond with words, but the look on his face spoke volumes. She hadn't heard anything about anybody being killed. Desi hadn't even known that a body had been found at the scene of the crash. No one had told her . . . that anyone had been shot.

"The night Lonnie was killed, Desi," Solomon quietly continued, "O. P. was at that motel."

Her gaze shifted to her fiancé.

"Jordan . . ." She whispered his name without meaning to.

"Jordan wasn't there," Solomon added. "He was gone by the time O. P. arrived. But O. P. had been called by someone—I had the number traced to a man named Edgar Beckman."

"Edgar?" she repeated, stunned.

"You know him?" Solomon asked.

Desi nodded. "He was Mr. J's friend," she explained, sounding almost like a child. "He used to come over to our house sometimes . . ." She swallowed. "Before Julian was killed."

"Beckman called O. P. after getting off the phone with Gatewood and told him to go there and remove any evidence that Jordan was ever there."

So, what kind of man was this O. P., really? she thought, staring at him. "You were there—before the police came?"

He sat there looking like a big, black stone wall. Where was that radiant smile of his now? Desi turned her attention back to Solomon. "How long have you known this?"

Solomon shrugged. "Not long, Desi," he said seriously. "O. P. and I didn't connect the dots until a few days ago when I mentioned Lonnie's name."

Gradually Desi began to connect some dots of her own and all of a sudden, there seemed to be a light glowing at the end of this long, black tunnel she had been in since she'd come back to Texas. "So, we can go to the police," she said excitedly. "Solomon, we can call Detective Randolph and tell him everything about that night." She looked anxiously at the two men. This was it! This was the evidence that they needed to put Jordan Gatewood at the scene of Lonnie's murder. That along with the fact that she'd told them the two of them had been lovers, and that he'd tried to kill her before, was more than enough to arrest him now, or at least, get real serious about investigating his arrogant ass! Desi hurried to her feet to get her purse and find Bobby Randolph's phone number, but she made the mistake of getting up too fast and if Solomon hadn't caught her when he did, she'd have fallen.

"It's not that easy, Desi," he said soothingly.

"Sure it is." How come the pool was spinning? He helped her back to her seat. "O. P., not the Mayberry kind, can tell him everything. Or we can tell him, Solomon," she desperately explained, suddenly realizing that O. P. didn't seem like the type who got along well with others, especially detectives. "He'll believe you. You're a lawyer."

Solomon knelt in front of her. "It's not that easy," he repeated tenderly.

He might as well have been speaking Greek, because Desi didn't understand a word he meant. "Why do you keep saying that?" she said, frustrated. "Of course it's that easy. Even if he doesn't want to talk." She motioned to O. P. "You can tell him what you know. You don't even have to mention your friend's name, Solomon. Just tell him that Edgar called someone." The idea came to her like a lightbulb suddenly appearing over her head. "Yes! Tell them that Edgar made a call, and they'll trace his phone records to . . ." She looked at O. P.

"No one," the man said simply.

The look on Solomon's face shut her up.

"We can't go to the police with this," he told her, squeezing her hands in his.

This wasn't what she wanted to hear. It wasn't what she wanted to know. They had something—something tangible and something that could finally implicate Jordan in Lonnie's murder and they couldn't do anything with it?

Angry tears clouded her eyes. "Why'd you tell me this, Solomon?" she asked, feeling more helpless than ever.

She knew that Jordan had shot Lonnie. She knew it with everything in her soul, and this man, this O. P., confirmed what she knew, but he was a fuckin' criminal and they couldn't take what he told them to the police because it would mean implicating him. He was Solomon's friend. And Solomon didn't want his friend to go to prison, because God knew, he looked like he belonged there, fine or not.

"Why'd you tell me if we can't do anything about it?" Desi asked, surprised by the fact that she had started to cry. "It doesn't help—it doesn't help—you telling me this."

"I told you because I felt you needed to know everything," he explained earnestly. "And I wanted you to know that I'm on it, Desi."

She stared, confused, at him. "What does that mean?"

"It means that Gatewood knows that I know."

She looked surprised. "You told him?"

"I want him to stay the hell away from you, Desi. I want him to back the fuck off and I let him know what could happen to him if he didn't."

But none of that helped Lonnie. Desi loved Solomon so much for wanting to protect her, but this wasn't about her. Jordan murdered Lonnie and he was going to get away with it.

Solomon got up and sat down next to her. "I swore on my life to protect you, baby," he said sincerely. "I meant that."

But who would protect Lonnie? Her memory? Who would make him pay for what he did to her? Desi looked over at O. P. staring at her from behind those dark glasses, looking almost as if he could read her mind.

Chapter 49

"*Now that you're back,* things can go back to being normal," Olivia said proudly, casually strolling into Jordan's office unannounced. She stopped just on the other side of his desk and waited for him to do the proper thing.

Reluctantly, Jordan stood up long enough for his mother to take a seat across from him.

"I assume you've begun making arrangements with the board to force Desi Green out of Gatewood Industries?"

Jordan didn't respond, but it didn't matter because Olivia continued talking as if he had.

"That girl's been a stitch in my behind since she got out of prison," she muttered more to herself than to him. "The society columnists—or bloggers or whatever they're calling themselves these days—had a field day with her showing up at the Investors' Ball. Did you read any of that mess they were writing?"

"My wife was dead by the time those stories were published, Mother," he said sarcastically. "So—no."

That strange look on her face, a mixture of empathy and offensiveness, was a warning for him to be cautious with his attitude.

"How long will it take?" she asked coolly.

"How long will what take?"

"To force Desi to sell her stock back to the company?"

Well, if her goddamned boyfriend hadn't burst into the executive gym the other night and threatened to turn over proof to the police that Jordan had been at the murder scene the night Lonnie was killed, it could've happened pretty fast. Jordan thought about saying it, but instead, he cleared his throat.

"I've started the process, Mother," he lied.

Solomon's "special delivery" had been the body of a man Jordan had never met propped up in front of his garage with a bullet through his head. Getting rid of the body had been like getting rid of any unwanted garbage, requiring nothing more than a phone call, but it had set a precedent.

"Have you set a price yet?" she probed. "How much?"

He just looked at her.

"She got Anton stock for damn near pennies," Olivia reported, rolling her eyes and crossing one dancer's leg gracefully over the other. "I don't want to have to pay any more for it than she did," she insisted.

Olivia was ridiculous if she thought she'd get the kind of deal that Desi got. But the truth was, she wasn't going to get any deal. Not until Jordan could figure a way to get rid of her ass without harming a hair on her pretty head.

"Mr. Gatewood." His assistant stood at the door of his office. "I'm so sorry to interrupt, sir, but there seems to be a commotion at the security desk," she explained, looking nervously back and forth between Jordan and his mother.

"Why on earth would you bother him with something like that?" Olivia fussed. "Have security take care of it."

Jordan ignored his mother. "What kind of commotion?"

"A man who says he's . . . He's insisting that he's your father."

Olivia looked mortified. "That's ridiculous! Tell security to call the police!"

"He says his name is Joel, sir. Joel Tunson? And he's insisting on seeing you. . . . I'm sorry but I don't know what to tell the security guards."

All the color washed from his mother's face. Jordan had to remind himself to breathe. If that was Tunson at the security desk and Jordan turned him away, all hell could break loose. Olivia seemed to be thinking the same thing.

"Tell security to bring him up," he instructed the confused woman.

She hesitated. "Um . . . Yes . . . yes, sir."

Olivia stared wide-eyed back at her son, and for the first time in his life, he saw that his mother was actually speechless.

Joel had never seen a building this big before. He'd never ridden an elevator past the fourth floor. He'd never had the police escort him anywhere. And he'd never been as determined as he was now. He marched behind that uniformed man, off those elevators, down a long corridor with floors as shiny as glass, all the way down to the end of the wide hallway, past a scared-looking, skinny white woman sitting behind a desk almost as big as Joel's house.

The officer stepped aside and raised his hand toward the door, sort of showing Joel that he was supposed to go inside the room. He went inside, expecting to see the boy, but he never in a million years expected to see her—his first wife—Olivia. Looking damn near as young as she looked back when he'd first met her. She was thin, though, too thin, long and bony. She'd always been light skinned, but Olivia looked like her face hadn't been kissed by the sun in years. There was no denying those eyes, though. Beautiful eyes that weren't quite brown but were as clear as marbles when she held her face to the sun.

"You can leave." Jordan spoke to the man in the uniform standing behind Joel. "Close the door behind you," he instructed him.

He could tell just by looking at the boy that he was none too happy to see old Joel, but it didn't matter. Joel hadn't come here to make any-damn-body happy.

Jordan went to his desk and pushed a button on his phone.

"Yes, Mr. Gatewood?" a woman answered.

"Take the afternoon off," he said abruptly.

The woman started to say something else, but Gatewood pushed the button again to cut her off.

"What the hell are you doing here?" Theodore—Jordan Gatewood—blurted out the question like he was ready to put fists behind those words.

Joel raised his chin at the challenge and stared across the room at this man. "I had to see it for myself," he said solemnly.

This was the second time he'd seen his son since he was just a baby and Olivia took him away, the second time in three months. The first time, Jordan had come to Joel's house, the same house he'd brought this boy home to from the hospital after Olivia had him. He'd come looking for Joel about some money—Gatewood money—that he believed Joel had asked for. But Joel never wanted that money. He never wanted anything belonging to

Gatewood except to have his son back. That day Joel suspected that his boy was gone for good. Today, looking at him now, he knew that to be true.

"To see what?" Jordan asked angrily.

"To see what kind of man would stoop low enough to do what you did to Frank." He shook his head in disgust. "He's your brother."

"What?" Olivia finally opened her mouth to say something. "Brother? Jordan? What brother?"

"I don't know what you're talking about, old man."

He lied with conviction. He lied without batting an eye or hesitating. And watching him tell that lie only added to the fire already building in Joel.

"I wouldn't have raised you like this," he said bitterly. "Naw! I wouldn't have raised you to be this kind of man."

"You didn't raise me at all, Tunson!" Jordan shot back. "You know, I'm sick of this shit!" Jordan came from behind his desk and pushed past Joel, heading toward the door, and swung it wide open. "Get your ass out of my office!"

Joel couldn't believe it. This wasn't the boy he'd held in his arms. It wasn't the same little boy he'd held over his head and flew around the yard like an airplane, who'd laughed so hard that Olivia would have to make such a fuss before Joel would stop. He could see himself in that man's face, even now—even after all these years and so many missed opportunities, and it broke his heart, but it angered him that he'd been such a fool as to ever let that woman take his son from him and turn him into this sonofabitch!

He turned to face Olivia, the woman he'd loved more than his own soul so many years ago, and he cringed. "You turned him into this?" he said with disbelief.

Olivia stuck out her chin, stood up, and looked down her nose at Joel, that way she used to when she wanted to make him feel that he wasn't worthy of her yellow ass. "You heard him, Joel," she said, sounding all high and mighty. "You need to leave before we call security."

Joel turned back to Jordan. "She turned you into this!" For the first time since he walked into that office he raised his voice. Joel had never been so angry in his life.

"Get the hell out of my office!"

"You would turn your own brother in for some shit you did? You would put the blame on him to save your ass—send him to prison for killing that woman when we both know he didn't do it?"

"What? No! Joel, Jordan didn't kill anybody!" Olivia made the mistake of putting her hand on him, and Joel jerked away from her, damn near knocking the woman over.

Jordan crossed the room in two steps to get to her, and to put himself between Joel and his mother. He turned to Joel with his fists balled. Joel squared his shoulders, stared that boy in his eyes, and dared him to strike.

"Get your black ass out of my fuckin' office," he said again.

The soul of that part of the boy that had once belonged to Joel was still inside him. Jordan—Teddy—had a soul. He'd just forgotten that it was there. But it certainly wasn't gone. He'd been born with it.

"What do you see when you look in the mirror?" Joel asked, pleading with God for some sign that his boy was still in there somewhere. "What lessons would you pass down to your own sons if you could?" Lord! Jesus! Please, let him be there. Please! "Are you proud of the man you've become, son? Would your father be proud of the man you've become?" The word "father" nearly stuck in Joel's throat, because he wasn't this boy's father. Gatewood had been his father in Jordan's eyes. But would that man have been proud of this one, because if he would've been, then Joel's son was truly lost.

"Go! Joel, get out of here!" Olivia squealed in the background.

Jordan slowly backed away from Joel, but not soon enough, not before Joel had seen a glimmer of conviction in that man's eyes. That was all he needed. God had answered his prayer, even if it was an answer that only lasted a moment.

"I won't let you do this to Frank," Joel continued sternly. "He didn't kill that woman and he doesn't deserve to go to prison for it."

Jordan slumped down in the chair next to where Olivia was sitting. "Frank isn't innocent," he retorted. "He did kill somebody."

"Then let them punish him for that. But not for another man's crime. I can't stand by and let that happen."

"But you could stand by and let her take me away," Jordan suddenly blurted out.

"Jordan?" Olivia whispered weakly. "Baby, no. It wasn't like that."

Jordan stood up and faced Joel again. "You can be there for Frank's sorry ass, but I didn't mean enough to you for you to stop her?"

There was pain in his boy's face that broke Joel's heart all over again. That pain had never gone away, though. He'd just learned to ignore it.

He swallowed the lump choking him. "She said I wasn't good enough for you. She said he could give you all the things I couldn't." He cleared his throat. "She said you deserved better and that if I loved you, I wouldn't stand in the way."

Joel felt like a fool for admitting these things to his son out loud, but he deserved to know the truth.

"Because I was right!" Olivia shouted. "You barely had a pot to piss in, Joel, and Julian came along offering me and my child the world, so I took it!" Her face turned that same shade of red that it had always turned when she got riled up, but her words didn't cut him as deep this time. Truthfully, Olivia sounded like a crazy woman to him.

"He wanted me and everything that came with me including my son! I told him—if you want me then you have to take my child too!"

"And he had you," Joel said, hoping that she was smart enough to catch the insult.

She glared at him with those pretty eyes of hers. "In ways you never did."

"I believed her, son, but by the time I stopped believing her, it was too late. You didn't want me to be your daddy because you already had another one."

Jordan raked his hand across his head. "Julian Gatewood was her husband," he said, pushing past Joel again to get back to his desk. "He was never my father."

"That's not true," Olivia murmured. "Jordan, that's not true. He loved you!"

"He loved something, Mother, but it wasn't me. And I don't even think it was you." Jordan sat down behind his desk looking as weary as a man who'd been in a fistfight.

"How much of what you did was for me and how much of it was all about you?" Jordan looked at his mother.

Olivia looked hurt. "I told you, Jordan, I did it for both of us."

Gatewood shook his head. "Somehow, Mother, I doubt that."

"Now's not the time for daddy issues, Jordan," she shot back unemotionally. All of a sudden, Olivia didn't look so hurt anymore. "But of course, if your convictions are getting the best of you," she said, turning up her nose at Joel, "you can go back to that shack with him."

There was a time when Joel would have been offended, but not anymore.

"It's a good thing you've always been so pretty, Olivia," he said, looking down his nose at her, "'cause Lord knows you ain't got shit else going for your sorry ass. From what I read in the papers 'bout you, that husband of yours knew it too."

If Olivia expected her son to come to her defense, she was disappointed.

There was nothing else to say. Joel had come here to give the Gatewoods a warning that Frank Ross wasn't in this fight by himself.

"Frank's going to tell the truth," he told Jordan. He turned to leave. He had hoped that Jordan would ask him to stay, but of course, he didn't.

Jordan sat there long after the man had left. He'd almost forgotten that Olivia was still in the room.

"Joel Tunson was the biggest mistake I ever made," she offered quietly. "The only good thing to come from him was you."

He looked up at her and stared at his mother as if he were truly seeing her for the first time. Olivia the beautiful. Olivia the manipulative. Olivia, his mother.

"I'd have done anything to get away from him," she continued. "Especially when Julian came into our lives. He saw me, Jordan, took one look at me, and he thought I was the most beautiful thing he'd ever laid eyes on and he wanted me—us, son," she said emphatically. "He wanted us and I knew almost as soon as he said it that I would've been a fool to pass on a man like him. I'd have done anything to be with him—and I did." Olivia's eyes filled with tears. She believed that what she'd done was the right thing to do. "We deserved better, Jordan, no matter the cost."

Watching her theatrics, a conclusion suddenly came to him.

Olivia was a desperate woman. She had never been anything else, and a question came to him.

"Did you try to have Desi Green killed?"

His mother wiped away the tears falling down her cheeks with the heel of her thumb, cleared her throat, and sat up straight. "It doesn't matter," she said dismissively. "It didn't work."

Chapter 50

Jordan stood in the corner of a room of his house with his back against the wall because that's exactly how he felt. It had been three days since he'd been back in his office—the day that Joel had come by. Forces bigger than him obviously didn't want him there and he was just drunk enough to oblige.

Fate had put all of the pieces of this puzzle together and forced them to fit, creating the perfect picture of him holding that gun in his hand, pointing it at Lonnie's heart, and pulling the trigger. It was as if it never mattered that he didn't actually do it. Somehow, even from the grave, Lonnie was getting her revenge. Even dead, she was the most fascinating woman he'd ever met, a female version of him, his soul mate. The best he could hope for was that the two of them might meet up again in heaven—or hell—more than likely, hell.

What do you see when you look in the mirror? Joel had asked.

When Jordan looked in the mirror he saw a powerful man with a ton of money, cars—things. And he was lonely. His whole life, he'd been alone.

"What lessons would you pass down to your own sons if you could?" Thankfully he had no sons. But he had a daughter, one he hadn't seen since she was young—so young. He sent her money, maybe he'd spoken to her over the phone a few times. How old was she now? Nineteen? Twenty?

"Are you proud of the man you've become, son?"

He was a proud man. A terrible and painfully proud, lonely man with lots of power and money, a daughter he barely knew, and a woman, no, two women, who were dead because of him. Joel Tunson had come to warn him that he wouldn't let Frank be railroaded, and to remind Jordan that he wasn't the man he'd always believed himself to be. There was no fight left in him, because there was nothing to fight for. There never had been.

His phone had been ringing off the hook, but he'd let all the calls go straight to voice mail.

"Jordan?"

He pushed away from the wall when he heard her voice.

"It's Desi. I need to talk . . . " Her voice trailed off.

Why the hell would she be calling him to talk?

"About . . . I want to make a deal on the Gatewood stock, and—I want to talk to you about Lonnie."

There was something about the sound of her voice . . . He'd been drinking too much, and Jordan felt raw and he felt . . . fuckin' needy.

"I'll be at the Ritz downtown. Just me. Ask for me."

No! Hell—no! What was this? Some kind of bait shit set up by Desi and Jones? Jordan shook his head, no. He wasn't falling for that shit! They were trying to set him up, but he wasn't that damn drunk!

He picked up the phone and hit the redial button.

"Hello?" she answered.

"What kind of fuckin' game are you playing?" he blurted out.

"No games, Jordan," she said coolly. "You want your stocks back, and I just need some closure about Lonnie. I think it's an even trade."

He hesitated.

"Randolph put you up to this?" he asked. She'd spoken to the man at least once about Jordan and his relationship with Lonnie. If Jones wasn't trying to set him up, that detective surely would.

"I'm here alone," she said.

"And you trust me enough to be alone in a room with me."

"I don't believe you'd do anything," she said. He could tell that she was lying.

"But you believe that I killed your friend? Doesn't jibe, Desi."

"I'm telling the truth, Jordan," she argued.

He laughed. "The truth? Between you and me, Desi, don't you think the truth is a little absurd?"

"Did you love her?" she asked softly.

The question sounded odd coming from her. It took everything he had in him to finally respond.

"What are you doing, Desi?" This wasn't right. He could feel it. "What are you trying to do to me?"

"I don't want anything except to talk about Lonnie."

"I've got nothing to say about her."

"I don't believe that."

"I don't give a damn what you believe, Desi."

"Then you pick the place. We could meet someplace else. I just need some closure."

She was lying. Solomon Jones believed that Jordan had tried to have this woman killed, so she had to have believed it too. And she was still willing to be alone with him? It wasn't adding up.

Every cell in his body warned him not to go anywhere near that woman. Something wasn't right about this.

"I just need answers," she argued convincingly. "She was my friend, and I loved her, and I miss her."

The pause between the two of them was deafening.

"Nobody knew her like we did," Desi continued. Why the hell was he still listening to her? Instinct warned him to hang up the phone. "I can't talk to Solomon about her, and I can't let her go either, Jordan," she explained. "I need to let go. I think you do too."

Yes. He needed desperately to let her go.

"I don't want to be a shareholder in your company," Desi said unexpectedly. "I never did, but it's nearly gotten me and my fiancé killed. I'm tired, Jordan." She sounded like she was crying. "I'm supposed to be getting married soon, and I don't want to do this anymore."

Jordan was tired too. This feud between the two of them had gone on too long and he was ready for it to end.

He had no business going anywhere near Desi Green, but emotions ran deep in Jordan where Lonnie was concerned. Desi believed he'd killed her. The detective believed it, Solomon Jones believed it. What if he could convince the one person who knew Lonnie as well as he did, that he hadn't? Why all of a sudden did it matter?

"I'll be there. You be ready to hand over those stock certificates," he warned.

Jordan hung up and made a mental note to pack his pistol.

An hour later, Desi opened the door to her hotel room. She had on a skirt and a plain white tee shirt and sandals. Desi stepped aside to let him in, but Jordan wasn't in any hurry to rush face-first into one of Jones's karate chops.

"He's not here," she told him, seeming to read his mind.

Desi wore her thick hair straightened and loose. He stepped inside, wondering if she had some sort of death wish, inviting him to be alone with her inside this hotel suite.

"Can I get you something?"

He held up his hand to quiet her, and then proceeded to search the bedroom, the closet, bathroom, and balcony before coming back into the room where she had started filling a glass with water for him.

He made up his mind that he wasn't drinking that shit.

Jordan stood over her. Desi had a bandage wrapped around one wrist, undoubtedly an injury she'd received from the recent car accident she'd been involved in.

"Stand up, Desi," he commanded her.

Jordan had one more thing he had to check. She understood. Without hesitating, Desi removed her shirt and stood in front of Jordan wearing nothing more than a white lace bra. She tossed her top on the chair and then slid her skirt down to her ankles, stepped out of it, and slowly turned a full circle in front of him.

She was perfect.

"I told you," she said, facing him again. "It's just me, Jordan." Desi picked up her shirt and began putting her clothes back on.

"This doesn't make sense," he said, finally sitting down across from her. "Why'd you ask me here?"

She didn't respond.

"Your boyfriend thinks I tried to have you killed the other day," he explained.

Desi stared back, unblinking. "Did you?"

He couldn't help feeling surprised by her response. "You'd ask to be alone with me, and you don't know the answer to that question?"

Desi dared to smile. "I'm registered in this hotel, Jordan. And you just asked for me at the front desk. They've got cameras in the lobby, so if anything happens to me, they'll know that you did it." She shrugged.

Damn. She'd thought this through. He was a tad bit impressed.

"I'm tired of all of this," she admitted again, leaning back and crossing her legs.

Jordan was still high, maybe, but the urge to touch her was almost overwhelming, and he couldn't understand why. But he resisted. After all, this was Desi.

"We know the truth about each other, Jordan. We know the truth about our parents, and our relationship is the result of their relationships."

"So?"

"Why do you hate me? Why do I hate you?" she asked, cocking one perfectly arched brow.

"You know I didn't kill Julian, and you know that Olivia did. You know that she set me up."

She was right. He knew all of those things, but a hatred that had lasted nearly thirty years, no matter the reason, was rooted too deep in history to just get over.

"You know that Julian wasn't your father, but that he was mine. So, I don't get it. It doesn't make sense anymore to me. Why can't you stand me?"

Jordan found himself paying attention to all the wrong things about this conversation. He found his eyes lingering too long on the shape of her mouth, the dark richness of her eyes, the curve of her breasts, and he tried not to think about his dick swelling in his lap. She was right. There was no real reason to hate this woman.

He needed to regain his focus, and to get this conversation on track. "You asked me here to talk about Lonnie."

"We both know that you won't ever see a day in prison for her murder."

"Because I didn't murder her," he interjected.

Of course she looked as if she didn't believe him. "I just—Why couldn't you have just left her alone?" She was careful with how she phrased her words. Maybe too careful?

Jordan began to get suspicious again, thinking that maybe there was a wire in the room somewhere, if not on her.

"I did leave her alone, Desi," he said coolly.

"I told her not to come back here, Jordan," Desi explained. "Lonnie was bent on revenge and I knew that it was a bad idea."

He didn't say anything. Desi was baiting him. He could feel it, and he was pissed for falling for this little ploy of hers.

"I wouldn't know about that."

"Did you love her?"

He was being set up. "I think everyone loved something about Lonnie," he offered casually.

"I think that in her own way, she loved you, Jordan."

Someone else outside this room was listening. Jordan had come here out of stupidity and on a fantasy and a whim that, somehow, he could finally say what he felt about the only woman he'd ever truly cared about. But that was the alcohol in him. He'd given in to a vulnerability that was foreign to men like him, and he'd let himself make this foolish mistake.

"I wouldn't know, Desi," he finally responded. Jordan had to think fast. He had to get out of this before he slipped up and made another mistake. "So," he eventually said. "About those stock certificates . . ."

"Well, of course I didn't bring them with me," she explained. "My accountant has them."

He nodded knowingly. "Of course." Jordan abruptly stood up to leave.

"You just got here, Jordan," she said anxiously, standing up too.

Jordan started for the door. "You wanted to talk about Lonnie, we talked about Lonnie," he said over his shoulder to her. "I asked for those stock certificates, and you don't have them." He stopped at the door, causing Desi to bump into him.

Without thinking, Jordan wrapped his arm around her waist and roughly jerked her body into his, then covered her mouth with his free hand. He stared hard into her eyes, turned her around, and pressed her back against the door, holding her body in place with his.

He lowered his lips next to her ear. "Nice try, baby girl," he whispered.

Jordan inhaled the scent of her hair. He pushed his knee between her thighs, forcing them open, lifted her off the ground, and positioned his throbbing cock against her.

Little Desi Green was the most intoxicating thing he'd held in his arms in a long time.

Desi scratched at his hand with one of hers, trying to force him to uncover her mouth. His thoughts drifted off into so many faraway places, and he wondered out loud.

"Is this how he felt about her?" he murmured, thinking about Julian and his obsession with Ida Green. "Is this what she did to him too?"

Jordan ground his hips into her, imagining what she must have felt like, remembering what it did feel like to lose his mind over a woman—the way Julian did with Ida—the way he himself had done with Lonnie. His mouth watered at the thought of swallowing her nipples. His dick flexed as he imagined what she felt like inside.

Everything about this woman was wrong to him, and yet, he hadn't been this excited since the last time he had touched Lonnie.

"I loved her." He finally managed a breathless whisper. "Damn, Desi." Jordan felt caught up in a wave of emotion so much bigger than he was. "Claire shot her," he admitted desperately. "She shot Lonnie to punish me. My wife killed my lover and I might as well have pulled the trigger myself."

Jordan finally came to his senses, stared back into Desi's terrified and confused eyes, and slowly lowered her to the ground. He didn't expect her to believe that he hadn't killed Lonnie, but at least he'd said it.

Jordan removed his hand from her mouth and expected her to scream, but she didn't.

For several moments, the two of them just stood there, locked in some unspoken communication about what had just happened, and about what he had told her.

"I didn't," he said one last time with tears in his eyes. "Believe it." He shrugged. "Or don't. I really don't give a damn."

Jordan gently pushed her aside, and let himself out.

Chapter 51

Solomon hadn't wanted her to do this, but Detective Randolph had begged Desi to do it, and she'd agreed because it was the only chance they had to keep this man from getting away with murder. Solomon waited to use what he knew about that night Lonnie was murdered as leverage to keep Jordan in line. Desi wanted him to spend the rest of his life in prison.

"We lost audio shortly before he left, Desi," the detective said, bearing down on her. "What the hell did he say?"

Desi was still shaking from the encounter. She had no idea how much time had passed after Jordan left and the detective and Solomon showed up in her hotel room.

"Calm the hell down, man!" Solomon warned him. He sat next to her on the couch holding her hand. "It's alright, Desi," he said reassuringly. "Did he hurt you? Did he touch you?"

Lord, yes! He had touched her. He'd touched her in ways she'd never imagined that Jordan Gatewood would want to touch her, and it hadn't helped that she'd practically done a strip tease for the man either. But his touching her isn't what had her so upset.

"Desi," Randolph said emphatically, taking a seat across from her. "I need to know everything he said to you," he repeated.

The thing that had Desi more upset than Jordan putting his hands on her was what he had told her. But even more than that, the thing that left her trembling long after he'd left was the fact that, in the moment when he'd said it, she'd believed him.

"My goddamned job is on the line here!" the detective said, raising his voice.

Bobby Randolph's eyes bulged from their sockets. An artery as thick as her finger swelled in his neck, and the man looked like he was about to burst.

"What the fuck did he say?" he shouted, pounding his fist on the table.

"What the fuck difference does it make what he said?" Solomon shouted, bolting to his feet. "You don't have the shit on tape, man! Even if he did confess to her, the best you've got is hearsay and with a powerhouse like Gatewood you know his lawyers will have that shit thrown out even if you did get a fuckin' trial!"

The detective slowly stood up, walked across the room to where he'd planted the microphone, stuffed it in his pocket, and headed toward the door. Before leaving, he turned to Desi one last time. "He's going to get away with it, Desi," he said solemnly. He swallowed. "Hell, he has gotten away with it."

Bobby Randolph quietly closed the door behind him as he left.

Solomon crossed the room and began pacing back and forth. "Did he put his hands on you, Desi?" he asked under his breath.

He expected her to tell him the truth, but for some reason, she couldn't.

"He didn't hurt me, Solomon."

"I didn't ask you if he hurt you." He stopped in front of her. "I asked if he put his hands on you."

"He said he didn't kill her," she finally admitted. Before she'd even realized what was happening, one of the hotel room lamps went sailing across the room and shattered into a million pieces as it hit the wall.

"What the hell did he do to you?"

Desi was on her feet before she realized it, staring at him like he'd lost his fuckin' mind! "He didn't do shit to me!"

Solomon's handsome face twisted in confusion. "You're defending him? Desi—what the hell?"

Unexpected anger rose to the surface in her that even she hadn't anticipated. "He didn't hurt me, Solomon!" she retorted.

"He touched you!" he said, marching toward her. "I don't give a damn if he hurt you or not, he had no damn business putting his goddamned hands on you!"

Angry tears welled up in her eyes. "Just who the hell do you think I am, Solomon?" she questioned defensively. "Who the fuck do you think you're dealing with?"

"What?" he bit back.

"I am not some fragile female who's going to break just because some fool touched me!" Tears were streaming down her cheeks.

Desi was livid and she had no idea where it was coming from but she wasn't helpless! "You think you need to protect me, Solomon, but I've never needed anybody to protect me! I can take care of my-damn-self—I always have!" She sobbed uncontrollably.

"Do you hear yourself, Desi?" he asked, obviously dumbfounded by her reaction, but Desi didn't give a damn.

"I did twenty-five years in hell by myself!" She pointed her finger at her chest. "I did that! And I survived and I'm here now because I was strong! I did that! I did it by myself, Solomon!"

"What did he do to you, Desi?" His expression softened. Solomon approached her slowly, but Desi backed away.

She didn't want him touching her. She didn't need for him to protect her or to fight this battle for her. Desi had forgotten who the hell she was and she needed to get that back. She needed to draw from the strength of that young girl living in prison who had lived every day as if it might be her last, who had fought hard to keep that part of her that nobody could take away. She needed that girl's mind, her soul, her strength.

"He told me that he didn't kill Lonnie, Solomon," she muttered, locking onto his gaze.

Jordan was evil. He was dangerous and he was a killer. Desi never doubted that he had taken lives. She never doubted that he would take hers. He'd gone so far as to try and have her killed less than a week ago, but she had agreed to do this, despite Solomon's protests, because it was the only way she knew how to trap him and to get him to pay for what he'd done. But the man she had been with in this room, that murderer, had been afraid. He had been convincing. And she hated the fact that he had given her room for any doubt that he'd killed her friend.

"He said he didn't do it!"

"What did you expect him to say, Desi?" Solomon asked sympathetically.

She was losing her mind. That concussion she got from the car accident must've made her crazy, because Desi was truly losing it. She backed over to the sofa and sat down, filing through each of her thoughts about her encounter with Jordan Gatewood.

"Claire shot her . . . She shot Lonnie to punish me."

"It was the look in his eyes," she said more to herself than to him, reflecting on that painful, desperate look in his eyes when he said it. Desi felt what he was feeling. She felt the loss, the regret that he felt. She felt his heart break, and his guilt. She took a deep breath as the realization began to settle into her that either she was crazy or Jordan was one hell of an actor.

"Am I really that stupid?" she asked herself out loud. "He said that his wife, Claire, shot Lonnie." Her gaze met Solomon's for a moment. "That she shot Lonnie to punish Jordan."

And for some strange reason that made sense to her.

Solomon, of course, didn't understand because he'd never been in a moment like that. But Desi had been there. She'd been held prisoner between the truth and a lie. There was nothing like holding on to the truth with both hands, fighting to keep it close, knowing that it was real even when everyone else chose to see the lie. How many times had she had that same look in her eyes when she tried to tell those people that she didn't kill Julian Gatewood? That's the look he had in his eyes.

"You believe him?" Solomon finally asked. "He tried to kill her before, Desi. He tried to kill you. And you believe him?"

Yes. But she would never dare say that she believed him out loud.

Chapter 52

Seeing Joel Tunson again after all these years had shaken something dreadful loose in Olivia Gatewood. She stretched out on the sofa in her home with her feet up and her head resting against Edgar Beckman's chest, reflecting on her past.

"He looked old, Edgar," she said introspectively.

"We're all old, Olivia." He kissed the top of her head. "Even you, my dear."

Edgar was right, of course. Seeing him again only served to remind her of that defiant young woman so many years ago who believed she'd live forever.

"I only dated Joel Tunson because I knew that my daddy would hate it," she confessed quietly. "The doctor had his standards," she said, referring to her father. "As cliché as they were, he owned them, and he believed in them like they were his religion."

"All young girls are rebellious, Olivia," Edgar chimed in. "It's the nature of the young beast."

Olivia had been more than just rebellious when it came to her parents and her upbringing. She had wanted to punish them, especially her father, because she was his perfect little princess and he'd loved the ground she walked on from the moment she was born.

"Joel was everything he despised." She continued taking the long road of her memory back to a time that seemed like she'd dreamed rather than lived. "He was this handsome mess, cool, with a car that he loved and had restored with his own hands. He had a job working at the corn mill and his hands always looked dirty. He smelled like cigarettes."

She closed her eyes and remembered the way Joel Tunson used to make love to her, like she was as dirty as he was. He wasn't gentle with her. He didn't coddle her as if she was made of glass and would break.

"I fucked him with such abandon," she admitted unabashedly.

His big, beautiful black ass manhandled her and drove into her so deep—so hard—that she had no choice but to love it. Nothing ever hurt so good before—or since.

"He was a monster," she murmured.

"Why were you with him, then?" Edgar probed.

A soft, sultry chuckle escaped the back of her throat. "Because he was a monster."

Edgar shifted uncomfortably. "But he was a poor monster."

She thought for a moment, struggling to find the memory that would answer that question. "I didn't plan on getting pregnant. Of course, when I told him he insisted that we get married, and when I told my father, he insisted that I get rid of it, bring my ass home, and act like I had some damn sense."

Her father would've done it. He'd have performed the abortion himself just to keep their business out of the streets.

"I wasn't about to get rid of my baby," she said solemnly. "So, I married Joel and moved into that shack he lived in. The place was so small that I had to go outside to change my underwear, but he kept promising that we'd get a bigger place, a nicer house, even if it meant that he had to work two shifts at the mill."

"Ambitious," Edgar responded dryly.

But Olivia had been touched by Joel's sincerity and by the love he seemed to feel for her. It just wasn't enough.

"My mother insisted that I come to their anniversary party. I hadn't seen or spoken to my parents in over a year, but for some reason she wanted me there."

"Did Joel go?"

"No. They didn't want to see Joel and he knew it. He was going to drive me there himself and drop me off, but Daddy decided to add insult to injury and send a car for me."

"You could've declined it, Olivia, and allowed your husband his dignity."

"It was a Cadillac," she stated, as if that made all the difference in the world, and at the time, it did.

"Julian was there in all his beautiful splendor," she said passionately. "Oh, he was breathtaking, a blond-haired, blue-eyed black man dripping with money and salivating all over me."

In the beginning, Julian could hardly take his eyes off Olivia.

"You are the most beautiful woman I've ever laid eyes on," he'd told her.

Soon he made it clear that he wanted her. When Joel was at work, Julian would come to the house, pick her up, and drive her to the next county, where he'd rent a hotel room. He and Olivia would make love for hours. Her neighbor Mrs. Davis would take care of Jordan for her.

"You deserve better," he used to tell her. "I can give you better."

"I'd been born into privilege, Edgar," she explained.

"I understand, Olivia," Edgar concurred.

"I suppose that the only man I ever truly loved was my son," she finally admitted. "I wanted Julian because—well, he was Julian, and he was everything my father had ever believed that I should have." Olivia swallowed. "But I wasn't leaving without my boy. I told him that. If you can't take us both, then you can't have me."

Thinking back to that moment, Olivia could recall the look in his eyes. He wanted her, but the last thing he wanted was another man's child.

"Joel had no business coming here to stir up trouble," she said resentfully. "Jordan is not his son anymore, he's mine! And that man has no claim to him! Hasn't had claim to him in years!"

"Jordan's not a car, Olivia," Edgar retorted. "He's a grown man and he doesn't belong to anybody but himself."

Olivia sat up and glared at Edgar. "I'm losing my son," she said plainly so that this fool could understand. "Jordan is slipping away from me, Edgar, and Joel Tunson might as well have just yanked him out of my arms!"

"He's his son too!" Edgar had the nerve to argue.

"You have no idea," she said, shaking her head. Edgar had no idea—no one understood how long and hard Olivia had worked to cultivate that child into the man he was now. Jordan was one of the most powerful men in the country because Olivia had been the engine behind him, pushing him and forging him to be strong and smart and to take the helm of Gatewood Industries and bring that company to levels that Julian never had the vision or the courage to fathom.

"He's my everything," she said passionately. "He's all I've got."

Neither one of them heard June come into the house. "Thank you, Mother," she said, standing there looking just like Julian. "I've been waiting my whole life to finally hear you say it."

June had the nerve to look like her feelings were hurt, but Olivia had no sympathy, not after what she had done to their family.

"Oh, I said it, Junie," she said coolly. "And I mean it."

June blinked back tears. "And here we all thought that you'd killed Daddy because he had another woman."

All emotion drained from Olivia's heart and she was through putting on airs for her daughter. "Your father was screwing a whore, making babies all over Texas," she said venomously. "He had it coming."

"Olivia," Edgar interjected.

"Maybe he knew that Ida Green loved him," June asserted. "Maybe she was more than just some pretty *thing* with no substance and no soul who only wanted him for his money."

"I worshipped him!" Olivia slowly stood up. "I would've done anything for that man, but he chose to lay up with that whore making nasty children with her, when I was here, June! I waited up for his ass every night knowing damn well that he was in her bed! I sold myself and my child to that man and we weren't good enough for him!" Olivia sighed. "I even gave him you." She stared disgustedly at her daughter. "And even that wasn't enough. If he was so wonderful, Junie, how come his own flesh and blood wasn't good enough for him to keep his ass at home?"

"Because being at home meant being with you, Mom."

Olivia watched her daughter turn and leave. The sound of the door slamming behind her served as a painful wake-up call to Olivia that her world was indeed beginning to collapse around her.

Chapter 53

Joel Tunson was sitting on the front porch of that tiny house of his when Jordan pulled his car up into the yard. A younger version of Tunson was sitting next to him. Neither man made any effort to stand up when Jordan walked up to the foot of the steps. His gaze drifted from Joel to the other man several times before Jordan finally said something.

He looked at Joel. "Who's that motha fucka?" He motioned his head toward the other man.

The other man glared at Jordan. "I'm your brother, bitch. But you can call me Malcolm."

Jordan had been driving, just driving for so long that he'd lost track of time, and eventually he realized that he wasn't driving in circles anymore. He was on the road headed here.

"Malcolm," Joel said without taking his eyes off Jordan. "Why don't you go on home now."

Out of the corner of his eye, Jordan could see Malcolm shake his head. "Nah, Pop. I think I'll stay here. I don't trust him."

Joel stood up. "I do." He turned to look at whats-his-name and waited until the asshole stood up and reluctantly started to leave.

He stopped as he was passing by Jordan. "He'd better look that good when I come back here," he muttered under his breath.

Jordan decided right then and there that as soon as he had his mind right again, he was going to put a bullet in Malcolm's dumb ass. Both Joel and Jordan waited until Malcolm backed his truck out of the yard before saying anything.

Jordan looked around the yard, stared up at that tiny house, then rested his gaze on the old man. "I don't even know what I'm doing here," he finally admitted.

Even now, after everything that the old man had said to him and about him, Jordan felt at ease with him.

"What can I say to you?" he asked, looking up at Joel.

The old man shifted in his seat. "What do you want to say?" he asked simply.

There was no judgment in his eyes. Joel was just . . . Joel Tunson. He was as simple a man that ever was because he had nothing to complicate him—except for Olivia and he'd gotten rid of her ass a long time ago.

"You married?" Jordan blurted out the question, then felt like an idiot as soon as he had. It was dumb and had no relevance to this situation at all.

Joel surprised him and smiled. "My wife passed a few years back. Breast cancer."

"You loved her?"

"Yes," Joel said. "She was mean as hell but I loved her."

Jordan slowly ascended the steps and sat down in the seat left vacant by Malcolm. From this vantage point, the yard looked so much bigger.

"They denied Frank's bail," Jordan finally said, suddenly feeling uneasy.

"I know."

"It seems that Frank's gone and hired himself one of the best defense lawyers in the country," Jordan told Joel. "Good lawyers don't come cheap."

"No," Joel responded introspectively. "It helps, though, when you got bags of money just lying around the house getting dusty." He smiled wryly.

For years, Joel had been receiving anonymous amounts of money every month. He'd suspected that it had come from Jordan. Jordan finally figured out that it had actually been coming from Olivia. Deep down, the woman had a conscience. But like any other secret in her life, money was the key to keeping it buried.

"The Dallas Police Department called me in for questioning," he admitted. "Seems Frank told them that I'm the one who asked him to call Lonnie."

"What did you tell 'em?"

Jordan shrugged.

"You lied and said you didn't?"

"I lied and said I didn't." He looked at Joel. "I did tell him that Frank was an acquaintance of mine." Jordan said it as if he expected Joel to turn flips that he'd told the truth at least once.

Joel just sat there. "Well." He sighed. "I suppose that's something." There was a long silence between them when Joel finally spoke up again. "Did you kill that woman, son?"

Jordan shook his head. "No." He came really close to calling Joel "sir." "But I was there when she was killed," he confessed. "My wife—Claire—caught us together and she had a gun and pulled the trigger."

"I read in the paper that your wife died recently."

Jordan just sat there.

"Kinda puts you in a predicament," Joel said casually.

"Kinda."

Jordan was forty-eight years old, and sitting here next to this man, he felt like he was eight and he'd been bad and owed it to this man to tell the truth about so many things.

"I never knew that I didn't have everything," he admitted, cursing himself for the way that must've sounded to a man like Joel. But it was the only way he knew how to put it. "I never knew that there were other things missing in my life."

"How could you know?" Joel interjected. "You got it all, son. Money, women, a big house or houses. Fancy job with a desk bigger than this whole place," Joel said. "That does sound like you have everything."

Jordan thought for a moment before responding. "I do and I don't."

"But you have plenty."

"No, Joel." Jordan shook his head. "I don't think I do anymore."

"Then you tell me, son," Joel said thoughtfully. "What's missing?"

Some things he never thought he really needed. Some things he'd always taken for granted, that he had them, but he never really did. "I'm a motha fucka," he said, swallowing. "Some men are just so damned honorable, all day, everyday. It's second nature and comes naturally to them." He looked at Joel. "Like they don't know how to be anything else." Jordan chuckled. "Don't look at me like that. I do the best I can. What do you do? I wear it like a tie. I can put it on when the occasion calls for it and I can take it off just as easily."

Joel frowned. "Then all you got is a tie, son," Joel eventually responded.

Surprisingly, Jordan laughed.

Joel just sighed. "A man needs honor. He needs integrity. Nothing else matters without 'em."

He was kicking down the door to fifty and Jordan was learning one of the most basic lessons of a man's life damn near at the end of his. He felt like an idiot, a fool.

"I'm too damn old to change now," he muttered, shaking his head.

Joel laughed. "Not as long as you have breath in you, son. Shit, I got one foot in the grave and I'm still learning new things."

Jordan cut his eyes at him. "Like what?"

"Hmpf! Like that new iPad your brother just bought me for my birthday. Now what the hell do I need the Internet for?"

Jordan laughed again. "Well, it's the thought that counts, I guess."

Joel shook his head. "Malcolm don't think about shit. He just does what he wants then begs for forgiveness afterward."

"Malcolm is itching to kick my ass."

"Yeah," Joel agreed. "But he'd feel bad about it later."

Both men hesitated before bursting out laughing. This wasn't how his life was supposed to turn out. Never in a million years would he have ever guessed that Julian Gatewood was anything more than a disapproving father, or that Olivia Gatewood was a helpless widow. He would've never dreamed that this small place was the house his life had started in, or that this old man sitting next to him would make him feel more accepted than Julian ever did.

"I am sorry that I ever let you go, son," Joel said sadly. "That's been my biggest regret and one that I don't think I'll ever forgive myself for."

Jordan didn't know if he could ever forgive him for it either.

"There's no excuse." Joel shook his head. "Not for that. Olivia didn't deserve you. Gatewood sure as hell didn't. And maybe I didn't either. But I have to admit," he said, nodding approvingly, "you did get one hell of a nice car out of the deal."

Jordan looked out at his vehicle and smiled. "Actually, I've got quite a few."

Chapter 54

Desi had read on the Internet that a man named Frank Ross was being indicted for Lonnie's murder and that he had implicated Jordan as the one who'd actually shot and killed her. But the Gatewood camp had emphatically denied the allegation. Desi knew this drill all too well. A team of expensive attorneys would form a wall around Jordan to keep the laws of Texas from even so much as brushing up against him, and that poor Frank Ross would likely die in prison over something he didn't do.

"Hey." Solomon came into the kitchen, stood behind Desi at the center island, placed his hands on either side of her, and kissed her neck.

"You all packed?" she asked, handing him her cup of coffee.

He took a sip and then nodded. "Yep."

"You sure you don't want me to drive you to the airport, baby?" she asked. Lately, she'd been sugary sweet to him because she'd felt bad about the way she'd talked to him after trying to get a confession out of Jordan. Desi had told him that she didn't need him to protect her because, in essence, she could take care of her damn self, but she was wrong. She needed Solomon like she needed air to breathe and he'd never failed to be there for her, whether she was too dumb to admit it or not.

"Nah," he said tenderly. "You just be waiting here for me when I get home."

She smiled. "I can't think of anyplace else I'd rather be."

Desi stood at the window and watched his car disappear down the driveway. She'd learned a long time ago that there were just some things in life that couldn't be changed no matter how much you wished them to. The fact would always be that Lonnie was dead and that the person responsible would never have to spend one second in prison for killing her. Jordan didn't point that gun at Lonnie and pull the trigger, but his actions compelled his wife to do it and because of that he had no right calling himself innocent. People like him treated other people like shit and got away with it. Lonnie was dead by association with him, and even in a lot of ways, she was dead by association with Desi. She'd have never met Jordan if she hadn't stepped in to take on this fight for justice on Desi's behalf in the first place. Circumstances had just unraveled in all the wrong ways and Lonnie had ultimately paid for it with her life.

"Apology has always been a dirty word in my vocabulary," he said to her.

The call from Jordan had come an hour after Solomon had left the house, and Desi couldn't help wondering if that had just been a coincidence or if he somehow knew that Solomon was gone. It was surprising enough that he'd called her, but absolutely unbelievable that he had somehow worked the term "apology" into a sentence directed at her.

"You're expecting an apology from me?" she asked guardedly.

He knew that she had tried to set him up. Jordan was no fool, and he'd made it clear the other day in the hotel room that he wasn't stupid enough to fall for that old "I'm going to trick you into confessing" trap.

"I have a habit of losing my temper," he continued casually. "I have a habit of overstepping boundaries."

Once again he was being careful with his words, but regardless of what he believed, she wasn't going to let him off the hook so easily.

"A good friend told me once that you weren't above a little rape every now and then," she said venomously, purposely pushing buttons that crossed his boundaries.

She waited for a response, but got nothing.

"Why are you calling me?"

"Can you come to my office?" he asked reluctantly.

Desi was shocked. "Your office?"

"It's hallowed ground, Desi," he explained. "Got a whole building full of people you can call on for help if you feel the need to."

"What's this about, Jordan? Why can't you just talk to me over the phone?"

"Because what we have is too damn personal for a phone conversation, Desi. Please," he said as earnestly as a man like him could.

She thought long and hard before responding. "An hour?" she finally said. Desi's curiosity was getting the best of her.

"I'll be here." Jordan hung up the phone.

Jordan's assistant was waiting at the security desk for Desi when she arrived.

"Miss Green," the woman greeted her professionally. "Follow me, please."

This was the first time Desi had ever set foot inside Gatewood Tower, and it dawned on her as her heels clicked against the marble floors that this was the company Julian had built. This was what he came back to every time he left Ida and Desi's small house. This is who he really was, his legacy and his power. This was her father's company and the walls of this place seemed to embrace her with every step.

They took the elevator to the twenty-fourth floor and the doors opened to another expansive foyer with gleaming, polished floors, expensive one-of-a-kind sculptures and paintings, lush plants and fresh flowers, and beautiful floor-to-ceiling windows on all sides with panoramic views of the entire city. The woman led the way to Jordan's office.

"Close the door behind you please," he instructed the woman.

So, this was his world. Jordan was a king sitting on a throne twenty-four floors up in the sky. This is what he fought so hard to keep. This moment right here, this setting, defined everything that Jordan Gatewood was, and all of a sudden Desi knew him.

He motioned for her to take a seat, which she did. Hate him, love him, there was no denying that he was physically one of the most beautiful men on the planet: tall, caramel-brown complexion, polished, with broad features that were just stunning. Desi would've had to have been blind to deny that. He took a seat on the sofa.

"Can I get you anything? Water?"

"Why'd you ask me to come here?" she asked abruptly.

Something about his features had softened since she'd last seen him, but then again, the last time she'd seen him he had her off the ground, pressed up against the wall, covering her mouth with his hand and looking crazy enough to snap her neck.

He looked introspective for a moment, thoughtful. If he'd have been anyone else, she'd have thought he looked kind.

"I made mistakes with Lonnie," he admitted apprehensively. "Too many."

"You got her killed, Jordan."

He locked onto Desi's heated gaze. "I got her killed, Desi," he confessed, unwavering.

Desi was speechless. Both of them were, and they sat there staring at each other for a time.

"Maybe we both did," Desi whispered, owning her role played in Lonnie's death. "If it hadn't been for me, Lonnie would never have met you."

"Oh, I don't believe that," he said adamantly. "Whatever fates exist drew me and Lonnie together, and in this case, it just happened to have been you. But if you don't believe anything else I say, believe this, that in my own way, I loved her, whatever that means. I wanted Lonnie more than I've ever wanted any woman, but because of . . . circumstances, I knew that I could never have her. And I had accepted that."

This was his confession and there was no doubt in her mind that he was telling the truth. But one question remained. "Why are you telling me this, Jordan? I mean, me, of all people. Why do you care that I know this? Did you forget that you hate me?"

He surprised her and smiled. "No, I didn't forget that."

A joke? Was that Jordan Gatewood's version of a joke?

"You and I are as much victims of circumstance as Lonnie was, Desi," he began to explain. "Our lives have been intricately entwined and designed by forces outside of our control by the people who claimed to care about us."

Jordan had a sincerity in his eyes that Desi would've never believed possible, but it was there, and empathy coming from him that seemed to break his heart.

"Neither one of us is who we believed we were. I'm not a Gatewood by blood, but I grew up believing that I was and that I was owed everything that I have."

He had just admitted that out loud?

"You, on the other hand—you are Julian's flesh and blood and you've been denied those rights your whole life."

"What are you saying?" she asked, stunned at the admissions this man was making openly to her.

Jordan paused again. "I'm saying that you shouldn't have to fight so hard for what's rightfully yours, and I shouldn't fight so hard for what isn't mine. The stock you own in Gatewood Industries belongs to you and I won't try and take it from you. You're his daughter, Desi. So, step up and be his daughter. Petition to have your name changed, and to make it legal—make it real."

Desi's heart beat in her throat. "You're kidding me?"

He shook his head. "I've never been more serious."

"What the hell is wrong with you?" she blurted out.

Jordan sighed deeply and said two words: "I'm tired."

The door to Jordan's office suddenly burst open and Olivia Gatewood flew in like a bat, with Edgar Beckman on her heels.

"Jordan!" she shouted.

The look on her face was so familiar to Desi, and instinctively she jumped up and moved across the room from the woman.

"Wh-what-what are you doing? Wh-what are you telling her?"

Obviously, Olivia had been listening on the other side of the door.

"You need to leave, Mother!" he demanded.

"No!" Olivia persisted. "I won't leave, Jordan—what are you telling her?"

"Olivia, you need to calm down," Edgar barked. "Sit down, Olivia. You're getting yourself all worked up—"

"I won't let you do this!" she shouted at her son. And then the woman turned to Desi. "I won't let you do this!"

Olivia Gatewood was that force Jordan had talked about. She was the "circumstance" that both Jordan and Desi had been victims of.

"Mother, you need to go!" he insisted. "Edgar, get her the hell out of my office!"

"I won't let you hand over my company to her!" Olivia shouted, marching toward Desi.

"She's his daughter, Olivia!" Jordan shouted. "You knew it the night you shot him!"

"The night you killed him!" Desi shouted, meeting Olivia Gatewood in the middle of the room.

Olivia slapped Desi hard across the face, and Desi slapped her back.

"No!" Edgar jumped in between the two women, pushing Desi until she stumbled back across the room.

Jordan's assistant stood in the doorway, in some kind of heated exchange with him about calling security.

Desi was furious as she lunged at Edgar, pounding him on the back and slapping him across the head. "You bastard! You fuckin' bastard!"

The next thing she knew, Jordan suddenly appeared between Desi and Olivia and Desi was being lifted off the ground and pulled away from both Edgar and Olivia.

Edgar shouted. "No! Olivia, no!"

A gun fired. Olivia held her gun pointed at Desi. And then she fired it again.

Jordan lowered Desi to the ground, and then sunk to his knees onto the floor.

Olivia gasped, dropped the gun, and wilted into Edgar's arms. "Nooooo!" she wailed, realizing that the bullets she'd meant for Desi had hit Jordan.

He dropped to his hands, gasping to breathe. Blood began dripping onto the floor.

What had he just done? Desi couldn't believe what he'd just done! "Jordan," she cried, stunned.

He struggled to raise his head and for a moment, he looked into her eyes.

"Jordaaaan!" Olivia cried out, reaching for him. "My sonnnnnn!" She looked helplessly at Edgar. "Help him!" she cried, then glanced angrily at Desi. "Do something—Edgar! Please!"

Security appeared as if by magic in the doorway of Jordan's office. Olivia cried hysterically and pointed her long, trembling fingers toward Desi.

Olivia had cried hysterically the night she'd shot Julian. She'd shoved the gun into Desi's hands and pointed that same bony and trembling hand accusingly at her, just like she was doing now.

It was déjà vu. This moment was happening all over again, just like it had unfolded nearly thirty years ago.

Chapter 55

The police questioned Desi for hours, and just like years ago, her version of what happened never changed. But they asked her the same questions over and over again, because this had happened before. Desi Green had been involved in a shooting involving a Gatewood and the media was going crazy.

Solomon had left thirty messages on her voice mail by the time they'd let her call him back.

"I'll be on the next flight out," he assured her.

"Yeah, because I really need you here," she cried.

And she meant it. He'd made a promise that it wasn't just Desi alone against the world anymore.

It was dawn before they finally finished their interrogation. Solomon was waiting to take her home. Edgar sat in the lobby next to him, looking every bit his age and then some. He looked up at Desi, forced a smile, and then let his head drop again and cried.

"Let's go." Solomon took hold of her hand and led her out of the building.

She spent the next several days inside the house. Desi had insisted on going to stay at a hotel, to keep the media attention away from Solomon, but he wouldn't hear of it.

"You're a drama magnet, baby," he said playfully. "Shit, I knew that when I proposed."

Olivia Gatewood had fallen back into her Alzheimer's/dementia routine big-time and was currently under the care of a physician who was closely monitoring her condition. June Gatewood was at the helm of Gatewood Industries, trying to salvage the fallout from the events that had unfolded in Jordan's office.

Desi kept playing the scene of what happened over and over again in her mind, astonished at the parallels between the time Olivia had shot Julian and when she'd shot her own son. Olivia had pointed her gun at Ida the night Julian died. This time, she pointed it toward Desi. Julian had jumped in between the two women and she'd shot him instead. Jordan was pulling Desi away from Olivia and her bullets hit him. Both men had fallen to their knees, and then to their hands, until they finally collapsed. It was all so eerily similar that there was no way Desi could believe that it was a coincidence.

Three days had passed since the shooting and despite her best efforts to stay away and to try and move on with her life, Desi had to see him one more time.

The first bullet had hit Jordan in his shoulder and passed through the other side. The second had hit him in the torso, missing his heart but piercing a lung.

She stood just inside the doorway of his hospital room. Neither of them had bothered with the formality of hello.

"You saved my life," she offered.

Jordan looked more than physically wounded. "The first bullet was meant for you," he stated simply. He swallowed. "But the second one . . ." He looked at Desi with tears in his eyes. "That was meant for me."

Olivia had wanted them both dead.

Desi shrugged. "So—we square?"

He nodded. "We square."

A week later, Desi was sitting at the desk in her office, talking to her assistant.

"Guess what?" she asked the other woman.

"What?"

"He still wants to marry me. Can you believe it?"

She laughed. "Still?"

"Yep," Desi said proudly. "I guess we've got a wedding to plan—you and me."

"I'm on it, boss. Let's get to it."

The night before, Solomon had held Desi in his arms and brought up the subject of marriage again. They hadn't really spoken about it since he'd proposed in New York City several months ago, and with everything that had happened, Desi had pretty much shelved the notion. A marriage proposal was one thing, but an actual wedding was something other people did.

"I'm going to need you to set a date," he had mentioned casually.

Desi played dumb. The truth was, getting married scared the hell out of her. What they had wasn't broken and she saw no reason to muddle it up with technicalities like marriage certificates.

"Oh, yeah," she said reluctantly. "I've been thinking about it," she lied.

"So, when do you want to do it?" he probed.

Desi searched through her mental calendar. Not only did she have to come up with a date for a wedding, she also needed to get back on track with her own business, Konvictions, which she'd all but ignored these past few months.

"I uh . . ."

"You haven't been thinking about it," he interjected. "Have you?"

"That's not true," she argued.

"So, pick a date."

"Well, it's not that easy, Solomon."

"Desi."

Pressure. He was all about the pressure. "February twenty-seventh," she blurted out.

February twenty-seventh was four months away. There was no way in hell she could pull together a decent wedding in four months.

"Okay," he said introspectively. "Why February twenty-seventh?"

"It's Momma's birthday," she said quietly.

Solomon kissed the top of her head. "February twenty-seventh it is, then."